BRIGHT
ARROWS

Grace Livingston Hill
America's Pioneer Romance Novelist

BRIGHT ARROWS

Grace Livingston Hill

America's Pioneer Romance Novelist

HOWARD
Fiction

The Classic Collection

Our purpose at Howard Books is to:
· *Increase faith* in the hearts of growing Christians
· *Inspire holiness* in the lives of believers
· *Instill hope* in the hearts of struggling people everywhere
Because He's coming again!

Published by Howard Books, a division of Simon & Schuster
1230 Avenue of the Americas, New York, NY 10020

Bright Arrows © 2006 by G. L. Hill, Ltd.

ISBN-13: 978-1-4165-3595-9

HOWARD is a registered trademark of Simon & Schuster, Inc.

Manufactured in the United States

Cover design by Smartt Guys Design
Interior design by Tennille Paden

This Howard Books edition of Grace Livingston Hill's book contains the complete text of the original edition. Not one word has been omitted.

To Learn the Intriguing Story behind
This Beloved Pioneer Romance Novelist,
Turn to Page 324.

CHAPTER ONE

EDEN WAS sitting in the library of the old house where she had lived all her life. She was going over some papers in the big library desk. Her father had asked her to give special attention to them as soon as she would get home from his funeral service and be alone.

She had eaten quietly and conscientiously of the delicious supper which the devoted sorrowing servants had lovingly prepared for her. She had tried to keep a cheerful face during their ministrations, and then had told them that she wouldn't need them any more tonight and they must go to their beds and rest, for they had had a hard day. They had blessed her for her thoughtfulness, and gone off to finish the few remaining household duties. Then they went silently to their rooms.

At least they had seemed to go, though they had not all gone to sleep. One of them did not even go to her room, but was still alert for Eden's movements. The old nurse

Janet, who had been a part of the household ménage ever since Eden was born, did not even pretend to retire. She merely sat down in the servants' dining room and waited with a listening ear for her young lady. Her sharp bright eyes were hiding quick tears which she had not dared to shed before the others, and her kindly old lips that carried and would cherish to the end a Scotch accent from the old country, were quivering with pain for the young girl left so alone in a world that had always been so satisfyingly filled with the presence of a tender father. Tabor, too, was sitting in the upper hall within hearing. So Eden was not really alone.

But Eden, having waited for this moment ever since her father had breathed his last on earth, thought she was alone now. She drew a sigh of relief, and went over to the desk, taking out the small key that hung on a slender chain concealed about her neck.

It seemed almost as if her father had a rendezvous with her. She knew he had planned it during those last few days of his illness, after his accident, when he knew that his hours were numbered. It was the thought of this last farewell message from her father that had kept her up during the hard hours after he was gone. It was as if she were under orders, and had not time to mourn for him yet, because he had left her something to do. He had said it would be something that would make it easier for her to go on.

Eden was very young to have to meet a crisis like this: the shock of an accident that resulted in the death of her only near and dear one, from whom she had almost never been separated. For she could scarcely remember her mother. Her father had been both mother and father to her. With old Janet to minister to her bodily needs, Eden had lived a happy carefree life.

And so she sat alone, with old Janet out beyond the hall and pantry and kitchen, on sorrowful, unsuspected guard.

Eden fitted the small key into the lock of the drawer to which her father had often directed her attention, turned it, opened the drawer. Catching her breath a little as one who understands a momentous thing is about to happen, she looked within.

And there, right on the top, was a folded paper bearing her name, in her father's beloved hand. For an instant it almost seemed as if she were looking upon that dear dead countenance that they had just laid to rest in the old cemetery. And then she remembered what he had said to her about this moment, and how when she unlocked that drawer she would find his last words to say good-by and comfort her.

She closed her eyes for a brief instant and then put out her hand for the paper and drew it toward her, handling it as one touches a very precious treasure.

Softly, carefully, she unfolded it. It was not long, but

3

very clearly written, somewhat like the letters he had written her during his few brief business absences from home, but her eyes lit with pleasure as she recognized the old sweet greeting, "Dear little lass." That had always been his dearest way of addressing her, even since she had grown into lovely girlhood.

She held the paper closer, and settled back to draw comfort from her father's last words. There was an earnest look of eagerness upon her young face.

It was just at that moment that the door opened silently and someone came into the room. He stepped so inaudibly that at first she did not sense his entrance.

Then suddenly with an inner sense she realized that she was not alone, and looking up she saw him.

He was a handsome young man with a very engaging smile, nicely camouflaging a flippant sneer on lips that were not tuned to gentleness.

She had not seen him for three years, but she had never liked him. As a child she had been afraid of his cruel jokes and petty torments. When her father found it out he removed her from his vicinity, taking her away with himself on a journey, till the obnoxious boy and his still more unpleasant mother had moved to a far city, with other interests.

He was not exactly a relative, just the son by a former marriage of a woman who had married her uncle for a few years before his death. But he called himself her cousin though it was not a blood relationship.

And now suddenly he was standing in the door-way looking at her with that gloating glitter in his eyes, masked by his old insinuating smile. How did he get in? The servants had locked up for the night. The night latch was on the door always. He had no key, and never had had one. Something cold and frightening clutched her heart.

For an instant they surveyed one another, and then the young man spoke:

"Eden! You lovely thing! You are more stunning look-ing than ever! I certainly am glad that I came!"

Eden lifted her chin haughtily, and there was no an-swering smile on her young lips. She tried to summon all her self-possession, and spoke in a voice of cool distance.

"Oh, you are Ellery Fane!" she said.

"The same!" said the young man, his hand on his heart, and bowed low. "I am flattered that you remember me. And now that I am recognized may I sit down? For I have something to tell you. I won't interrupt you long for I see you are going over some important business papers. I'll be glad to help you if you think you are equal to doing them tonight after such a strenuous day as you must have had."

Eden suddenly remembered the dear letter she held in her hand, and with a quick motion she lowered the pages out of sight down in her lap. Then with swift stealthy fingers, she folded the letter softly, and slid it into the drawer, snapping the drawer shut, and turning the key softly. Her experiences in the past with this slippery would-be cousin had proved to her that nothing precious was to be trusted in his sight. Instinct had taught her this from her first knowledge of him when she was a mere child.

So, as he talked on with his insinuating voice tuned low, obviously on account of her recent sorrow, her fingers were swiftly at work extracting the little key and folding it close in her hand. Then she lifted her eyes haughtily to meet his insinuating gaze.

"Thank you, I do not need help," she said coldly. "I feel that your coming, especially so stealthily, and at this time, is an intrusion. But since you are here, what is it you want? I am in no need of help at present, and certainly not from you, when I remember under what circumstances you left this house last, at my father's request."

"Oh, now Eden, you're surely not holding that against me. I was a mere boy then, and I did make a mistake or two in my accounts at the bank. Of course I've learned better now, and I suppose I ought to be grateful to your father for being so severe with me. It taught me a much-needed lesson. I've forgiven him long ago, of course, and started out to be a real man, the kind of man he wanted me to be. I've been studying high finance and am really an expert now, and I felt it was not only my duty but my pleasure to come and offer you my advice and skill in settling your estate. Of course you are inexperienced, my dear, and I have an idea there will be many things about business that will be most puzzling to you. I'll be glad to put my financial knowledge and abilities at your disposal. I have several letters with me that will show you I am all that I say in these lines, and it certainly will be greatly to your advantage to have my advice."

Eden's voice was still cool and quiet in spite of her mounting anger, and she looked him in the eye steadily.

"That will be entirely unnecessary," she said coldly. "Such matters have all been attended to satisfactorily, and I have no need for advice. My father arranged everything for me before he left me."

"Yes, of course, I understand he would," soothed the honeyed voice. "He was always kindness itself, and thoughtful, most thoughtful for the welfare of others. But my dear, I had not been in his bank long, even when I was a mere lad, before I knew perfectly well how unworldly he was, and how almost criminally ignorant he was of the best ways of managing a fortune, and making the most of what he had, you know. As I began my studies and went on to wider knowledge, I kept looking back to what I knew of your father's business matters, and I knew what advantages he was missing by some of his oddly fanatical ideas about right and wrong that were simply nonsensical. And so I thought that it was my duty to come and tell you what I had learned in the world of finance, and offer to set matters right for you, so that you might become almost fabulously rich in your own right. It will merely mean straightening out a few matters, and exchanging some of your father's foolish investments before it is too late."

Eden, white with anger, rose from her chair, the little key clutched tight in the palm of her hand, the other hand leaning hard on the edge of her father's desk, her eyes flashing indignation.

"That will be all I care to hear," she said freezingly. "You can go now. I certainly want no help from *you ever*, in *any way!*"

Eden in her excitement did not realize that her fingers had automatically touched the little switch on the edge of the desk by which her father had often called for the old butler to do some errand for him. But suddenly the bell responded quickly through the silent house, making the unwelcome guest start in surprise and look cautiously around. That bell was something he had not known about as it had been installed after he had left that part of the country. But Eden was so coldly angry now that she paid little heed to the bell. Besides she thought that the servants had all gone to their rooms and were probably asleep. And she was not really afraid of this would-be cousin, anyway, just furious at his insufferable impudence toward her wonderful father. She felt that she could handle this situation herself. She would let him know that he was not wanted.

But the young man sat still watching her intently.

"You don't understand, my dear! I mean all this in utter kindness. That is why my mother and I talked it over and decided that she and I would give up everything else and devote ourselves to you. Mother will arrive on the early train in the morning. She had to come from the far West, you know, and could not get here in time for the service today, but we talked it over on the telephone, and arranged it all. Mother is coming here to live with you and chaperone you of course. You could not think of living here alone. It would not be respectable. Your father would never approve of that, I'm sure, and so it was up to your nearest relatives to come to your rescue—"

"Stop!" said Eden, tense with anger now. "I do not wish to have either you or your mother here, and besides I have other arrangements—"

"Oh, really? Who is going to stay with you?"

"I don't wish to discuss that matter with you, either now or at any other time. My affairs are my own and you have nothing to do with them. If you will leave at once that will be all I shall ask of you."

The door into the hall had opened so quietly that neither of them realized that there were two other people standing in the room. It was the old butler who spoke firmly—his old voice sounded almost as young again as when he first began to serve his beloved employer.

"You rang, my lady," he said, standing at attention, with even his white gloves on his hands, giving an air of formality to his hastily donned uniform.

And just a step behind him to one side, stood old Janet, her eyes wide and angry, her lips shut thinly and her hands folded flatly across her stomach in her most formal servantly humility, just as she had been accustomed to serve all her life.

The young man stood up, startled into embarrassed awkwardness for an instant. But he quickly rallied to what he called his "poise"—though there had been others who called it merely "brass"—and smiled an ingratiating smile.

"My word!" he said with a note of forced delight in his voice. "If there isn't dear old Janet. Alive yet! I remember how I used to delight in her gingerbread, and chocolate cakes. And old Tabor, as faithful as ever. Say this is a wonder. Eden, you ought to—"

But Eden was talking in a clear firm voice that cut like a knife through Ellery Fane's paltry prattle.

"Yes, Tabor, I'm glad you came. Will you kindly see this person to the door, and make sure that every door and window is carefully locked? And Janet, could I have a cup of tea?"

But the young man broke in upon her orders:

"Oh, but I'm not going out again tonight, Cousin Eden. I had planned to stay here all night. Didn't I tell you? You see my mother is expecting to arrive here in the morning and I thought we could talk it over and settle about our rooms—"

But Eden spoke coolly and firmly again.

"No," she said forcefully, "you are *not* going to stay here tonight, and your mother is *not* coming here tomorrow. If you know how to reach her on the train you had better wire her when you get to the station. It will not be convenient for me to have either of you stay here *at any time*. You had better go now, Ellery. I wouldn't like to have to call the police." The young man grinned impudently, as if it were a joke, but Tabor announced carefully:

"I've already called them, my lady! Your father made me promise to do so, if ever there were intruders—and I think I hear the police car at the door now."

"Thank you, Tabor," said Eden pleasantly, as if he had just announced friendly callers. Ellery saw by the set of the girl's shoulders and the lifting of her head, that this was no joke, and without further adieu he turned to the hall door.

"Oh, well, if you feel that way about it," he said, and vanished into the dimness of the dark hall, retrieving his hat and coat from a chair near the front door, and pausing only to shout back:

"I'll send you a card with my address, and any time you

need me you can send for me. I'm sorry you took it this way, when I merely intended to help you. Good night."

So the unwanted caller left the house, even as Mike, the big policeman, entered the kitchen door. Eden stood quietly until she heard the front door shut and Tabor, after a short conference with Mike, returned to the library again. Then Eden sank slowly into her chair and dropped her face down on her folded arms on the desk. It was then that old Janet noticed that her nursling's face was wet with tears.

Quietly Janet slipped over and put a tender arm around Eden's shoulders.

"There, my little one," she said tenderly, smoothing the soft hair and patting the beloved shoulders. "How ever did that little rat get intae the hoose I'd like tae know? I didna sight him at the service. He surely wouldna had the impertinence tae coom openly. He allus useta work on the sly everything he did. He's not tae be troosted."

Then Eden lifted her tear-wet face and smiled.

"It's all right, Janet. It just upset me for a minute, but I'm glad it's over. And now, Janet, I think we had better keep this room locked, at night especially, because I don't like the idea of anybody being able to steal into daddy's special room where he kept all his important things."

"Of coorse not, my wee lamb. We'll see tae thet right away," said Janet, with a look toward Tabor.

"Yes, my lady," said Tabor capably. "And I'll have a

word with the police to keep an eye on the place. In fact I'm not sure but they intend to anyway. Your father may have mentioned it to McGregor when he was in to see him the other day. I thought as much for the answer he gave me when I spoke with him early this evening."

"Oh!" said Eden, looking startled. "But father did not know where Ellery was, I'm sure. I knew he distrusted him, but we haven't heard from him since father sent him away that time he made all the trouble for him at the bank. I shouldn't think he would dare to come again."

"That rat would dare onything," said Janet. "He's just been bidin' his time till there wasna onybody tae stop him. But don't ye worry. We'll see thet you're looked after."

"Why, I'm not worrying, Janet." Eden gave a vague little smile. "Only it was so dreadful to have him come in just when I was reading some last words from daddy. Janet, I think I would like to take that second drawer up to my room. It's just letters, nothing really valuable except to me, but I wouldn't like to think of anybody like Ellery getting his hands on them."

"Of coorse not, my lamb. We'll take it right up tae yer room, an' I'll be sleepin' across the hall the night. Tabor will make oop his bed at the end of the downstairs hall, so ye'll be weel guarded, blessed child!"

"Oh, I'm not afraid, you know, Janet. But it will be nice to know you are near at hand. It *is* lonely this first night of course."

"Is it this drawer you want, Miss Eden?" asked Tabor, stooping to lift it out. "But it's locked."

"Yes, Tabor. Here is the key."

The man unlocked the drawer and drew it out.

"Is this the only one you want, Miss Eden?" he asked.

"Yes, I think so. Wait. None of the rest are locked. I'll see if I need others."

Swiftly she drew them out one at a time, and glanced over the orderly contents.

"No, they are just routine things. Records, receipts, things that aren't very important." She closed them all and they started up the stairs, Tabor carrying the drawer, and leading the way.

"Just put it down on the table by my desk," said Eden, "and thank you, Tabor. Now don't you two worry any more about me. I shall be quite all right, and I hope you won't lose any more sleep over prowlers. I'm quite sure Ellery Fane is the only one who would dare, and I think you thoroughly scared him off with your promise of the police."

"Right you are, Miss Eden. I'm positive you'll be entirely safe from any intruders from now on."

So the two servants were presently gone, and Eden locked her door and sat down to the reading of her father's letter, entirely assured that this time she would not look up to see Ellery's hateful eyes looking at her.

Sitting there in her own pretty room, in the luxurious

chair that had been her father's gift on her last birthday, with all her pretty belongings about her, she could take a deep breath and really enjoy this last little conversation that her father had prepared to help her through the first hard evening after he had left her finally.

And so she began to read:

Dear little lass:

I promised you a last few words, so you could feel this first night that my love is still with you.

Because I have felt for a long time that you had missed the most beautiful thing out of your little-girl life when your mother was called away, I have been casting about in my mind to find something that will partly make up for it. So I am now leaving you a packet of her own letters which have for years been the most precious possession I owned, and which nobody else but myself have ever read. Of course I have told you a great deal about your dear mother, but even at its best the telling of a thing is never as good as the thing itself. Just hearing about what a mother you had could never be like growing up from childhood under her loving care. It is for this reason that I have left you her letters, that you may gather from them the atmosphere of the home into which you were born, and really sense what a wonderful mother you had.

We talked a lot about you before you came, and afterward before she went away. You have a right to know what we said, and how we loved you, and what we hoped for your future. You will gather much of that from these letters, which are now yours, dear lassie. Don't weep when you read them. Just be glad to know we are safe with our Heavenly Father, who is also watching over you.

Good-by, little one, till we meet in Heaven, and don't forget we'll be counting on your coming Home when your work down here is done.

Your loving father,
Charles Hamilton Thurston

Eden did not weep as she read the last words and let her eyes trace the precious familiar signature with tender glance. But her cheeks were flushed and there was a wonderful light in her eyes as she lifted them for an instant to look into a far distance, as if she were trying to send a smile beyond the gate of Heaven to let her father know that she was being true to her promise that she would not let herself grieve for him.

A great swelling of her heart came as she folded up her father's letter and slipped it inside her blouse just over her heart. It seemed to her when it was there that she could feel his dear hand resting on her head, his voice telling her to be strong and not think about her disappointments, but just trust and not be afraid.

Then half shyly she put out her hand to take the first letter of her unknown mother, whom she could scarcely remember, except as a sweet presence who was always smiling. How glad that mother must be now that her dear husband had come to be with her in Heaven. But it was all so vague. Did people live and feel and think and rejoice in Heaven as they did on earth? Sometime when she found some very wise person who had studied about Heaven she would ask about that.

Then her glance came down to the letter, as she took it out of the delicate envelope, and scanned the beautiful writing. Oh, she had seen her mother's writing before of course. There was a lovely little white book, her own baby record, written in this same charming chirography, but somehow this was different. The book was a formal record with an occasional little merry account of some quaint child saying, or bright idea.

But this letter was different. It was going to be like listening to her darling mother talking with her precious father.

"Dear Charlie:"

The words thrilled the heart of the young girl, and for the first time some faint realization of what it must have been to her mother to be in love with her father, as he must have been when he was young. Then she settled down breathlessly to read that sweet wonderful letter, the first real love letter that Eden had ever read. Oh, she had read love letters in novels of course, just fiction. But this was real life. This love letter had been *lived,* and by special dispensation was so linked to her life that she had a right not only to read it, but to cherish it as a very part of herself.

Breathlessly she read the lovely girl-thoughts. More beautiful than all the dreams of romance that had ever visited her imagination—waking or dreaming.

On she read through the sweet impassioned words, which grew only more tender and delicate in expression as she went from one charming epistle to the next. Reading a rare continued love story, through the first days of a beautiful courtship, and on to the wedding day.

Then came a letter that told of a visit to relatives. It was most enlightening—Aunt Phoebe in a pale gray silk with blush roses in her little gray bonnet tied under her sweet little trembly chin. Eden remembered her only as a little old woman with tired eyes and a skin like old parchment and a way of falling asleep in her chair. Grandma Haybrook with snapping black eyes that couldn't brook a fault in any but herself. She almost laughed aloud as she read about Uncle Pepperill, who would continue to take a pinch of snuff, even at a wedding.

There were fewer letters after that, save now and then a note written just for the joy of saying, "I love you." For she sensed that the two were continually together now, seldom separated except for a day or two occasionally for some business reason. But ever was that perfect flow of harmony and love in the very atmosphere, even of the brief silences between the letters.

There were little notations on the envelopes to mark these absences of letters. One read: "The first letter after Eden was born, while I was absent for a day at a banking conference."

Eagerly she opened that letter and found a wee snapshot of herself as a tiny baby, and a tender line:

I never knew or even dreamed what it would be like to have a little new soul entrusted to our care! And to think our little Eden has such a wonderful father! I shall ever thank God for that! Oh, how can we ever hope to find a man as good as you, my beloved, as fine and strong and tender, and worthy to marry her? We must ask God Himself to prepare one for her.

It was just then that Janet's quiet footsteps came down the hall with a tinkle of silver and china from the tray she carried. She tapped softly at Eden's door, and Eden was suddenly recalled to the present from a very faraway past that represented her own beginning on the earth.

"Yes, Janet, what is it?" said Eden quickly.

"It's joost a wee drap o' tay an' a scone, my lambkin. Ye mustna make yersel' sick wie yer grievin'!"

Eden sprang to the door and let in her faithful friend:

"But I'm not grieving, you dear faithful friend," she said, taking the tray from Janet's eager hands. "But the tea smells good, and I really believe I'm hungry. Thank you, Janet! But you didn't need to worry about me. I have been having a wonderful time reading these letters that my father prepared for me this evening. Letters from my own dear mother, Janet. See what pretty writing. And they are wonderful letters. Someday I'll read you some bits of them, especially those about my coming. You were here before I was, Janet. You knew my mother."

Janet stooped and looked sharply at the envelope Eden held out.

"Aye! Weel I knew yer dear mither, my lambkin. An' thet's her writin'. I had several letters from her mysel', afore I came tae her while I was still in the auld country."

"Oh, did you, Janet? How nice. You never told me about that."

"Didna I tell ye? Weel, ye were a wee mite, an' ye missed yer momma somethin' turrible. I didna wanttae worry ye. And noo, ma bairnie, let me holp ye tae undress an' get intae yer bed. It's verra late, an' ye've had a hard day."

"No, I want to finish reading the rest of the letters," said Eden looking wistfully toward the drawer beside her, that still had more letters remaining.

"Why not let thim remain until the morn?" asked

Janet practically. "Ye're lookin' verra fagged, an' I'm quite sure yer feyther would advise thet."

Eden looked up and drew a long breath.

"Why, yes, I suppose daddy would tell me to go to bed now. But it's been so wonderful to read letters from my own mother to my father, and to think he planned for me to read them now, so I wouldn't feel so lost and alone."

"Yes, my bairn. He was a wonnerfoo feyther, an' she were a rare mither. Ye're greatly blest thet ye had them, even though ye air lonely the noo. But noo, let me brush yer hair for ye, and get ye tae yer cooch. There'll be people comin' in the morn perhaps, an' ye'll wanttae be good an' rested tae meet them."

"Yes, I suppose you're right, Janet," said the girl, yawning wearily.

And soon Janet had her tucked comfortably in her bed, the light out and the door shut for the night. So thinking the pleasant thoughts about those letters, as her thoughtful father had known she would do if she read them before she went to bed, she soon fell asleep.

Then the faithful Janet went quietly to her bed, and Tabor, on his makeshift bed across the library door, planned to be quietly alert to any sound.

So the moon rose, then sailed behind a cloud, and later drew heavier storm clouds about her and slipped down her way to rest also, and the world was very dark.

Then when the night was at its darkest a dim figure

stole across into the deepest shrubbery at the side of the Thurston house, and disappeared near a little-used window of the old library. But the family slept on, and not even Tabor with all his wakefulness heard a sound.

In the morning, however, when Tabor opened the shutters and dusted the room he found that the other drawers in the master's big desk had been thoroughly searched, the contents stirred up and everything left in heaps!

He studied the whole situation thoroughly, and then went to the kitchen and called up the police station. It was early and no one abovestairs was stirring yet. This was something that must be settled without the young lady's knowledge if possible. He had promised his beloved master that he would guard Miss Eden as his own.

So Mike and Tabor went into the library and examined everything very carefully, and very silently. Then all the papers were put back, the drawers locked, and they went around searching for the place where the entrance to the house had been made. They found it soon enough in the long window on the side piazza that opened into the library. It was always kept locked. Ellery must have been the intruder, and had probably unfastened the window as he stood by it during that last brief altercation before he left.

A few questions Mike asked of Tabor, and then took himself away to start a search for Ellery Fane.

Chapter Two

QUITE EARLY the next morning Lavira Fane alighted from a western plane, took a taxi from the airport to the railroad station, and after a refreshing cup of coffee and a pile of well-buttered toast with jam, boarded the train for Glencarroll, the city suburb where the Thurstons resided.

Finding no liveried chauffeur to meet her, no taxi at the early hour in the morning, and not even a station agent whom she might blame, she walked, with angry, disapproving strides up to the house, reflecting on her hard lot. She did not spend much thought on her lazy son for not attending her, for well she knew his ways. He had probably been up late the night before and was now sleeping the sleep of the shiftless. That was the way she had brought him up. Why should she blame him?

So she blamed other people for whatever he had not done, and assuming that Ellery had told Eden that she was coming, she blamed Eden for not having sent her chauffeur to meet all trains until she arrived. Hence she stalked along growing more and more irate as she drew nearer to the house, which by the way seemed to have removed to a far greater distance from the station than she remembered.

In due time however, angry and tired, and thinking incessantly of the fine breakfast she anticipated that would be served her soon after her arrival, she marched up the stately stone steps, and rang the bell.

This was while Tabor was conversing with the policeman, and Janet had not yet come downstairs.

Tabor heard the bell and frowned, glanced at his watch and frowned again. The policeman gave him a quick glance and said he had better leave.

"Wait!" said Tabor. "I don't know who that would be unless it's that pest of a mother of his. He said she was coming this morning."

"Mmmmm!" said the policeman in an undertone. "You go ahead. I'll stick around."

So Tabor went reluctantly to the door, and silently Janet began to descend the upper stairs.

Thus re-enforced Tabor opened the door.

"Well! So you decide to come to the door at last, did you?" blatted the undesired guest. "I shall certainly report this to the family. Are you the same servant that was here the last time I visited?"

Tabor met this tirade with a stern countenance.

"Whom did you wish to see, madam?" he asked, in his most butlerish tone. "What is your errand?"

"*Errand!*" sneered the would-be guest. "I've come to *stay.* The family must have known I was coming. Stand aside and let me come in. I think it was most unfeeling of them not to have met my plane at the airport, they with their chauffeurs and butlers and other servants!" She fairly snorted out the last words, but Tabor stood immovable.

"Madam, I'm sorry, but I was told not to let anyone in until further word, and we are not disturbing the lady of the house at this hour. She has been through a heavy strain and needs the rest."

"Lady of the house!" snorted the irate Lavira. "Who's that? You don't mean that conceited Janet with her queer Scotch lingo, do you? Because if you do I'd have you to know that no person like that can keep me out. I belong to the *family!*"

"Yes, madam, that may be so, but you see I have my orders, and I am not able to go beyond them."

"Why, you unspeakable outrageous fool! The very idea of your daring to keep me out of this house! I insist that you take my name up to Eden or whoever she has put in charge of the house. If you don't do so I'll push by you and go right upstairs to her room myself. I simply *won't* be treated this way, when I've only come to be of service here, and I'm practically being turned out of the door. You go at once!"

"No, madam. I have been told not to disturb Miss Eden on any account. Perhaps you do not know, madam, that there has been a death in the household, which has made it very hard for everybody, and we are doing all we can to give Miss Eden a chance to rest. In fact her father, Mr. Thurston, asked me a few hours before he died to especially guard her from all intruders these first few days after he was gone, for he knew they would be more than hard for her."

"But this is ridiculous!" spluttered the woman. "I shall appeal to the authorities!"

Then suddenly Mike stepped into the picture.

"Just what is it you wanted to appeal to the authorities for, madam? I belong to the police force and I have been asked to look after the comfort of this house. Suppose you come with me and we can talk it over."

Mike was enveloped in a brusque politeness, and his sudden authoritative appearance so startled the woman that she fairly gasped.

"Oh! A policeman!" she ejaculated. "Why, what has happened? Are things in such bad shape here that they have to be guarded by a policeman?" she questioned, yielding to the firm pressure on her arm and the authority of the law, as she backed down the steps and was propelled down the front walk and out to the street.

"Why yes, madam," Mike said in a well-guarded whisper. "Last night after they had all retired and the house was carefully locked, somebody broke into the library and went through the late Mr. Thurston's desk, and all his private papers!"

The announcement was made solemnly and filled the woman with awe.

"*How-how perfectly terrible!*" she exclaimed. "Of course I didn't know about that. No wonder they were all so upset. But you see I'm one of the family, and came here to help. I ought to go right up and comfort Eden."

But the hand of the law was still firmly upon her arm, and she did not go back. In fact the alarm that this big Mike had suddenly raised within her was on the increase. She felt she should learn more about this supposed robbery that the man said had been going on. She must find out if her son had been caught in any such mistaken escapade. It would not be beyond his powers to try something like that, she knew. And it was all right of course if he found such measures *necessary* to carry out his plans. He and she had hoped to be able to work quietly from inside the house as members of the family. But anything was all right if he could get away with it, and hitherto he had always got away with it. Still it was rather frightening to think that there was a possibility that this time he might not get away with it.

She looked up pleadingly to Mike's stern face, with slippery unmotherly eyes.

"I really ought to go right away to Eden. She will wonder why I didn't come."

Mike looked down at her with his wise penetrating eyes.

"What did you say your name was, madam?"

"Fane," said Lavira eagerly. "I'm Mrs. Lavira Fane. And I got word—that is, I had notice of the death, and I started right away to come, for I knew the dear departed man would have expected me to be here at once. I took the first plane and came right out here as quick as I could."

"You say your name is Fane? I see." He took out his notebook and flipped over the leaves with one hand. "Fane. Yes, Fane. Have you any relatives in the city or near by, by the name of Fane?"

A quick wary look came into the woman's eyes as she met the stern gaze of the big policeman.

"Relatives? Oh no, none by the name of Fane. That is, no relatives at all in this part of the country except the Thurstons. You see my name is really Thurston. I was a widow with one son and I married a brother of the deceased, Mr. Thurston, so my name is really Thurston, and I certainly ought to go right back and be with Eden. It is my duty, you know."

But Mike McGregor walked steadily on, with his grasp

still firm on the woman's arm, and suddenly he looked down into her shrinking frightened eyes.

"Your son's name is Ellery?" he asked, quite casually, and pierced her through with those eyes that did not flinch.

"Why yes," she simpered, trying to hide her astonishment, "did you used to know him when he was here before? He was only a child then. I never heard him speak of you. He'll be here in a day or two, I guess. He had some business matters to settle up before he left the West, but he'll be coming on soon."

"Your son is here now," said the policeman calmly. "He must have arrived sometime yesterday, or perhaps earlier, but he is here now."

Lavira gave him a frightened glance, and he could see that her lip was trembling.

"But how would you know that?" she asked, trying to appear casual. "Where is he? I want to see him at once!"

Mike paused beside a big red police car and opened the door.

"Get in," he said coldly, "I will take you to him."

Lavira turned toward the car and suddenly caught her breath, stepped back a pace and looked the bright red car over.

"But I can't get into *that* car," she said haughtily.

"Why not?" asked Mike sharply.

"But a bright *red* car like that! It looks like a police car!"

"It *is* a police car. Get in!"

"But I can't ride in a car like that! I never was in a police car in my life! I couldn't endure to ride in that. I would be ashamed all the rest of my life. I couldn't get over it."

"People have been ashamed all their lives for less than that," said the policeman grimly. "Get in!"

"Oh, no, no, *no!*" said Lavira. "I simply couldn't do that! Tell me where you think my son is, and I'll get a taxi and go there, but I can't go in a police car!"

"Sorry," said Mike, "if you want to go to your son you'll have to go with me in this car. This is my car, and I'm taking you. Get in!"

There was that in Mike's voice that made the woman know she must obey. Slowly she turned and got in, forcibly assisted by Mike's big insistent hand.

"But, but, *where* am I going? I can't do a thing like this without knowing where I am going."

"You're going to the police station, madam," said Mike. "Your son is there. You wanted to see him. That's where he is."

"Oh!" she gasped, "but what is he doing there?"

"He's being questioned for breaking into the Thurston house last night and ransacking Mr. Thurston's desk drawers."

"Oh, he didn't do *that*," pleaded the mother. "I *know* he didn't. He wouldn't do a thing like that. Besides he wasn't here last night. He was to come in on the afternoon train and meet me here. We had planned to come right on and take care of Eden. We knew she would be so lonesome!"

But McGregor rode on in silence, not even noticing by so much as the lift of an eyelash, the flow of words by his side, and the freely flowing tears which he told himself grimly were only crocodile tears. For McGregor knew his crooks, and didn't often make a mistake.

It was so that Lavira was ushered into police headquarters, where she was greeted by the sight of her misguided son sitting in one corner of the room, in close confab with two stern-looking policemen. He sat there before his inquisitors filled with assurance, his one long wavy lock of hair hanging gaily over his handsome dejected face, like a banner, to which he occasionally gave a careless toss, but his mouth was grim and sullen as he tried to explain to the police how it came about that his fingerprints were on the window that had been jimmied open in the Thurston house, and what he was looking for in the Thurston desk drawers; also how it was that he came to have several old cancelled checks in his pocket that bore Mr. Thurston's signature, and what he had been planning to do with them. His excuse for the latter that he wanted the checks for souvenirs of his beloved dead uncle did not seem to go down with the police, as they knew well by now that Mr. Thurston was neither his uncle, nor beloved.

Meanwhile, back at the Thurston house, Eden lay in her own quiet room, getting a much-needed rest. All that day she was watched over by her faithful servitors, careful that nothing should disturb her.

And then next morning, all too early for the careful plans to guard her, it was the telephone by her bed that roused her from her long refreshing sleep.

CHAPTER THREE

HELLO, BEAUTIFUL! How are you?" breezed a voice out of the past. "How are you fixed for the day? Ready to run off for a few hours and have a jolly time? I'm here on leave for the day, and I want to make the most of it if it's okay with you."

Eden was silent for a minute or two, blinking at the instrument in startled bewilderment, unable for an instant to identify the voice, it seemed so much more mature than when she last heard it. Then it came to her. He would be older of course than when he went away to war two years ago, or was it more?

"Oh!" she exclaimed in amazement. "Why, it's Caspar Carvel, isn't it? But I thought you were away in the Philippines somewhere, or even in Japan. How grand to know you're home. How did you get here without letting us know? And where have you been all this time?"

"Oh, here and there," said the laughing voice.

"But you never wrote to us but once!" reproached Eden.

"Well, I know, I never was much of a correspondent, you know. Besides they kept us awfully busy in the army. I just didn't have time. But anyhow, I'm here now, and I have to leave tonight. I'm due up in New York to do some broadcasting, and I can't tell when I can get back, so I thought I'd call you up. How about it? Can you give me the day, and perhaps part of the evening if we can find some good show or a nice dump for dinner and a dance? Will you go? You know it's a long time since we went gadding together, old girl, and I don't want to waste any time. Hurry up and say yes. I haven't got another nickel handy and I want to get this settled. I'll come for you in three quarters of an hour. And make it snappy. Can you be ready in that time? Wear something pretty smart. I may want to introduce you to a coupla the fellows if we happen to meet them. This all okay?"

Eden caught her breath. Could this really be Caspar Carvel? He didn't sound in the least like her old friend and playmate. The handsome boy who had been her playmate in high school, and who had been almost daily running in and out of their house. She hesitated, and the voice on the other end of the wire grew impatient:

"I say! Are you there, Eden! Didn't you hear me? I'm in an awful rush, and I haven't got another nickel handy."

"But—are you *really* Caspar Carvel? Somehow your

voice sounds so different! I didn't recognize it at first. You seem so grown-up!" There was a little sad reproach in her tone.

"Well, good night! One does grow up, you know. And I guess there's no place to accomplish that quicker than in the army. Do you mind?"

There was a sharp challenge to his tone now.

Eden still hesitated.

"Why, no, of course not," she said, trying to speak naturally. "It's quite to be expected of course. But somehow you startled me. I wasn't expecting you."

"Well, are you coming with me? Get a hustle on. I only have this day and I want to make the most of it."

"Why, Caspar, I want to see you of course, but I couldn't go with you. Nor do all those things you suggested."

"What? You mean go dancing? You mean your dad would object to that? But surely he doesn't attempt to lord it over you the way he used to. You're of age, aren't you? Or almost. I should think you had a right to do what you want to now. But anyway, if you think he would kick up a row we could steal away some place he wouldn't know about. Would he really make a fuss now? It's time you made a stand against such petty domineering. If you're afraid of him I'll tell him what I think of him. Just wait till I get out there."

Eden's voice was choked with sudden tears.

"My father is not here, Caspar."

"Well, then, what's the matter? He needn't know where you went. Where is he? Will he be away all the evening?"

Eden took a deep breath and choked back the tears.

"Caspar, my father died four days ago. His funeral was day before yesterday." There was deep sorrow in the girl's voice, and Caspar's gay tone suddenly hushed.

"Oh!" he said, aghast. "Oh, you don't *mean* it! You see I didn't know it. I ask your pardon for barging in this way. I'm sorry! Was he sick for long? Somebody ought to have told me. But I really haven't seen anybody from over this way in a long time. I hope you'll understand. Of course I don't suppose you feel like making gay right away. I understand. Perhaps you'd rather I didn't come over today."

"Oh, no, I'd like to see you," said Eden gravely. "I have been wondering what had become of you. Nobody seemed to know."

"Okay, I'll be over for a little while. By-by!"

Eden dropped back on her pillows and lay there staring up at the ceiling. Was that really her old friend Caspar? How strangely different he seemed. Even after she had told him of her father's death his voice was hard and unsympathetic. The words were all right, but he sounded as if he were in a world that was not hers. Of course that was what people were saying war did to the boys, though some that she knew had come home quite changed in another way, more reliable, more gentle and sometimes grave.

Well, but this wasn't fair to Caspar. Judging him before she had really seen him at all. It would be natural that one would change to some degree when taken out of a home environment and put among a lot of tough fellows. Although of course they were not all tough. Well, she would put such thoughts aside and try to wait until he came, and then perhaps she wouldn't feel he was changed so much after all.

But as she rose and went about the matter of dressing, the brief conversation over the telephone kept lingering in her mind. The way Caspar had spoken of her father, so disrespectfully, suggesting that she get out from under his care. How terrible for him to speak that way! Why, he used always to admire her father, to look up to him! And her father had always been so nice and kind to Caspar. Had he forgotten all that? Didn't he remember how her father had gone with him to see the man at the apartment house after he broke two of their windows in the basement, and paid for the windows, and then let Caspar pay him five cents a week out of his allowance until it was all paid for? And Caspar had been so pleased, and had understood why dad didn't pay it himself, because it wouldn't be good for Caspar to get away without paying for his own carelessness. Caspar used to be such an understanding boy. Oh, he couldn't have changed that way. He used to come to dad for help in things instead of going to his own father, because his own father simply got angry with him and took away his allowance for a while. Well, anyway, she mustn't judge Caspar until she saw him face to face, and talked with him, and found out whether he was really the fine upstanding boy he used to be in the days when she thought he was everything a young man should be.

Of course she had been much upset that he hadn't written to her as he had promised to do, but she had excused that because she knew Caspar hated to write letters. And gradually she had learned to forget the heartaches that had come at first after he went away, and told herself that she was too young to break her heart because a school boy had forgotten to write letters when he was off fighting battles. And so the days had gone by and the memory of Caspar had gently faded from her thoughts. And now, suddenly, with the sound of his voice, the whole vision of his handsome vivacious face, his fine flashing eyes, his alluring smile came over her, and in spite of all her common sense, and her definite resolutions that she was done with Caspar, she couldn't help an excitement thrilling in her veins. Somehow it was great to have her old friend coming back just when she was sad and lonely over the loss of her dear father. She hurried in her dressing to be ready when he should arrive. If he had not much time she must be ready to see him at once, and of course she must hurry down and tell Janet that he was coming and would likely stay to lunch.

Then right into the midst of her thoughts the telephone rang again.

"Hello, Eden, this is Cappie again. I'm sorry as the dickens, but I find I'll not be able to come this morning. I've just met some old friends, and they are determined I shall go to lunch with them. One of them is my old buddie in the army, and he's going back overseas tonight, so you see I've simply got to stay with him and see him off."

"Oh!" said Eden coldly. "Then I'm not to see you at all. Is that what you mean? Well, I'm sorry, but of course it's all right."

"Oh, no, I didn't mean that," said the young man amusedly. "You didn't think I'd come all this way down from New York just to see you, and then go off without seeing you, did you?"

"It sounded like that," said Eden with dignity.

"Well I always was a bungler when it came to talking. Of course I'll be around as soon as he leaves. I haven't found out what train he takes yet, but I'll be seeing you. How about early this evening?"

"But I thought you wanted to go dancing," she said sweetly. "Don't let me hinder you."

"Oh, see here now, that's all off. Of course I wouldn't expect you to go out having fun when you just had a death in the family. I'm not that crude. And I certainly do want to see you like the dickens. I've been thinking about you all the way home. Yes, I'm all kinds of sorry I had to meet up with this buddie of mine and be hindered in coming directly to you. But you see I kind of felt under obligation to him on account of things he did for me when I was wounded. But say, are you going to be in this evening?"

"Why yes, I think I probably shall. Yes, of course, come when it's convenient to you. I'll be very glad to see you." But her tone was cool.

"All righty, I'll be there, and I'm just crazy to see you."

So with a hasty "So long," Caspar hung up and Eden went back to her precious letters.

The last letters of Mrs. Thurston were written from a hospital. They were full of tender love for her husband and anxious premonitions for her little Eden. And now Eden could read between the lines, and sense that her mother knew that her health was in danger, and that she might soon be taken away.

There were only a few letters left now and her heart was longing to read them all and get to know this mother who had gone from her so long ago that she could not remember anything about her but a vague lovely face, and a gentle touch.

Curiously enough the last three letters were filled with a kind of exultant joy in her love for her husband, and an overwhelming longing that her little girl might grow up to have such a wonderful life as hers had been. And in one letter she said:

I have been praying lately that our little Eden when she grows up may find as fine a man as you are, my beloved. I have been praying much about that, and hoping that as she grows up we may be able to teach her that she must take time to be sure about choosing a mate. That she must not be taken by the first handsome face, or a man with wonderful manners, or social standing, or riches, or honor, or physical charm. She must wait and be sure before she joins her life with another life. I shall try with all my heart to make her understand what real love is, and that she must not hastily fancy herself in love with somebody who may turn out to be utterly selfish and bring her nothing but sorrow. Oh, I pray that may never be for my little rosebud of a girl. A girl that has such a wonderful father as my beloved, should also have just such a wonderful husband.

And now the letters brought a new note, a foreshadowing of change, as if the mother were trying to prepare her dear ones for her going.

In the very last letter she said:

And if it should be that I may have to leave our baby girl before it is time to make her understand how important it is that she should choose the right companion for life, I am asking you my beloved husband that you will tell her most carefully, warn her, impress upon her that she must go cautiously, and not make too quick decisions. That she must not think of marrying anyone whom she does not love implicitly. And even then, she must not accept a love that is not from a man who is good and right and true.

Eden sat for a long time, reading that letter over again, and looking off out of the window, thinking. And then the vision of the handsome boy who had been Caspar Carvel came to her questioningly. Suddenly she realized that when Caspar went away to war she had looked upon him as the man she would eventually fall in love with. Not that he had ever said a word of any such thing to her, or that she had ever put such a thought into logical form even in her own mind, but she had viewed him in her innocent thoughts as a young man who would some-day be a friend of whom to be proud. That was how she put it. And why, now, since this brief talk over the tele-phone, should there be any question in her mind of his suitability as her close friend? She couldn't quite tell, but the very form of his address had seemed crude and over-familiar. And yet that was absurd of course, for they had been very close friends as children, as students in high school, a merry, friendly companionship. Nothing senti-mental about it. And he hadn't even written her, just a gay little scrap of a letter, mostly jokes couched in army slang. Well, she would have to wait and see what he had become before she let him take even his old informality with her. She could be friendly, yes, but that was all till she knew him well.

But having gone so far in the analysis of her old playmate, she had a definite feeling of sadness, a sense of loss. Something that she had taken for granted was gone, something that had belonged to her, that had been of real value. Or *was* it?

Then she gathered up some of the letters that had touched her most and read them over again; as if, were her mother alive, she might have gone to her for advice. What would her mother think of the present Caspar? That would be something that she might always ask when she had any important question to decide. What would mother say?

It was almost like having come suddenly into possession again of her own mother. Having read all those letters of hers, she knew pretty well what would be her advice, her decision about a great many questions of the day.

And now as she got up from her chair and went and looked out the window at the beauty of the day, she was glad in her heart that Caspar had not come immediately as he had first suggested, for now she would come to meet him with the wisdom of her dear mother's judgment upon her.

For she had to own to herself that the little talk she had

had with her old friend had not reassured her about him.

Could it be that it was just because she had been close to death, and a thought of the other world had made her more critical? She could not be sure. Of course her heart was sore, and Caspar had revealed a great lack of respect for the father she loved. She had supposed he loved him also, and that failure to show any love had gone far toward opening her eyes to what he might have become. Certainly she could never be very friendly with one who, having once known what her father was, and benefited by much kindness from him, could speak disrespectfully of him, even though he did not know of his recent death. With a sigh she turned away from the window and went back to put her letters into safe keeping, where no prying eyes could ever bring them out and go through them. She did not yet know that someone in the night had tried to do that very thing to other drawers in her father's desk.

So she got out a lovely capacious writing desk of quaint old-fashioned design, made of exquisite polished wood, that had been her mother's, and carefully packed her letters within, locking it and stowing it away on a wide shelf in her own personal clothespress safely hidden behind a row of hat boxes.

And just then she heard the doorbell. Could it be possible that Caspar had come so early? But no, he had said he had to see that soldier friend of his off on a train. Well, perhaps he went on an earlier train than was first planned.

Eden's heart began to give anxious little uncertain flutters. Would she know just what to say? How to act? Had her mother's letters made her self-conscious? That was not good. She must have perfect poise and dignity if she were to use right judgment, and she must of course be friendly and kind as an old schoolmate would naturally be. She must be back exactly where they left off when he went away if she were to judge if he had changed, and if for better or for worse.

And then suddenly Janet broke in upon her thoughts with a gentle knock.

"Miss Eden," she said in a low voice, "Mr. McGregor is doon the stair. He says there are some important questions he must ask ye and would ye kindly coom doon the stair an' let him have a few words wi' ye?"

"McGregor?" said Eden. "Oh, you mean Mike. About the burglar, I suppose. Why of course I'll go right down."

So Eden went down to meet the big friendly policeman and the man he had brought along with him. They were sitting stiffly in the little reception room next to the front door, and just in front of the library, as Eden entered wondering, a bit startled by the stranger whom she had never seen before.

Chapter Four

Eden looked with shy surprise at the stranger who had come with Mike. He didn't look like a policeman. He was dressed in an ordinary business suit. He was young and good-looking, a gentleman, that was entirely obvious even before Mike said:

"This is Mr. Lorrimer, Miss Thurston. He's interested in this case of the young man who entered your house last night. He wants to ask you some questions. He's got a right to ask 'em. He's a federal agent as well as the lawyer representing your bank, and he's here at your Mr. Worden's request to check things over for us."

Eden gave the young man another startled glance. It sounded rather frightening. Federal agent! Lawyer! Surely she didn't know anything that a federal agent would want to question her about. But another good look at the clean-cut face, the steady dependable, trustworthy eyes, reassured her.

"Yes?" she answered, watching his eyes keenly, trying to still the frightened beating of her heart. He didn't look dangerous.

Then the young man smiled.

"Thank you. I'm sorry to have disturbed you, but it is necessary for me to learn some facts from the head of this house, and I understand that you are the head of this house."

He gave her a quick glance that sized up her youth quite accurately.

Eden answered with a grave smile, and a nod of assent. She hoped her lips were not trembling, so she held to the smile rather determinedly, to keep them steady.

"Very well, then can you tell me just who this person is that calls himself Ellery Fane? Is he related to you?"

"No, he is *not,*" she said quickly. "He was the son of my uncle's second wife by her first husband. I know my uncle, my father's brother, never knew of the boy when he married Mrs. Fane. But he was too kind-hearted to turn the boy out, and soon after that my uncle died. Then my father tried to be kind to Ellery, but he was rather awful. He forged some checks in father's bank, when father tried to give him a good job. He was a torment as long as he stayed here, and finally he ran away. Soon after that his mother disappeared. This is the first time I have seen them since Ellery was sixteen. Father took me away with him on a

47

long business trip. When we came back they were gone. I think that is about all I know."

"Thank you," said the young man, looking up from the quick shorthand notes he was taking. "And now, what about last night?"

"I was sitting in the library going over some letters of my mother's that father had left for me to read, and I looked up and saw Ellery standing by the door. I don't know how he got in, or when, he just stood there and called me 'cousin,' and began to talk to me. He thought I was going over business papers and offered to help me. I told him I didn't want any help from him. He said he and his mother were coming to live with me and take care of me, and that he was going to teach me how to change Father's investments and make me a rich girl. He was very insulting to my wonderful father. Then the servants appeared, and when the butler said he had sent for the police, Ellery slid out into the hall, got his hat and coat, and vanished. I think that is about all I know."

"Thank you," said the man. "And now, Mr. McGregor, where is the butler, and the serving-woman, that you said had more to tell?"

"Right here, sir," responded Tabor, entering immediately, with Janet like a shadow just behind him. Janet slid quietly in and Tabor stood at attention near the door.

Tabor told of the night's invasion, and his calling for the police. He told why Ellery had been at once suspected, and how his fingerprints, taken after he was caught, had corresponded with those on the library window that had been jimmied open.

Eden listened in wonder as the story unfolded, and then as Janet arose stiffly in response to her name and went on to tell of Mrs. Fane's arrival, and Mike's carrying her away protesting in his police car, she leaned forward and listened amazed.

Oh, what had been going on about her while she was asleep! How wonderfully her guardians had protected her! Bright tears flashed into her eyes.

But suddenly the stranger turned to her again and asked several direct questions. Just what had been the actions of this Mrs. Fane during her first stay in town that had made Eden dislike her, and how had the matter terminated? Eden told briefly of her unpleasant and insistent attempts to get a foothold in the house. Then he asked if she knew whether her father had a financial agreement with Mrs. Fane that made her leave?

"Oh, no, I think not!" she said, very sure of her facts now. "Father didn't believe in bribes. That would have been bribing, wouldn't it? No, he simply made me pack up in a hurry one night and we went off to Europe, leaving no word behind except with Mr. Worden at the bank, father's friend you know, who has my affairs in charge. And of course Tabor and Janet knew how to get in touch with us. But they would have never told. They were our own family, you know," and she cast a grateful little flash of a smile at the two old retainers that was not lost on the lawyer.

"Yes, of course," agreed Mr. Lorrimer, with a quick glance taking in the looks that passed between Eden and her servants, and appreciating the beauty of the sentiment between them all, realizing that on the surface, at least, there was nothing suspicious here.

"And now," said Lorrimer, settling back, his pencil and notebook in hand ready for any item that needed jotting down, "Miss Thurston, I wonder if you can tell me about business matters? Was there anything valuable in that desk besides what we know about? Have you a list of what it contained?"

Eden thought for an instant, and then sprang up.

"Why yes, I think perhaps there was a list. I'll get it. It's up in my room in my desk. Father gave it to me after he was first hurt, but I was so worried about him that I'm afraid I didn't give much heed to it at the time."

"Of course," said Lorrimer sympathetically.

"Couldna I get it for ye, Miss Eden?" asked Janet, as Eden turned to hurry away.

"No thank you, Janet. You wouldn't know where to find it. I won't be long," and Eden hurried upstairs, while Mike and Tabor conversed in low tones about the way the room had been found that morning, and Janet stood with folded hands and waited. The young lawyer poised his pencil over the notes he had already taken, and seemed to be summing them up and pondering.

But Eden was back in a moment with her hands full of neatly folded papers which she handed over to the lawyer, small groupings of them strapped with rubber bands.

"These are some properties owned by the estate. He kept most of his important papers in the bank, of course. But these are a few securities he was going to explain to me about selling them, and so on."

The lawyer took them bunch by bunch, looked over the headings, glanced at them all and noted down something about each one.

"I'll just have these checked over with the list we have at the bank," he explained to Eden. "That way we can tell if anything has been tampered with, or if there is anything missing."

"Oh, yes," said Eden, "but I don't think my father left anything down here that would matter. He usually put valuables in the bank."

The lawyer looked at her thoughtfully and then said:

"It won't do any harm to make sure of course. Your father wasn't able to get down to his library and make any changes in the contents of his desk after the accident, was he? Might not something have been forgotten?"

It came to Eden as she listened that this young man was keen, and didn't take anything for granted. But she answered, still thoughtfully:

"Of course it is possible, but I don't think it likely. Dad sent me downstairs twice to get special papers for him, and had me seal them in envelopes and send them to Mr. Worden at the bank at once."

"Yes? Well, now I wonder if I could look at that desk, and examine the room that was broken into?"

So they went a solemn little procession into the library, a room literally lined with books.

"I wonder," said the lawyer after he had gone through the drawers and noted down the contents carefully, "whether there is any possibility that there might be a secret compartment in this desk? Do you know, Miss Thurston? Such a place does not usually manifest its presence for a casual glance like this."

"Oh, yes, it seems to me I remember father saying something long ago about a secret compartment but he wouldn't likely have left anything valuable there, would he? Or I should think he would have spoken of it. Tabor, did you ever hear about that? Did you know of a secret drawer?"

"Yes, Miss Eden, I'm sure there was. I remember he spoke to me about it once when he put some papers away in it. I'm not sure where it was but I think in behind some drawer."

"It's worth looking for, anyway," said Lorrimer. "Could it be possible that if there is one, that that Fane boy knew of it?"

"Oh, no, sir. I don't think he would be likely to," said Tabor. "He was not allowed in this room. I had my orders when he was about."

Then Janet spoke up.

"Don't ye be too sure!" she said heatedly. "Thet lad was a little rat, and there was no room too locked-up tae keep him oot. I found him in here once meself, and he was always fussin' around wi' locks an' ketches. If there was a secret drawer he'd find it!"

The lawyer looked at her sharply, and then walked over to the desk, tapping expertly in different parts of the desk, listening for hollow sounds.

"Here!" he said, "let's try this side, behind this first drawer. Pull it out will you, Tabor. Look! That drawer is not long enough for the whole depth of the desk. That's where it would be. Behind the end of the drawer perhaps. These compartments are very cleverly hidden. Have you a flashlight, Mike?"

"Yes sir, here!" and a fine clear light pierced the dark recess behind the drawer.

"Yes! Here!" said the lawyer. "Pull out the next drawer. The compartment must be behind both of them, or perhaps even three."

They pulled out the next two drawers, and at last came to the hidden spring that released the little high narrow door, and showed a generous space, with just a few scattering papers, none of special value, but all of them mussed and looking as if they had been hastily stuffed back for a hurried departure.

"Yes," said the lawyer thoughtfully. "And here is a thought, perhaps. This place is not in the careful order that seems to have been maintained throughout the rest of the desk, or the room. If we only could be sure of what was originally kept in this compartment we might be able to check up. Perhaps Mr. Worden may be able to give us some light on this when he gets back. I'm looking for him to be home tonight or perhaps sooner. I'll ask him at once. By the way, let me feel back into that compartment. I have a hunch that there is still something more in there. I didn't reach all the way to the bottom, did you, Tabor?"

"Why, yes sir, I thought I did. But there didn't seem to be anything down there. It was all smooth. It almost seemed like it had been varnished."

The lawyer was down on his knees again beside the desk, turning on the flashlight, and examining every inch of the way most carefully. Then his hand went down into the compartment again and searched around. He seemed to be lingering longer than was necessary just to make sure that there was nothing further there. It almost seemed as if he were struggling with something, and then he reached out one hand.

"Get me a screw driver," he said from under the desk.

Tabor gravely produced one and laid it in the reaching

hand, and the rest of them stood watching, wondering if he had found anything.

A moment more the lawyer worked away out of sight, and then drew back and brought forth a white box, just the length of the lower part of the compartment.

Then he rose, dusted off his hands and knees and sat down in front of the desk, the white box still in his hands.

"There!" he said triumphantly. "The box is covered with satin paper and feels like a smooth varnished surface. That's what fooled us. Could there possibly have been other such boxes in there?" He looked speculatively at Eden, but her eyes were full of wonder.

"I don't know," she said, shaking her head. "I don't remember daddy ever saying anything to me about it. Isn't there some writing on that box? It looks like it. Yes! See!"

The lawyer handed her the box and she turned it over and read.

For Eden. Your grandmother's pearls.

"Oh," she said. "And that is my mother's handwriting! She must have put this here a long time ago, and then perhaps it was forgotten."

"I mind," said Janet. "I mind weel when she writ thet, an' stowed it awa' in the wee bit drawer. But I'd thought it was tuk to the bank this lang agone! Is the pearls in the bit box yet?"

"Open it, will you, Miss Thurston? This is something

we must understand if we're to go searching for a possible thief."

Eden took the box in trembling hands, untied the white ribbon with which it was bound, and opened the box cautiously. The little audience watched her and the box breathlessly.

There was tissue paper folded neatly on the top, and then soft pink cotton, and more tissue paper. And at last she brought to light a double string of fine lovely pearls with a delicate clasp set with tiny diamonds.

"Oh!" said Eden with great awe upon her, and then suddenly the tears rolled down her face, and she could scarcely hold the box for trembling.

The young man leaned over and lifting her hands set them down on the desk, box and all, and Janet stepped up with a delicate handkerchief for Eden. In a moment more the young girl was smiling, in spite of her shaken emotions.

"I'm sorry I had to be such a baby," she said, half giggling, "but I'd just been reading some of my mother's letters, in this same handwriting, and it sort of broke me up. It was as if she had suddenly stepped into this room and given me these pearls, that must have been her mother's."

"They were, that," said Janet in an undertone. "She'd often spoken tae me of thim, an' once she showed thim tae me. They is rare pearls."

"It's quite understandable that you should be broken

up at finding them, Miss Thurston," said the lawyer. "I'm sorry I had to be the cause, but I'm glad for your sake that we found them. And now I don't want to bother you any longer than is necessary. If you'll just answer a few more questions we'll be done. Do you have any idea whether there were other things, more jewelry perhaps, in the drawer, and what they were? Would there be a list anywhere?"

"No," said Eden, "I wouldn't know. Perhaps Janet would, and of course the rest might be in the bank if there were other things."

"Yes," said Janet decidedly. "There were ither bits. A diamond bracelet, a lovely pin wi' rubies, an' some rings my leddy couldna wear ony mair since she got so thin they kept slipping off."

"You're sure of that?" asked the lawyer, and wrote down carefully every little item Janet could remember.

"Of course these may be in the bank. I'll check that over when Mr. Worden gets back. These things may have been the booty the young man was after. Do you know whether he knew about them? Could he have known of the secret drawer?"

"I couldna answer thet," said Janet reverting to her native tongue, "boot I dootna he mightov foond it. He was thet nosey. Leave him in a room, he'd get tae the bootum ov it in no time, an' things would be missin' and naeboody to accoont fer thim."

The lawyer looked up at Mike.

"Better get Hiley on the phone at once. Tell him to search the boy before he gets a chance to make away with anything. Search the old lady, too. He may have managed to hand something over to her. Here's the list. Tell him to make a *thorough* job of it, before he gets a chance to hide anything."

Eden listened in wonder.

"Did Mrs. Fane know of the existence of this jewelry?" asked Lorrimer.

"I don't know," said Eden, and he turned toward Janet.

"She might have known," said the old nurse, "although Mrs. Thurston was thet ill after she coom thet she seldom wore jewels. Still this Fane woman was thet much of a snoop thet somehoo she'd smell oot a thing an' pry around till she got a sight of it."

The lawyer nodded, showing that he was getting a pretty good idea of the Fane woman's character, and that of her boy also.

Eden was sitting by the desk with the fine old pearls dripping through her fingers, and the young man as he looked up could not but think how fitting such jewels were to go around a lovely throat like this young girl's.

He gave her an admiring glance and an apologetic smile.

"I hope you'll forgive me," he said, as he got up to take

his departure. "This really was necessary, and I shouldn't wonder if these pearls would help a lot in solving our problems. It's been nice to have you and your servants co-operate so well. I thank you."

"Oh, I'm glad if we helped any, and I'm grateful to you for finding the pearls," said Eden. "Perhaps I never would have known about them if this hadn't happened." She smiled into his eyes and he thought again how sweet her young eyes were.

"Well, I'm glad we could find them, and I'll find out from Mr. Worden at once how much he knows about the contents of this secret drawer. You know it just may be that this little box fitted so tightly into the bottom of the compartment that it escaped notice when the other things were taken out to go to the bank."

"Yes, of course," said Eden. "I wish I knew just what those things were, the rest of the valuables. Somehow I never took much interest in them while father was alive, and while I was in college. I just thought of them as some old family relics. But I guess I ought to go down to the bank and look the rest over. Should I do it right away?"

"Don't worry yourself now. If Mr. Worden hasn't returned yet I think I'll call him on the telephone. This is important, to get hold of the facts in the case before anything more can happen. If I get any more information I'll call you."

And so with a smile and a quick friendly clasp of the

hand he went away with Mike, and the household settled down to what they hoped was going to be peace and quietness.

Eden, standing at the window, watching the young lawyer walk down to the street, thought how very kind his voice was, and how respectfully dependable he seemed. Of course she didn't know him at all, but he seemed very nice, and she felt almost comfortable knowing that he was working to protect her interests.

Then Janet suddenly appeared on the scene.

"Coom ye oot an' heve yer loonch!" she commanded. "Ye hed niver a bite o' breakfast, an' verra little dinner the night before. We didna want ye to blow awa' wi' the first little breath of air."

"Oh," laughed Eden, "I didn't realize I hadn't had my breakfast. I was just so excited over what they were talking about. Isn't it awful that anybody tried to break in? Do you really think it was Ellery, Janet?"

"*Think!*" sniffed Janet. "I shud say there's na doobt aboot it. Little snake in the grass! I only wish he would be put where he couldna be botherin' the likes of ye ony mair. An' tae think of thet old sneak of a mither of his coomin' aroond sayin' she was goin' tae be yer chaperone! I sure would like tae see her bashed in the face the way Mike talks aboot doin' tae soom of the criminals."

Eden laughed a merry little ripple of a relieved sigh.

"What did she say, Janet? Did she talk to you?"

"Sure she did, an' I give her gude-an'-plenty back agin. Her wi' her sham tears, and her pretenses! But noo, coom ye out tae yer loonch. It's already settin' on the table, and the cook's fair frantic fer ye tae eat afore it gets cold. Coom noo an' I'll tell ye the rest whilst ye eat."

So Eden went to her lunch and heard the full tale of Lavira Fane's attempt to get into the house earlier in the day.

"And where do you think she went?" asked Eden, with still a bit of trouble on her brow. "Will she try to come back here tonight do you suppose and plead that she hasn't any place to sleep?"

"Na, she'll nae do thet. Mike said he would see thet she was safely hoosed."

"You—don't mean they've arrested her, do you, Janet?"

Janet gave a significant shrug to her shoulders.

"I canna say what they've doon wi' her, but I'm certain they'd niver let her run at large. They've places tae keep people they don't troost, ye ken. Perfec'ly respectable places, thet is, so tae speak, where they can keep an eye on her, an' ef there ever was a wumman needed an eye kep' on her, that Fane wumman's the one."

"Well, I shouldn't like to be the cause of her going to jail," said Eden with a troubled look.

"Why not, ef it's the only place ither folks is safe from her? But don't ye fret, dear cheeld. Mike's a discernin' mon ef there iver was wan, an' he can be troosted. An' besides all this, don't ye know the law has ways of findin' oot aboot folks? He's loikely, as he says, 'got a line' on her an' her crooked son, by this toime. An' ye see the matter is not in *yer* wee hands. It's the law has it the noo, an' ye can't do onythin' aboot it."

"But maybe I ought to telephone Mike to get them to promise to go back West where they came from and we won't say anything more about it. Wouldn't dad have wanted me to do that?"

"No, my leddy, he would niver want thet. He was allus fer joostice. A good business mon is allus fer joostice. And what right would ye tae send them crooked folk back tae steal frae ither folk? No, me leddy-gurril, ye've naethin' more tae do wi' it. Just rest yer heart, my lamb. An' ef ye wanttae talk wi' onyboody mair aboot the matter, go call yer feyther's friend, Mr. Worden. Belikes he knows all aboot it by now. Thet yoong lawyer-mon seemed mighty fine an' oop-comin'. He won't let the grass grow onder his feet. He'll get the right kind of advice, an' stan' by it. Jest ye rest."

So Eden ate her delicate lunch.

"A wee drap o' soup," to quote Janet's description of it, "a cooppla crispy bits o' toost, a bit o' the brist of chookie, a cool little slice o' pineopple ice, an' a shred o' angel cake. Don't that soond gude, my lamb?"

So Eden began to plan what she would tell Mr.

Worden when she called him up. Would he be at the bank now? And would that Mr. Lorrimer have talked with him yet? Somehow she felt that that young man would have a right, just view of things. He wouldn't be hard on people unless it were necessary, for the safety of others. She would wait a little before calling. Mr. Worden usually went out to lunch at one o'clock. Perhaps she would be able to catch him a little before one. A glance at her watch told her that there was a good half hour yet before she should try to speak with him.

Then her thoughts reverted to Caspar. How fortunate that he had changed his plans. If he had come this morning it would certainly have complicated things. Caspar would have been impatient. Would have wanted to know what was going on. Would have recalled all his unpleasant memories of the trouble Ellery had made her father, and would probably have advocated vengeance on the Fanes to the limit. She was glad he was not there. And as for keeping it quiet, keeping Caspar in ignorance of what was going on, that would hardly have been possible. Not with police and lawyers coming to question her, especially when he was wanting to see her without any hindrances to talking.

Then she began to look forward to the evening. Would the troubles be settled by that time? Or would some more policemen come barging in and want more interviews? She hoped not.

Up in her own quiet room again she found it impossible to rest. She tried to call Mr. Worden, but found he had not returned from his business trip, and would probably not be back until the next day some time. There had been a wire from him saying so, and there seemed to be nobody in the bank just then who could take his place.

She hung up the instrument and sat down perplexed. Oh, if her father were only here! How strange that all this should have to come just after he had left her! And he had tried so hard to make everything plain and straight in her little world for her, so there would be no perplexities.

Just then the telephone rang again and it was Mr. Lorrimer.

"Is that you, Miss Thurston? I'm Lorrimer, your lawyer. They told me you had just called for Mr. Worden so you know he has not yet returned, and that I have not been able to talk with him except briefly on the telephone, just as he was catching another train. But I did learn that he knew of the secret compartment in the desk, and that there had been articles left there for you, things of your mother's, meant for you. They were to be taken to the bank, after you had gone over them, and selected what you wished to keep here. He told me where to find the list of these things, and I have gone over it carefully. None of them are in our vault. Of course we cannot check definitely until Mr. Worden returns, but I have been comparing notes with the police headquarters, and so far they have discovered a handsome jeweled pin fastened in the coat of the young man, under the sleeve lining. He claims that his girl gave it to him when he went away to war. But so far we can find no record of his having been accepted in either the army or navy, and his mother's stories and his do not agree. We are holding them for further questioning, and to give them a more thorough searching. The woman is wearing a very handsome bracelet on her upper arm under a heavy sleeve. It might be the diamond bracelet but she claims it is rhinestones, and that *you* gave it to her."

"No!" said Eden. "I never gave her anything."

"I have not seen it yet," went on Lorrimer. "We will have it examined of course by an expert. Just how she would have gotten possession of it if the young man stole it during the night we have not yet figured out, but it might have been done. The list names some unmounted jewels, three emeralds, a ruby, and four sapphires, one a star sapphire. They seem to have been part of your grandmother's dowry. We have tried to find them in the bank, but they are not there. They are things that can be easily hidden in clothing. I suppose there will have to be a trial, I am not sure. But be assured we will do our best to keep you out of this whole matter, so please do not worry."

Eden turned away from the telephone at last with a degree of peace in her heart. At least she was assured that her affairs were in safe hands, and she could rest on that.

And after all what were jewels? She could live without them. She had been happy before she knew of their existence. Of course she would like to have articles of value that belonged to her family but why should she make herself miserable over their loss? She found herself exceedingly weary of the whole matter. So, telling Janet she was going to take a nap, she went up to her room, and curling up on her bed fell into a deep sleep.

CHAPTER FIVE

CASPAR CARVEL turned up before dinner after all. He had been used to barging into their house whenever he liked to a meal, when he was a lad, and he figured that times hadn't changed even if there had been a war.

Eden was in the big living room curled up in a chair, reading a book she had found among some mail that had come to her father since his death. She had unwrapped it, and sat down to find out what it was, when the door opened and Caspar walked in, just as if it were yesterday that he went away.

"Hello, Lovely!" he said, "my buddie took an earlier train than he had expected. He went up to New York to get his boat, and so that let me out. I figured perhaps you'd be here anyway, so I came. Think they'll have dinner enough for me too, or will I have to take you out to a restaurant?" He finished with his well-known grin, and suddenly it did seem only yesterday that he had gone away.

Eden looked up smiling, trying to put a note of gaiety into her voice, for surely that was what he, a returned soldier, deserved. He must have seen plenty of hardship and sorrow and horror; and was just trying to put it all out of his thoughts, as of course he ought to do if he was to return to living.

"Come in," she said brightly, holding out her hand to greet him. "Of course there'll be enough dinner for you. Did you ever get turned away hungry from this house?"

"No," he responded heartily, "I never did!" and he grasped the hand she held out, possessively. Before she knew what was going on he had drawn her close within his arms and kissed her most thoroughly on either cheek, her eyes, and then her mouth, as if he had all the rights in the world, as if she had been his always. He did not seem to notice that her lips did not respond to his in the kiss. He was the master of the situation and was entirely satisfied with the way he was conducting the scene.

But Eden gasped, and struggled back away from him.

"Caspar! Don't! Please don't!" and she turned her head away from his attempted repetition of the kiss.

"Why, what's the matter, Beautiful? Aren't you glad to see me? Don't tell me you don't like to be kissed. Every girl likes that. And I have a reputation for being good at it." His possessive hands reached out to draw her close again, but Eden in quick alarm backed off definitely from him and drew herself to her full height.

"I do *not* like it," she said decidedly.

"But—but *Baby*, don't be *stuffy! All* the girls kiss the army boys, and all the army boys kiss the girls. It's the custom, you know. It's a part of patriotism. Why, they all kissed up when we went away, and of course now we're back we kiss them, and *they like it.*"

"Oh," said Eden coldly, retiring from his near vicinity. "Was this supposed to be an army regulation? A sort of mass salute? Well, you see, I'm not like the rest. I do *not* like it. Won't you sit down and be yourself, Caspar? Where have you been and what have you been doing?"

"Oh, for gosh's sake, Eden, do I have to recite my exploits to you? Wait till next week and hear me over the radio. That'll be enough. And now suppose we talk about you. You certainly haven't wasted any time growing up. I doubt if I would have really known you if I had met you in New York, say. You're quite sophisticated, too. You're not a dowdy little kid the way you used to be. You're *gorgeous*. You really are more than pretty. I never dreamed you'd get to be so good-looking. Of course I missed you a lot when I first went away, but they kept us so darned busy out there I didn't have much time to think about you, and then in between we used to have a lotta fun. The girls everywhere we went had dances for us. I've learned to dance you know, and I'm pretty swell at it, they tell me.

You and I will have to try it the next time I come back. How long do you have to stay cooped up here before you can go out again and get around among was 'em? I'd like to take you up to New York and show you around. See life, you know."

Eden smiled distantly, "Thank you, but I've been to New York, you know, quite a good many times," she said. "I used to go up with father every time he had business up there, and we always had wonderful times together."

"Oh, yes, I suppose you did," said Caspar contemptuously. "Symphony concerts, and lectures and stuffy things like that. But *I* mean see *real life*. I'm crazy to take you to night clubs and shows."

"Oh," she reminded him with dignity, "night clubs are not at all my style. I wouldn't care for them."

"Oh, but you don't know. You've never been out and seen real life. You don't know what you're missing. Wait till I get you to a few places I know, you'll be crazy about it. Don't be stuffy, Eden."

"Thank you," said Eden in a really cold voice now, "I do not care for that kind of life, and I do not want to see it. I like *real* things."

"Aw, ye gods! If I ever saw such puritanical notions. Anybody would think you were an old woman in your dotage. Be your age and have a good time. I thought of course you'd get over those silly notions when you got away from your puritanical father."

"Well, I haven't, Caspar," she said with flashing eyes. "I'd rather not talk any more about it. I certainly don't think you have improved when you talk like that. You always *used* to be respectful to my father."

"Oh, sure, he was a good guy, and all that. But he's gone now and it can't hurt him any if you have a little good time."

"That isn't my idea of a good time," said Eden quietly. "Suppose you tell me some of your experiences abroad. What countries were you in? Italy? Oh, you saw the Forum, and all those wonderful buildings. I've always been fascinated by Rome. And were you in Switzerland at all? Tell me about it."

"Oh, that!" said the young man contemptuously. "Mountains of course, and wonderful sunsets, and castles, and all like that. But I'm not keen on scenery, and I was glad to get back to city life. I enjoyed Paris most."

He rattled off into a description of a few gay gatherings and told some jokes he thought were funny, that Eden didn't appreciate. She was glad when Tabor came and announced dinner and they could go out to the table.

Caspar was talking a lively stream of reminiscence as he drew back Eden's chair for her, and then sat down, but Eden waited quietly till he came to the end of a sentence and then she said shyly, "Caspar, you used to ask the blessing when we were children. Will you ask it now?"

Caspar grinned, looked at her as if she were joking, and then grew red.

"No, I don't believe I remember any of those little old prayers," he said. "You get away from all that sort of thing when you go to war, you know."

But Eden did not smile. She quietly bowed her head and said quite simply as she had been taught to do in childhood:

"Lord, we thank Thee for this food, and we ask Thy blessing upon us tonight, Amen." The two servants stood at their places for serving with bowed heads, just as Caspar remembered they did whenever he came over to dinner, only it was usually Mr. Thurston who asked the blessing in recent years. Nevertheless, there was something impressive in the whole little ceremony, something distinctly admirable and quaint in the young girl who had taken her place in life even as she had been trained to do. The annoyed young soldier bowed his head reluctantly. Maybe it wasn't so ridiculous as the world would think it was. It was rather sweet in a way, and Eden was awfully pretty, with all her quaintness. Besides she must have a mint of money. People with money could get away with oddities. He had never thought of money very much before. But getting back from war and seeing all this quiet elegance made him feel that it wouldn't be bad to have a part in a life like this. He must take care not to antagonize his old friend. And of course it would be easy to *train* Eden, and get her away from her religious fancies when he had her under his control. He had always been able to influence her, he flattered himself.

Then the excellent dinner was served, further strengthening his faith in money and its powers. Caspar roused himself to be agreeable, and fall in with her "prejudices" as he called them.

Janet from her humble position as servant was in and out, bringing dishes, and messages to Tabor from the cook; and Caspar chatted on, asking questions about their old school friends, exhibiting a wider knowledge of some of their moves than even were known by Eden, who had lived near them while he was away.

"Cassie Howard got married, and then got herself divorced, didn't she?"

"Oh," said Eden thoughtfully, "did she? I didn't know. I never knew Cassie very well, you know."

"Oh, well, you didn't lose much, I guess. You see her first husband was in my regiment, and he had all kinds of tales to tell me, including some pretty rotten facts about the fellow she married next. You know he was a bomber, and was killed in a crash. Nobody knows what Cassie will do next. She's pretty thick now with a married man. Rich, he is, too, and not much reputation."

"Oh," said Eden with a shiver. "What terrible things are happening!"

"Well," said Caspar with a careless shrug, "that's war for you. When you see people getting killed on every side you think, 'To heck with right living! Tomorrow we die! Why not have a good time while we're at it?' It really has that effect on you a lot."

Eden gave him a troubled searching look.

"I know people it has not affected in that way," she said shyly.

"Then they were softies, I'll bet!" said the young soldier.

"No," said Eden, "they weren't softies. One was a man with all kinds of wonderful citations to his credit. Another had completed a long list of missions, and wore a silver star and a medal for special bravery. He told me himself that the whole thing gave him a different view of life and he felt life was more serious than he had ever thought."

Caspar's lips went up in a sneer, and for a moment he forgot that he had planned to agree with her.

"Not *me*!" he said, shaking his head. "You'll find all that talk some of those would-be-heroes give you, is just a line they see is popular with some of their home folks, so they are working it for all they are worth. I say they are softies when they talk that way. I say live like a sport and die like a hero. That's all there is to it."

Eden looked at him aghast.

"Why Caspar! You talk like a heathen. Didn't you join

the church when I did? You believe in God and Christian standards, don't you?"

"Oh yes, I joined church. But it's all a lot of poppy-cock. Kid stuff, you know. Nobody believes that line today. We've wised up. Science has taught us a lot. We've worked out a better line of behavior today, more fitted to the times. We've left the days of self-sacrifice behind, and have come to the time when it's every man for himself, and the best man wins the race. How else would you think they would have got us fellows to go out and fight if it hadn't been for that? I tell you times have changed, Edie, and you'd better get wise to it or you'll be good and left behind. It's time for you to get busy and have some fun before you get old. You've got a good complexion and a pretty face, and if you'll just drop your traditions, put on some make-up and get into things, we could team up and have a great life. How about it, girl? I'm for it if you are!"

He had almost finished his dessert now, and was about to ask if he might have another piece of pie, as he would have done in the days that were gone. But Eden was not eating hers. She had scarcely taken a bite. She was watching her erstwhile playmate in consternation. And as he finished his extraordinary proposal she stiffened in a kind of fury.

"Stop!" she said. "Don't speak another word like that. If you feel that way you are no friend of mine. You are despising all our beliefs of the past. You are trampling on God! I am ashamed of you. God who has brought you through the war unscathed."

"Not on yer life He didn't," said Caspar with a sneer. "I brought myself through. What did God have to do with it? If I hadn't been courageous and gone out to kill, and not to be killed, if I hadn't studied out ways to find easy-street when I was sent on a mission, and let the other fellows take the raps, do you think I'd have been here today? How about all those others that got *killed?* What did God do for them?"

"*Stop!*" said Eden excitedly. "You shall not talk that way about God in this house. If my father were here he would put you out for that, and I will not hear another word. Go away! I don't want ever to see you again, not unless you find how terrible you are and go to God and apologize. Get down on your knees and tell God you are ashamed and sorry. I don't see how I can ever forget what you have said, or count you my friend. I think you are *awful!*"

Eden was very beautiful as she stood there in her righteous anger and flashed her lovely eyes at her former friend. And Caspar was suddenly realizing what a fool he had been to let her see what he felt so early in the game. He rose with a wistful look toward his empty pie plate, and realized that he must placate this angry girl or his plans for the evening would be all upset. So he put on a wheedling tone, the tone by which he always used to be able to coax her to do anything for him.

"Aw, Eden, forget it! I didn't mean all that stuff of course. I just want you to see you're getting hayseeds in your hair, and it isn't done today. Your father didn't realize he was making you an old woman before your time by feeding you such antediluvian ideas as he did. Of course a lot of people believed that way when he was young, but he was sick and getting old, and he didn't see how the modern successes were growing away from all those fool ideas. Of course those things are very becoming in a lady if she does not carry them too far. Eden darling, forget what I said. I love you, Eden, can't you see that? And I want you to be just perfect. Darling!" The young man came quickly near to her and letting his arm steal about her softly, put his clean-shaven cheek close to hers in a loving embrace, with intent to kiss her in a regular way that she would not forget.

They were standing in the hall doorway now, and Eden, startled, furious, gasping, struggled away from him, even as she brought her right hand about in a quick swing and dealt him a ringing slap across his amorous mouth, followed by another stinging blow across his eyes. Then turning she flew across the hall and up the stairs as if on wings, calling back from the head of the stairs to the young soldier below her who was bent in pain and struggling to overcome the effect of the blinding blows she had dealt him.

"Go away!" she called, "and *never* come back again!"

Then she went into her room, shut the door sharply and turned the key in the lock.

Both Janet and Tabor were in the offing, having heard it all of course, though discreetly in the background. Now Tabor came forward with the young man's cap and coat in his hands:

"You'd best be going!" he advised in his most severe and unfriendly tone, and helped Caspar on with his coat, handed him his hat, and opened the front door for him.

So Caspar Carvel staggered blindly down the steps, pausing a moment at the walk, with his hand over his eyes, to recover his poise and self-assurance, and then vanished down the street and around the corner.

Upstairs Eden in her quiet room threw herself on her bed weeping her heart out for an old friend whom she felt was utterly unworthy and had gone out of her life forever.

In an interval as her sobs subsided Eden heard Janet's gentle step, and then a soft tap on the door.

She was still a minute, and then as the tap was repeated she quieted her sobs and got back her voice:

"Yes?" she said. "Who is it?"

"It's juist old Janet, my leddy. I merely wanted to enquire ef you would want the perlice sent for again."

"The police?" said Eden, opening the door and presenting an astonished face. "Come in, Janet. What do you mean?"

"Wull," said Janet as Eden let her in, "I thought as ye had throwed out two young gentlemen, mebbe ye was expectin' a third yet, the night?"

Then suddenly Eden went off into a peal of laughter.

CHAPTER SIX

BUT TEARS and laughter did not entirely banish the trouble from Eden's thoughts. She kept going over and over what Caspar had said. Did he really mean all those terrible things? And how had she answered him? Was it right to send him away like that never to return?

But of course it was enough to raise her righteous wrath, just the way he had spoken of her father. Her wonderful father! Even if Mr. Thurston had been old-fashioned, which he wasn't in the least, Caspar had no right, just after death had taken her father away, to come into the home where he had always been welcomed and bring him into scorn before his own daughter. She was right to feel it was outrageous. She was right to rebuke him for that. But when he not only did that, but brought her father's God into contempt also, what could she do but strike? Send him away?

And now there came to her memory of other days.

Why! Caspar had been as earnest as any of the others in their young people's meeting which they all attended. He even made good speeches, and sometimes led in prayer. She always used to be so proud of him for he had a way with him when he was president of their society, and said so many good things, so fitting to the subject. Was it possible that he had so utterly changed? It almost seemed to her that he must have been drinking or he never would have talked like that, though the Caspar of old never drank. Had he learned to do that too, as well as to despise holy things?

Not that Eden herself had ever been particularly spiritual, but she had been regular in her church attendance, conforming always to the lines laid down by their church, and the requests of their nice old pastor, being most active in all the activities of the church. But now it suddenly occurred to her that there was something more than mere church activity required to meet a situation in which God Himself had been challenged, and somehow she felt she didn't have it. At least she didn't know how to answer one who talked as Caspar had done. Somehow she must find out what to say if anybody ever talked like that again in her presence. She just couldn't stand it. There must be an answer to such blasphemies, or her father, her good wise father, would never have believed. It wasn't thinkable that such triflers as Caspar could actually dare to flout the tenets of the Christian religion. Oh, she had of course heard of unbelief before, but she had always thought of unbelievers as low-down vicious people who had no culture or education.

So carefully her father had guarded her that she had been sent to schools that did not spend their time in breaking down respectable religious beliefs that had carried generations of good people along in a placid faith and trust. So now Eden was bewildered that her old playmate who had been brought up in what she had always thought was a respectable way had gone back on basic doctrines and beliefs. Somewhere she would have to find a way to answer this if he ever came back to discuss the matter with her—or if anybody else from such a war experience as Caspar had had should come her way. Probably her father knew ways to answer such things, and bring unbelievers to see the right, but she couldn't recall that he had ever given her proofs to store in her mind. Yet she was sure beyond the shadow of a doubt that her father had believed in God, and had gone to Heaven, trusting in the blood of Christ. She was sure he was expecting to go straight to God in Heaven, when he said good-by to her, and that her dear mother would be there also. She knew from her mother's letters that her father and mother had often talked these things over and agreed, and were expecting to be together for all eternity in the presence of God. That was enough for her. She believed it because they did. But that was not enough to help her tell other people about it. She had to know why wise Christian ministers and saints believed these things. It had never troubled her before. It was the accepted belief of her family, her church, her Christian friends.

But now a new group had come to her knowledge. Not just low-down heathen in far foreign lands, nor even gangsters who had never wanted to be good, but a group of whom Caspar, at present, was a representative—a group of young fellows, who, before they went to war, worked in churches, made speeches and prayed in meetings. And now that they had come back from facing death they had come to the belief that there was no God, no salvation, no right; that it was all a line of talk. She hadn't talked with others who said so, but Caspar seemed to take it for granted that she knew that all who were not softies felt that way about religion now, and she *had* to know. She had to know for sure how to prove that God was still God, and could save, and Heaven was real, or else she could not go on even for herself. And how else could she help others to find the way back to right living? How could she ever help Caspar, suppose he ever came back again after the way she had treated him? There must be a way to find out why reasonable people believed all that.

She decided finally that she would go to church next Sunday and see if anything was said that would bring her light on the problem. And if she couldn't get anything out of church she would go to the minister and ask him questions.

It was not that her own faith in God was shaken. She believed in her father's God too much to be troubled on her own account, but now that the question had been brought up she felt she must understand it. It was doubtless true that her father had talked about such things long ago, when she was very young, and had merely supposed that she had understood it, and so said nothing more. Just as a teacher would not be continually harping on the alphabet after one had learned to read.

So thinking it out Eden went back to the book she had been idly looking through, the book that had come to her father since his death, evidently ordered by him from the publisher.

And now she noticed for the first time the subject of this book, whose perusal Caspar's entrance had interrupted; it was religious. Ah, perhaps this was just what she was looking for. Perhaps this would give proofs and arguments that there was a God, arguments that she could use if she ever had to talk again with Caspar. Eagerly she began to read and was amazed at the simplicity of the wording, and the startling truths that were set down as facts.

For the first time in her life, although she had gone to Sunday School since she was a little child, and to church every Sunday—sometimes twice or three times a day—she began to take it in that God considered everyone a sinner. Of course she had heard about sinners, but she had never realized that people like her father classed in such a category. For the first time she took in the great thought that ever since Adam's sin, everybody was born with a dead spiritual nature. That all of Adam's children had inherited a tendency to sin, and that Satan was using that sinful tendency of mankind to turn men, even Christians, against the Son, Jesus Christ. And where he failed to turn them actually against Christ, he was engaged in trying to make it appear that *he* was doing Christ's work, or more subtle still, trying to make the world believe there was no devil and no sin.

Eden read on, fascinated, because the book was written most simply and originally, yet it touched on themes she had never before heard discussed, or if she had, she had never taken any notice of them. There was "original sin" that seemed to belong to everybody. She had never thought of herself as a sinner. She had always tried to do right, to please her father and mother, and do the things expected of her, yet here was this strange book saying "*All* have sinned and come short of the glory of God." Emphasizing it, as if this not only was meant for gangsters and low-down people, but as if it might have some kind of meaning for good right-living people. And another phrase, "Ye must be born again." But surely that did not mean church members! Strange! What was this doctrine, anyway? Why did her father send for this book? Or was it just sent to him to advertise it? Yet she couldn't lay it down, and kept on reading till little by little she began to wonder if all this could be true.

What was being "born again," anyway? There had been a Sunday School lesson long ago in her childhood about a man who came to Jesus and wanted to know how to be saved, and He had told him that he must be born again. But she had always supposed that that man had been a very wicked person, so wicked that Jesus saw he had just to begin all over again. And wasn't he wealthy, too? It seemed she remembered that about him. She had never thought of this advice as applying to good right-minded people. She couldn't help feeling a little outraged that anyone should think she herself—well, at least her father, anyway—needed to be born again. Perhaps this was some sort of heretical book that she ought not to bother with. Yet because it had been sent to her father she felt she must know more about it. Besides, the book itself was intriguing. It seemed to speak to her very soul, to make her suspect things in her heart that she did not know were there, that she had never dreamed were objectionable to God.

So she went on reading, until suddenly Janet knocked at the door.

"Are ye asleep, Miss Eden? I'm sorry to disturb ye, but a mon downstairs seems tae think he ought tae see ye richt away. It's that lawyer mon from the bank, and he says there's something important ye ought to know at oncet. Could ye coom doon juist a meenit? He sayed he wouldna keep ya lang."

"Why, of course, Janet. No, I wasn't asleep. I was just reading one of daddy's books."

Eden jumped up, her finger in the page where she had been reading, and hurried down the stairs.

The young man was standing in the hall, glancing at his watch.

"I hope I haven't disturbed you, Miss Thurston. Mr. Worden has telephoned again and he wanted me to get in touch with you and tell you what has been discovered so far."

"Oh, you haven't disturbed me," said Eden pleasantly. "I was only reading. Come into the living room and sit down. Of course I'm anxious to know if there are any new developments."

"Well, yes, there are," said the young man. "They've found some more jewels sewed quite neatly in the lining of the young man's coat. Also several concealed in the woman's hat, and even some jewelry fastened into her clothing. They were so cleverly concealed that they were not discovered at first, and so have just come to light. Of course the woman claims that you gave them to her, but in view of the fact you knew nothing about some of the other things she said you gave her, we felt you should see them at once. Also most of these things answer to the description of the articles in the bank list as from that secret compartment. Now, will you look at them? See, I have put them out here on the piano so they won't confuse us. Here's the diamond bracelet. Do you remember ever seeing it before?"

Eden shook her head.

"I'm not sure," she said. "I dimly remember sitting on my mother's lap and putting my hand on something on her wrist, and saying 'Pitty, pitty.' At least there is a story in the family to that effect, and I've heard it so much that it may be I just imagine I remember it. And it might have been the bracelet. I don't know."

"It *were!*" announced Janet arriving quietly in the room. "Ye was settin' on yer mither's lap, an' playin' wi' her bracelet, an' they was one o' the verra first words ye spoke. 'Pitty, pitty.' An' yer feyther was that pleased! An' thet's the verra bracelet. I mind it well."

So they went down the line of jewels. Some Eden vaguely remembered having seen before, others she knew nothing about, but all of them were familiar to Janet who had often helped Eden's mother put her treasures away carefully.

"Well, that's about the crop so far. All single jewels in the list are found, except a few rubies, and they may turn up in the possession of the two crooks. We are going to search them again carefully. But they have enough on them already to definitely put them in jail. In fact it will be necessary, for we have checked on their movements out West, and find that the boy had once before escaped from confinement there, where he was being held for trial for forgery and complicity in robbery. I'm afraid they are really hardened criminals."

Eden shivered a little and looked distressed.

"Oh, why do people want to be like that?" she said. "I never did like them, nor enjoy having them around, but why do you suppose they *choose* to be that way? Were they born so?"

"Well, yes, I suppose they were. That is, they were born with a sinful nature," said the young man thoughtfully, "the same kind of nature we all have of course, only some of us choose to sin in more respectable ways," he smiled disarmingly. "People don't have to be crooks unless they choose to be. We don't have to follow every evil thought that comes to us. They know the things they plan to do are wrong, but they *want* to do them. They take a chance that they can get away with it. This time they didn't get away with it."

Eden looked at the young man with interested eyes.

"That sounds a little like something I was reading just now in this book that was sent to my father."

"Why, yes, I suppose it must. I was just noticing the book in your hand. I've heard of it and often wanted to read it. As soon as I get settled into real living since army days I want to do some reading. Just now I haven't time, but from what I've heard about that you'll find it a great book. Don't you?"

"Oh, I haven't read but a few pages yet. I was just looking it over and it seemed quite new and strange to me. If it hadn't been sent to father's address I wouldn't have known whether to trust it or not, but I rather think he had ordered it himself. You see I was really wishing for a different kind of book when I first opened it, and then I got interested. But perhaps you would know of a book I could get to answer someone who doesn't believe in God any more. Is there such a book? Surely there must be somewhere. There are so many good people and so many fine churches."

The young man looked at her with quick surprise and a gentle pity.

"Oh, yes, there are books, plenty of them. Of course the Bible is the crowning book. But did your friend ever believe in God?"

Eden cast him a puzzled look.

"Why, I suppose he did," she said as if she were trying to think back to the past. "He joined the church at the same time I did. Aren't all church members supposed to believe in God?"

"Yes," said the young man sorrowfully, "*supposed* to believe. But they do not always do it. Sometimes they do not even know what it is to believe. They are just accepting a general belief that is popular among their friends. Jesus Christ means nothing at all to them. I know a lot of ex-Christians like that myself, some of them were never taught, or had never been introduced to the Lord Jesus. Of course that is the best proof that there is a God, if you *know* Jesus Christ. When one really knows Him he can never doubt again. Do you mind my asking if you know Him?"

"Oh," said Eden with distinct trouble in her eyes, "I don't know. I—supposed I was all right. I never really heard anybody put it that way. I didn't know it was possible to know the Lord till you got to Heaven. How could you know Him on this earth?"

And it was just at that moment that Tabor, who had answered a ring on the telephone, came in to say:

"Beg pardon, sir, but there is a call for you on the telephone. They said it was urgent. The speaker was about to catch a train."

"Oh, will you excuse me a moment, Miss Thurston?" said the young man, and hurried to the telephone in the hall.

Eden stood pondering what he had been saying, amazed that a young man of his age and standing should be so earnestly interested in religious matters. Perhaps he would be able to help her perplexities. Then he hung up the receiver and returned to her:

"I am sorry to interrupt our conversation just at this

point, but this message was urgent and I must go at once. May I talk to you again sometime about it?"

"Oh, yes," said Eden. "I want to know very much what you were going to say."

"Very well then, I'll be seeing you later. Soon, I hope. Good night!" and he was gone, leaving a great wonder in her heart and an intense admiration for a man who could speak in this assured way of the things of God. Then she went back to her book, and somehow it became more alive and real than before she had had that talk with the lawyer.

CHAPTER SEVEN

"JANET, WHAT d'ye think? Will that impertinent boy Cappie come back again, or are we rid of him fer good?"

"Weel, Tabor, I dootna he'll coom back soom toime, if not richt at oncet. But he was pretty weel astonished at the way my leddy treated him. I canna blame her, fer he was juist awfoo' talkin' thet wy about the master an' the master not dead a week yet, an' him allus sae kind tae the lad 'fore he wint awa' tae war. He showed no tender feelin's at all, either fer my leddy, ner him. An' as fer his Maker, it cowes a', hoo he could lift oop his head an' speak like thet. Do ye nae think he'd been drinkin', Tabor?"

"No," said the old serving man, "he gave no sign of drink. That is, I didn't smell it on his breath when I he'ped him on with his topcoat. Besides, it's not likely he would come here with that on his breath, knowin' how the family feels about young men drinkin'!"

"Weel, he kens juist the same hoo they feel aboot God,

an' yet he spoke oot like a regular heathen."

"Yes, I know, but that's the way a lot o' the kids are talkin' now. They learn that in school. They think it's smart. My niece's boy was talkin' some like thet the last week end when I was home, an' he's only a high-school kid. He said the teachers okayed talk like that. That is he said *some* of the teachers talked that way right in class. Though when I narrowed it down, he owned up there was only *one* teacher of the whole lot talked that way, and laughed at the Bible."

"Dear me!" said Janet, "whut air we coomin' tae? Nae wunner the master dreaded tae leave his wee bairnie alane in a worl' like this. I hoop thet Carver lad stays in the army. We dinna want him around here, mooch as I useta loike him when he was a slip of a lad. But he niver was a match fer oor young leddy. I'm certain bein' in the war hasna improved him ony, though I will say there are some as is quite fine an' different since they coom back."

"Yes," agreed Tabor, "I reckon it has improved some, made 'em more thoughtful-like an' considerate. That young lawyer seems a nice sort. Where does he come in? I don't seem to remember him around here before the war."

"Nae. He wasna. Marnie the oopstairs maid says she heard he's the soon o' an ole friend o' Meester Woorden. He was stoody'in' law afore he enlisted, an' whin he goot back Meester Woorden sint fer him, an' took him intae the firm."

"So! That's the way of it! Well, he's some man. I'd like to see our young lady get a man like that."

"Weel, he do seem loike a braw laddie. But it'll be the way the Lord plons," said Janet with a sigh, as if she were a little dubious how that would turn out, and would fain get her own hands on the planning.

But over in her own room Eden was deep in her book, and as she read farther and farther she kept recalling the words of the young lawyer, and was more and more impressed by what he had said, wishing he were here now so that she might ask him a few questions. Strange it was how a young stranger had been able to impress thoughts upon her just when she was exercised about these things. How very different he was from Caspar. It somehow seemed more and more as if Caspar hadn't really grown up yet, or perhaps she should say he had grown undesirably.

And a few blocks away in a small pleasant room on the tenth floor of a modest apartment house young Lorrimer was preparing for rest after a long hard day. He was reading his Bible, jotting down a few notes in his small diary, thinking of the sweet girl who had asked him such unexpected questions, looking up a book he thought she might like to see, and at last kneeling to pray for her, his heart more deeply stirred for her than perhaps it had ever been stirred for any other person. And that was strange, because he scarcely knew her at all, and from what he knew of her station in life, and her fortune, she wasn't at all a girl on whom he would have felt he could fasten his interest.

He puzzled over that idea for a moment as he prayed, and then he said to himself, "Of course not, but that need not hinder my interest in her salvation, and I don't believe she quite knows what it is all about. Teach her, dear Father!"

Those were strange days that followed. Eden spent much time in her room reading the wonderful book that she had found, growing more and more filled with interest in it.

But often she was interrupted by the coming of old friends. Three sweet old ladies who used to know her mother, and who, though they had not kept much in touch with Eden since she had grown up, felt a duty toward her for old friendship's sake. They all talked of the old days, and fairly purred over her state of loneliness, and wished she would come and see them. It was all a little hard to bear.

Then there were a few older men, intimate friends of her father's. These she knew better because they had been often at the house when he was living and she liked them and was glad to see them. But through it all she was thinking now and then of the book she had been reading, and wondering if these people knew the doctrines the book had talked about so simply, as if everybody knew.

There were other callers in the afternoon, girls she knew well, some coming shyly in, some boisterously, because they hated the idea of death, and didn't exactly know what to say, especially because Eden had always been so devoted to her father, and they felt she must be now in the depths of despair without him. They spoke of having seen Caspar, wondered if he were still in town, or had gone back to New York. Some of them had hoped perhaps Eden would be out, and so the day of calling on her might be postponed. Eden was such a reserved girl, and seldom reacted as they would have done. They were sure she would not burst into tears and weep hysterically, or would never be giddy nor gay. But they felt uncomfortable. Of course they were sorry for her, but they did not feel they knew her well enough to be sure how she would meet them. Of course they were relieved when they found she was just her old sweet self, with no sign that she had met with a hopeless disaster, no mark of shock on her lovely face.

A few of her old boy friends came in the evening, in groups of two or three. They made a good deal of noise and rollicked quite a little to cover up their embarrassment, but Eden understood. They had been good friends of her father too. Some of them had been in the bank. She knew that they mourned for her father who had always been so kind to them, and she was smiling and pleasant with them, trying to act as she knew her father would wish her to do, and make them feel comfortable. She appreciated their coming, and knew it had been hard for them.

Then there were two or three of the older fellows from the bank who came, singly; most of them had something pleasant to tell her about what her father had done for them, some pleasant remembrance of him while they had been working under him.

Each time when it was over and they were gone, Eden had a lovely warm feeling that she had been with her father for a little while. It was so beautiful to hear them praise him, and show that they so fully realized his worth. It spread a healing balm over the sore wounds that her former friend Caspar had so thoughtlessly caused.

It was four days later that Mr. Worden, her father's confidant and friend, returned. He came at once to see her. After she had had a talk with him she felt greatly strengthened to go on in the way that her father had planned for her, and not at all apprehensive concerning the Fanes. Mr. Worden assured her he would look after them. Their trial was to come off in a few days now and he personally would talk with them both and see if he couldn't knock some sense into them.

It was while they were talking together, however, and she was just feeling so happy and comforted that the telephone rang and Mr. Worden was wanted at once. It was young Lorrimer talking, and though he tried to make his words most guarded, Eden, who had followed to the hall to give a message to Janet, could not help hearing a little, and so she stood with wide-open eyes, and a frightened expression on her face, her hands clasped over her heart.

"Oh," she said as Mr. Worden hung up the receiver and turned toward her, "something more has happened at the police station, hasn't it? I heard the word 'escape.' Tell me, please, what it is. You needn't be afraid. I don't get frightened, you know. But I like to understand thoroughly and then I won't make so many mistakes."

Her old friend smiled.

"I know, Eden. You wouldn't be your father's own daughter if you weren't like that of course. But this is nothing that need worry you anyway. It only concerns the police. It is entirely out of your hands."

"But who has escaped?" insisted Eden. "Ellery or his mother?"

"Well, both of them," admitted the man, "and they haven't quite figured out how it happened. They thought they had them safely guarded. But they'll soon be caught of course, and then we'll see that there are no more pranks played on the law."

Then the telephone rang again and this time it was Mike.

"Miss Eden, could I speak with Tabor a moment? Somebody seems to be using the kitchen telephone and this is urgent."

Tabor was on the spot at once.

"Tabor speaking, Mike. What? You don't say. Right-o, Mike, I'll check on the cellar, and the garage and the outside shed. Yes, there might have been some old coats and other things that were used by the gardener. Do you think they would dare come here again?"

"Shure. They'd think that was the last place we would look for them. Where else could they go in a hurry? No hideouts around here that aren't watched. That old lady is clever. She got around her keeper by pretending to be very sick. She asked to have her son sent for. Thought she was dying. Two guards brought the guy over, and she had another bad spell with her heart, almost died. Manda, our guard-woman, went for water quick, and when she got back they were gone. How they managed to get out is a mystery. They musta had this all planned before they began this show. Better check on your place right away. Put Janet wise too. And take it easy; they're smooth. They aren't new at this job. Better keep yer gun handy, but watch out how you use it. I'm sending two of my men over. They are on their way now. So long!"

Tabor did not wait to convey the intelligence. He vanished toward the kitchen. But Eden and her caller had heard enough to understand.

"Oh!" said Eden. "How terribly daddy would have felt if he had known we were to have a thing like this to go through!"

"Well, it's a mercy he didn't know. It would have distressed him of course, but we'll take care of you and your interests, child!"

"Of course! I know," said Eden smiling. "Only it seems so awful that two people we have known, no matter how disagreeable we thought them, should turn out to do things like this. Do you know, Uncle Worden, I never realized what sin was before, nor how much of it there could be all about us when we didn't see it ourselves."

"Yes, that is certainly true," said the man thoughtfully. "But you, kitten, ought not to have to think about sin. It will never touch you. You are not a sinner."

"Oh, but I *am,* Uncle Worden, and I've just found it out!" exclaimed Eden. "I found a book of daddy's, one he had just sent for, and I got to reading it. I think it is a theological book. Father was interested in such things, you know, and I've been very much interested in it myself. I find that the Bible says that we have all sinned and come short of the glory of God, and that nobody is able, in themselves, to please a just and righteous God. That Jesus Christ was the only one who never sinned. Of course in a way I knew that from Sunday School when I was a child, but I never realized it before. But the thing I can't understand is why people when they get old enough to understand should deliberately *choose* to be sinners instead of wanting to follow God, and be saved. Why, for instance, should Mrs. Fane start out to do what she must know is wrong, instead of teaching her boy to do right and doing right herself?"

"Well," said Mr. Worden, somewhat perplexed and very much embarrassed over her questions, "I don't know that I can answer that. Your father was always one who could study up deep problems like that and find the answers, but I always had to be content with just following out the line the church has marked out for us. That seemed easiest and best. But maybe this Mrs. Fane did this because she loved her son and wanted to save him. Or maybe he and she both wanted things they couldn't afford to buy and so they took the dishonest way to get them. That must be the explanation. However, don't you think maybe we ought to call up and see if there is anything more we can do to help find these people? We certainly don't want them hiding around this house all night. I wouldn't think of allowing you to stay here under any such circumstances. There! There goes the phone again. Perhaps that's my man Lorrimer again. Shall I answer?"

It was Lorrimer. He had been to police headquarters and had a bit of news. It seemed that Ellery Fane had somehow possessed himself of a knife brought with his dinner. It was dull, and not very effectual as a weapon, but he had managed to pry up a stone from the corner of his cell, and worked away carefully and cautiously until it had assumed alarming sharpness. That wasn't the first knife that Ellery had practiced the same act upon, and he had developed some skill in the art. Ellery was still missing and so was the knife, but one of the guards left behind unconscious on the floor in front of the empty cell had a deep slash scientifically placed which testified to the ugliness of the knife, and now that the guard was being brought back to consciousness he would more than likely be able to add details to the story of the escape. But in the meantime, just before the incident took place, the prison authorities had discovered another jewel sewn cleverly into the lining of the prisoner's coat, which had, of course, been taken from him. Naturally the young man had fled without his coat, and the jewel was still in the possession of the prison authorities. But the peculiar thing about it was that this jewel was not one listed among the Thurston lists. It seemed to be a rare diamond, probably guarded carefully, and possibly stolen from some other person, unless Mr. Worden could remember, or find some record of such a stone.

Eden as she listened began to feel that she was living in a wicked fairy tale. And then Mr. Worden came in with troubled face.

"Tabor has been hurt," he said and his voice was much troubled, for he had known Tabor for many years and knew how they all regarded him. "They are bringing him in. They found him lying unconscious in front of the tool house with a knife in his back. Eden, can you telephone for the doctor quickly while I bring a mattress down for him to be laid on? I'm afraid this is serious."

Eden flew to the telephone and fortunately got the doctor, who promised to come at once.

Eden found she was trembling as she went back to the dining room where they had put Tabor down. He was lying on his side on the mattress, and the knife, the crude prison knife, was still sticking in his back, a stream of blood making a crimson stream down his immaculate white linen coat.

"That's a prison dinner knife," said Mike, who had helped carry Tabor in. "That settles it. He must have been hidden in the tool house."

Eden's eyes were wide with horror. To think that all this could happen in their quiet home, and just after her father had gone! She felt unnerved. But quick as a flash she saw something she could do that took her mind off herself and her fright. She slipped down on the floor beside the mattress where Tabor lay and took his still hand in hers, just quietly, and was there when a moment later the doctor arrived and knelt to feel the pulse, and listen to the heart.

While this was going on Janet wasn't missed by any of them at first, till the doctor asked, "Where is Janet? Tell her I need her," and then they looked around and couldn't find Janet, who had always been on hand in any special crisis.

"Where did she go?" they asked, and Eden answered quickly, "Oh, I think she went out the back door. She would think she could find the Fanes. Janet was always like that."

It was Mike who slipped out the back door at once and gave a command to look her up, and then was back in the house again doing everything he could find to do devotedly.

Meantime Janet had gone out to the little conservatory behind the garage, for that was where some old garments hung that the gardener had been told he might give to a poor family who needed them. It was only a few days ago they were put there, and Janet remembered it, so armed with her flashlight Janet went that way. If the Fanes had come back to the house to hide, these little outbuildings would likely be where they would seek shelter, so reasoned Janet. And though she sighted several policemen near the house, she did not tell them of her suspicions, but marched boldly around the end of the garage and stepping quietly on the grass to drown the sound of her footsteps, she arrived in the doorway and silently turned on her flashlight from the enveloping shelter of her ever-present apron, and plunged it into the darkness of the little greenhouse, centering its light full on the hook where she had hung the garments. Her first object was to find out if they were still there or had been used as a disguise. Janet had a very good mind for reasoning, helped out by the many detective stories she had read in her leisure hours.

Janet did not yet know what had happened to Tabor or unquestionably she would have been back in the house helping to bring Tabor back to consciousness. But not knowing, she was here, engineering another dramatic scene for herself.

So she stood in the doorway, looking into the familiar little glassed-in room. And at first sight as she let the tiny pencil of light focus on the hook by the opposite door, the garments appeared to be hanging there just as she had left them a few days ago. She was about to turn away and try some other possible hideout, when it seemed to her in the wavering light that she saw or heard a slight movement over by those shadowy garments.

Janet was a courageous woman, and afraid of nothing, even the uncanny, but the idea of movement over in that corner sent a thrill up her sturdy old backbone, and her ever-alert mind leaped to the thought of what she could do all by herself, if it should prove that one of the Fanes was hiding there. She should have brought a policeman with her of course, but stuff and nonsense! He would only have laughed at her notions, and no real policeman would stand for a woman's idea of course, so she swiftly searched her mind for a way to catch whoever was there, if they were there, before they could get away. If anyone *was* there and should get away she would never hear the last of it from Mike for not telling him what she was going to do. But of course she must make sure, so she turned the flashlight full upon the hanging garments which even now showed a slight movement, as if someone or something were alive inside the clothes. Then the bright pencil of light played full upon the place, and there she saw as plain as day, a pair of feet, peeping out from a fold in the long old coat. It took only an instant to recognize a crouching figure, flattened behind those worn old garments, a bony hand clutching the coat across. The rest of the figure was hidden behind the dark green skirt that hung behind the coat. That would be Lavira Fane. Janet was sure of it at once. But how to catch her, that was the question, and there was no time to waste.

Down beside Janet's feet lay a coil of hose, already attached, and at her right hand was the small iron wheel that controlled the water supply. Could she do it? She had used it before at times when the gardener had been sick or away, and had asked her to water some special plants. But this, this was something different. She knew she was being watched by a desperate woman, and there was no time to spare.

But Janet was not one to hesitate when she had a job to do, she did it. Quick as a flash she stooped and silently caught up the nozzle of the hose, even while her other hand sought the wheel and gave it a twirl. With relief she heard the quick rush of water, and gave her swift attention to the flashlight, directing its rays straight at a pair of desperate eyes now peering out, relieved to see the swift stream plunge straight toward its goal. She turned the full force of water toward the gasping prisoner as the woman flung the disguising clothes aside and tried to get away. But Janet had the water turned on in full force now, and it knocked the trapped woman flat to the ground, as she groveled and struggled to get her breath and get away from that terrific force.

But now suddenly a great light burst over the place. Someone, perhaps a policeman, had heard the rushing water, and turned on the searchlight from the back porch. Then Janet's achievement was revealed, and two policemen came rushing to her assistance. They lifted the dripping Lavira to her feet, making her fast with handcuffs as they did so, and now she was screaming anathemas to the men, and declaring that they had no right to touch her, that she was a relative of the family and sent out there to get some garments that were to be given away.

"Anything around here we can put over her to carry her away, Janet?" one of the men asked Janet, wondering how they were to get this dripping woman back to jail.

"There's an old robe from the master's car back of you in the garage," said Janet crisply. "I'll get it."

She was back in a moment with a heavy old blanket, and they wrapped Lavira in it, and compelled her to the police car.

"Get you back to the house, Jan," called one of the policemen, as they propelled the reluctant prisoner toward the street where their car waited. "We'll look after this party. You done your work well, an' now you'll be needed in the house. Old Tabor was pretty bad hurt."

"Tabor! Not *Tabor*?" ejaculated Janet aghast, and sped with all her might back to the house.

Chapter Eight

As the result of the doctor's examination of Tabor it was found that he had been struck on the head and suffered a concussion in addition to the stab from the knife.

At last he had been restored to consciousness, and was resting quietly, watched over by the doctor and a hastily summoned nurse. Janet, after a quick consultation with Eden, and afterward with the cook and the chambermaid, hastily transformed the servants' dining room into a comfortable hospital bedroom. Willing skillful hands helped, the table and most of the chairs vanished as if by magic, a comfortable iron bed from an upstairs servant's bedroom was brought down, and in no time Tabor was tenderly transferred to the other bed, where he promptly fell asleep.

"Bless his heart, he'll sleep comfortable now," meditated Janet, speaking half to Eden, half to the cook who stood near brushing the tears away. "He wouldna have been happy in the big dining room. He would juist have got richt oop so soon as he kenned whar he was an' whisked awa' tae his ain room. Thet's Tabor. He would niver presoom. But here, he'd feel at hame, an' not thenk he was presoomin' or puttin's aebody oot. He'll be mair tae hame here."

Eden smiled.

"Yes, that's right, Janet. But he'll have to be watched even here, or we'll find him getting up and trying to serve dinner. There never was anybody like Tabor."

"Yes, that's right!" agreed the staff of servants, the doctor included.

A little later the house began to settle down to quietness. Then the telephone rang, and Mike informed Eden who answered it, that Lavira Fane was safely secure where there could be no further menace from her, and that a posse of men were out after her son, following every clue possible, but as yet they had found no trace of him.

Then young Lorrimer arrived in company with Mr. Worden, who said he had arranged with Lorrimer to stay in the house all night and keep him informed if there was any change in Tabor's condition, as he himself had to be with his wife who was ill and needed him, and he was worried not to have a responsible person at hand whom Eden could call upon in necessity.

"Oh, that won't be necessary," protested Eden. "It's awfully nice of you to offer, but I'm not at all afraid."

"No, of course you're not afraid," said the young lawyer, "but I want to stay. I shall feel easier in my mind if I can be at hand for possible service, even if you don't think you need me. And I won't be any trouble at all. I'll just drop down on that leather couch in the library, or anywhere else you suggest. I'm used to sleeping in a chair if occasion demands, so don't worry about me."

"Oh, that is nice of you, and I'm very glad to have you here," said Eden with a sudden welcoming smile that left no question.

It was while they were still sitting in the living room talking with Mr. Worden that Janet arrived with a goodly tray. Crackers and cookies, and even a few sandwiches, and tea. For in any stress of circumstances Janet considered tea a panacea for all ills, and couldn't bear to let an occasion go by without it.

While they talked there came a message from Mike. They thought they had a clue that led to the woods north of the town. There were woods all about the town of Glencarroll, so it was quite a proposition to hunt a fugitive in an area like that. Mike said they were getting bloodhounds, using some of the young man's clothes that had been in possession of the police department. They felt reasonably sure by this method they might find him. Unless of course he had been able to get away on a train, or hitchhike a ride. Although the highways were being watched at every cross road, and cars stopped and searched.

Eden caught her breath.

"Oh, this all seems so dreadful. How father would have hated to have things like this happen."

"Yes," said her father's friend, "I certainly wish it could have been prevented, or at least that we could have kept the knowledge of it from you."

"Oh, but you couldn't!" laughed Eden. "It began with me. Ellery Fane walked into the library where I was going through some letters father had told me to read, and began to say that he and his mother were coming to take care of me, and that he would help me go through all the papers of the estate, and get better investments! He said he was a financial expert!"

"The insufferable egotist. It sounds like some of the stuff he got off when he was a mere boy in the bank, carrying on his forgery schemes. Well, child, I guess we are fortunate that this has all come out in the open now, instead of having it smolder along out of sight. The whole trouble is that Ellery Fane did manage to get a good deal of information about your father's estate while he was with us, and he has never forgotten that there might be a rich mine for himself if he could only manage to get an entrance here. Well, I'm sorry, but I do hope the fellow will be caught, and soon. Now I must go, but I'll be over early in the morning, Eden, and Lorrimer will let me know sooner than that if anything more happens meanwhile."

When Mr. Worden and the policemen were gone, and while Janet was fixing a comfortable couch with blankets and pillows for the lawyer to sleep on, Eden lingered for a moment to speak to him.

"You know we have plenty of comfortable sleeping rooms upstairs where you could rest better than in the library," she said, with a troubled look. "It doesn't seem right for you to have to sleep on the couch when you are so kind as to stay here."

"Oh, no," he said, "I really prefer to be down here tonight. I want to see if anything more goes on, and also I want to check up on Tabor every little while. I've talked with the doctor and the nurse, and I want to make sure that there are no mistakes made."

"You are very kind," said Eden. "I do appreciate what you are doing tonight. And also I want very much to ask you a question about something you said the other day. You said it was possible to know the Lord Jesus Christ, now while we are living on this earth. Isn't that what you said?"

"Yes, I did," said the young man with a sudden eager light in his eyes. "Are you interested in that? I'm so glad. I've been praying that you would be."

"You *have?*" exclaimed Eden eagerly. "Well, I felt as if somehow somebody was helping me, and it must have been your prayers. Thank you. But now, would you please tell me how I can get to know Christ? I've been to church all my life, and Sunday School, but I can't remember ever to have heard that question discussed. Perhaps it was my fault. Maybe I just wasn't listening, or perhaps I was thinking of something else, and missed what was said, but I really can't recall anybody telling me I could know Christ. Maybe my father just took it for granted I understood, for I'm sure he must have known Him."

"I'm sure he did," said the young man solemnly with a lovely smile in his eyes, "from all I've heard about him, and I'm sure that he is happy to be with Him now today. I'll be glad to tell you about it."

"Will it take long?" asked Eden anxiously, "because I don't want to keep you up late tonight and I can wait until some more convenient time."

"No," said the young man, "it needn't take long, and there is no time like the present. Come sit down here by the fire and I'll try to make it brief and clear."

Eden dropped into a low chair covered with faded blue velvet, and the firelight played over her lovely hair spinning some of it into threads of gold, and touching the long dark lashes on her soft cheeks. In her simple dark blue dress that hung in graceful lines about her, she seemed just a lovely child, yet there was in her face a mature eagerness that spurred the young man to do his best to make plain the wonderful truths of eternity for her.

He sat down on the other side of the fire where he

could watch her, and with a quiet prayer that the Holy Spirit would guide him he began.

"To begin with," he said in a quiet voice, "I think you told me that you believed in Christ. Does that mean that you accepted Him as your own personal Saviour?"

Eden looked up shyly, perplexedly.

"I don't know," she said. "Does it? This book I have been reading, and perhaps only half understanding, had made me feel that I am a terrible sinner, and I never thought I was before. I thought if I just kept the Commandments, and lived as right a life as I knew how that I was pleasing to Him, and would of course belong in Heaven. But this book speaks as if everybody was a sinner, as if there were nothing pleasing to God in anybody, and it talks about Adam's sin. I've always heard about Adam's sin but it never seemed to me it had anything to do with me, and now it seems to have. I am afraid I just don't understand it at all. I am terribly confused."

"Yes? But it is very simple after all. When God made Adam and Eve and put them in a perfect surrounding He gave them only one commandment or law: they must not eat of the tree in the midst of the garden. It was their testing, to show whether they would be willing to obey God, and choose His way. He told them if they did not obey they would bring death into the world on themselves and all their children. And that first man and woman broke God's law, and brought upon themselves and their children the tendency to sin, so that everyone born of Adam entered the world with a sinful nature, a nature that *wanted* to please *itself* rather than God. That was how death came into the world through Adam.

"But God loved the world, and so He made a way to be saved. He Himself, in the person of His Son Jesus Christ, came down to earth, and took a human body, and though He had no sin Himself, He took on Himself the sin of the whole world, that anyone who would believe on Him and accept what He had done for them might be saved, and be free from sin before the just God, who must keep His word, for He had said: 'The soul that sinneth it shall die.' So He took the death penalty for all who would believe, and thus accept Him as Saviour. And then God raised Him from the dead as proof that He was satisfied with the atonement Christ's blood had made. God reckons that all who believe have died to sin and self with Christ when He died on the cross, and they may fully share life in His resurrection, even now in these bodies. The condition to enjoying the fulness of His life and power is that we are willing to reckon ourselves dead with Christ, saying with Paul, 'I am crucified with Christ; nevertheless I live; yet not I, but Christ liveth in me: and the life which I now live in the flesh I live by the faith of the Son of God, who loved me, and gave Himself for me.' In that way, although we still have that sinful Adam nature which continually wants to do evil, we have also a stronger nature that is Christ's own. As we yield to that His Holy Spirit makes us hate sin, and gives us the power to please Christ."

He looked into the sweet earnest eyes of the girl as she eagerly drank in his words, and the voice of his heart became a prayer, as he went on to speak.

"That is the story very briefly, and perhaps rather crudely told, but believe me it is true. When we have more time perhaps you will let me tell you how I came to experience these truths in my own life, and to *know* that they are true, as little by little I went on to study God's Word, and yield myself to Him in prayer.

"God will talk with you through prayer you know, and through the reading of His Book, and you will get to know Him so that you will trust your life utterly to Him, and be willing to die to self and the desires of the flesh. That might sound like a dismal life. It would be to unbelievers, but as you go on to know Him you find out that the joy of knowing Christ and being one with Him far outweighs any sacrifice. I have found it the happiest life that can be lived. Just go to Him and tell Him you accept what He has done and rest on that. I would like to tell you more about it, but I know you have had a hard day, and you ought to get some rest."

Just then Janet appeared in the doorway.

"Yer bed is riddy, Meester Lorrimer, an' I'm certain ye're riddy for it."

So with a bright smile the young man turned to the girl:

"Good night," he said, giving Eden a quick handclasp. "We'll talk again about this if you like, and—I'll be praying for you."

"Oh, thank you," said Eden with a lovely smile. "You don't know how you've helped me. I think I understand, a little at least. And I do want to know Him. I really do!"

"Thank the Lord for that!" he said fervently, and Eden went away to her rest with a warm feeling around her heart.

As she lay down to rest she went over all that the young man had told her, and somehow the book she had read began to grow plainer. Sin was in the world, and sin was in her, that is, the tendency to sin, but there was a cure for it. Christ Himself would live in her and guide her. That would be wonderful! Why did nobody tell her that before? When she understood it all she would be able to tell other people who did not know about it yet. This must be the resurrection-life that the book spoke of. It said a crucified Christian had a right to it because Christ rose from the dead. A resurrection life!

She went to sleep on that.

Word about the robbery and the excitement began to get around and newspaper reporters arrived and wanted to be told everything, but Mr. Worden and Lorrimer and Mike had strictly forbidden them all to give out any information. They were just to answer, "I have nothing to say," and refuse to let anyone talk with Eden unless it was some well-known friend she could trust. And even then they were to say nothing about the excitement. That would be the best way to let the matter die out.

So Janet put the morning newspaper away out of sight, and Eden didn't think to ask for it. She came down to breakfast quite rested and ready to begin a new day.

She knew there would be duties to perform. She had an appointment with Mr. Worden and the lawyer to sign some papers about the estate, and that would likely occupy a good part of the morning.

Soon after breakfast two or three of her girl friends called up and said they were coming to see her right after lunch. They had just come home from extended summer vacations, and were quite eager and excited over the news they had read in the papers. Wasn't it awful for her to have to go through a thing like that? Was she much frightened? They were most determined to get an answer even over the telephone.

But Eden managed very well.

"Oh yes, we had a little excitement," she said, "but it's about over now, and I believe the whole matter is well taken care of. Why yes, I'll be delighted to see you girls." That was all, and then she turned to greet the lawyer who had arrived ahead of Mr. Worden, having refused to stay to breakfast, as he said he had some matters to attend to before he met Mr. Worden.

So the two young people had a few minutes together before the conference began.

The young man looked into Eden's beautiful dark eyes and at once saw a cloud of anxiety in them.

"What is it you are troubled about? Has something happened?" he asked in a low confidential tone.

Eden flashed a quick look at him, and smiled shyly.

"Why, no, nothing exactly *happened*," she said hesitantly. "Some of my girl friends called up and are coming to see me this afternoon, and they are so excited about our robbery that I just know I'm going to have a terrible time answering them. They tried to get me to talking over the telephone but I put them off. I know it is going to be dreadful to refuse to tell them everything, and I don't want to talk about it."

The young man smiled sympathetically.

"No, of course not," he said. "But I suggest you put it all in the hands of your Heavenly Guide. Just tell Him about it as you have told me, and ask Him to take over, and show you what to say and how to courteously avoid answers. I think you'll find your worries will vanish."

"Oh, could I do that? About just *little* worries like that! Wouldn't He mind if I troubled Him about such trifles?"

"Of course He would not mind. Remember He has

loved you and taken over your life, and shared with you His own resurrection life, and He has promised to take over everything, if you let Him live your life for you. Don't you know the verse 'Casting all you care upon Him for He careth for you'?"

"Oh," said Eden, her eyes shining with wonder, her cheeks flushing sweetly, "why, that is wonderful! How grand life is going to be now if I can always do that."

"You most assuredly can," said Lorrimer, "only re-member that old nature is still in you, and your enemy Satan will try to stir it up to persuade you that it isn't true."

Then the doorbell rang and Janet let in Mr. Worden and their quiet time together was over for the present. But before Lorrimer went away she said in a low tone as he took his hat to leave:

"Thank you so very much. You have helped me a great deal."

"I'm glad," he said, giving her another smile like a ray of sunshine. So Eden went into her afternoon with new strength and comfort, feeling that she had not only found a real Saviour who could give her victory over self, but she had also found a new earthly friend in her lawyer. He was somebody she would not be afraid to ask about her perplexities.

The conference with Mr. Worden was brief and

friendly. She learned that Ellery Fane had not as yet been found, but that his mother had been safely placed where she could not do any harm. Court would be in session in a few days, and meantime she had been taken to the near-by county seat and taken care of until the trial. They had been looking into her case and found that both she and her son were wanted for fraudulent acts in the far West, so there was no need for further worry about any trouble from them. At least unless Ellery should turn up again, which was not likely.

The telephone rang as the lawyer went back to the library to get a paper Mr. Worden wanted, and Eden went herself to answer it, for Janet was busy. When she returned Lorrimer was standing in the hall waiting for Mr. Worden to answer some question of Tabor's.

Eden had come back with her face shining.

"This is wonderful," she said. "I didn't want those girl friends of mine to come to see me right away while all this excitement is so new. They would just talk and talk about it, and I didn't know how to keep them from asking questions that I've been told not to answer. And now they have called it off themselves. They have been asked to help out getting ready for some servicemen's party to-night, and they have to spend the whole afternoon making favors. So now by the time they do come perhaps a lot of my perplexities will be straightened out, and I won't find it hard to answer their questions. Besides, they will have forgotten a lot of it and won't be so interested by that time."

The young man's eyes shone.

"That's it," he said. "You'll be surprised. I've had many experiences like that. Some of my friends when I told them about it have laughed and said it was my imagination, but you'll find it doesn't work out to be imagination. It is real. The Lord cares for His own, even in little things."

"Do you mean nothing ever happens against your wishes and prayers?" asked Eden almost breathlessly.

"Oh, no, but I mean that when you leave it all to Him He works it out marvelously. I don't mean it always comes the way you have planned it, or want it even, but that if it doesn't you know it will work out in the end to be even better than what you wanted, if you are patient and rest in Him. The condition of course is that you leave it all to Him and rest. You know His wish for you is that you shall become like the Lord Jesus. Whatever hinders that, He does not allow."

"I see," said Eden slowly, trying to think it out. "But that is almost unbelievable. It is like living a charmed life."

"Yes, isn't it? But it is true. It is the kind of life He wants His own to live if they are willing."

When he was gone Eden spent much time thinking

over what he had said, and went shyly up to her room to pray. She had never before felt shy in approaching God, but now it seemed she had really just been introduced to Him, and was so filled with wonder and gratitude that her natural self-assurance seemed to desert her.

By and by Janet came up to tell her that the doctor had come and that he found Tabor's condition much improved. The wound was not deep, and was doing nicely. Tabor had roused to ask once what had happened and why he was in the servants' dining room, and then dozed off again. The doctor had said the concussion was clearing up. He hoped it would not be a long siege for him.

Eden asked if she might go to him, and the doctor said yes, if he waked again, and seemed to want to see her. So toward evening when he woke and was being given nourishment, she went and sat by his bed, and put her small smooth hand in the old faithful one that had served her so many years, since she was a mere baby.

At her touch old Tabor opened his eyes, and smiled, perhaps thinking he might have died and this was an angel come to meet him. But when he saw her, comprehension dawned in his glance, and he smiled again, and pressed her soft fingers respectfully. "Miss Eden!" he said, "my lady!" and smiled again, and closed his eyes sinking away to sleep with an expression of content on his old lips.

Then Eden went up to her room again, this time to pray for Tabor.

Just after dinner a neighboring woman came in for a few minutes, and brought some lovely flowers and Eden felt she should see her for a few minutes, so she came down to the little reception room near the door and thanked the woman for the flowers.

"But, my dear," purred the neighbor, "I was so horrified when I found out what you had been going through, and right after the sorrow of your father's death, too. It was cruel! Now isn't there something we could do to cheer you up? Wouldn't you like to come over to our house to stay a few days until the excitement is over? It will be quite convenient, really, and it must be so horrid to have policemen coming and going all the time. I've seen them come in, you know."

"Oh, thank you! That wouldn't be at all necessary," she said quietly. "The policemen don't bother me. It just seems pleasant to think they have been protecting us at night. And most of them have been friends of mine since I was a little girl. They used to direct traffic when I was on the way to kindergarten, you know, and always took my hand and led me across the street, so I know them all quite well. And besides, of course, I couldn't be away anywhere till Tabor is well and up and about again. I couldn't think of leaving for anything just now."

"But my dear! You don't mean to tell me that serving

man is still here? Why didn't you have him sent to the hospital at once? That would have been the natural thing to do. Surely he is well enough to be moved now! Would you like me to call for an ambulance and arrange about his being moved?"

"Oh, no, Mrs. Mattox," said Eden in horror. "Why! Tabor is a part of our family. He has been with us since I was born. I wouldn't think of letting him be taken away. It would grieve him terribly. He has cared for us for years, and he is very dear to me and was to my father. He is being cared for quite as well as if he were in the hospital. We have a nurse, and Janet and the other servants are much attached to him. They are all anxious to do all they can for him. Besides, the doctor feels he is getting on very well, and I know he'll be happier here than anywhere else."

"Oh, but my dear, don't be silly! He's only a servant. He would be very well cared for in the hospital, you know. That's what hospitals are for. And it must be so very gloomy to have someone so ill in the house. You have to keep so still and it must react on you. You're looking pale, my dear. I'm sure your father would want us all to take better care of you than to let you harbor an old worn-out servant in your home, when you must be having a hard enough time without anything more."

Eden sat up with more than her usual dignity and lifted her pretty chin.

"Thank you, Mrs. Mattox, but I couldn't think of having Tabor taken away, and my household arrangements are very comfortably settled. We have a good doctor you know, our old physician, and a fine nurse. No one need feel any responsibility about me. I am quite well taken care of, and I should feel very unhappy to have Tabor away."

"But that is just sentiment, my dear child! Don't be silly."

Eden looked up with a smile of dignity:

"Sentiment is what we feel for the people who are near and dear to us, isn't it? But it really doesn't matter what you call it, Tabor stays here in his home, or what has been his home ever since I was born. But it certainly was kind of you to bring these lovely flowers to me, Mrs. Mattox. They are beautiful."

"Well, I'm glad you like them," said the lady stiffly. "But I do wish you would come over, my dear. It wouldn't be like going out. Of course I know you don't feel like being gay with your father just gone, but this would be just our family, and my niece, Rilla Wattrous. She is about your age, you know, and you certainly would have things to talk over in common. It would be better than being all alone with just servants."

"Thank you, Mrs. Mattox," said Eden, relieved that the lady had arisen as if about to leave. "You are most kind, but I'm sure you will excuse me. I really don't feel like going anywhere just now. I prefer to be at home for the present."

The woman studied her quiet poise for an instant before she finally left and when she got back to her home she remarked to her husband, "Poor child! She seems utterly crushed. She is just determined to sit down in the dust and be gloomy. Imagine a young girl being willing to stay at home with just servants!"

But it was with a sigh of relief Eden went upstairs to pray for Tabor and his swift recovery.

CHAPTER NINE

THE NEXT day some of Eden's girl friends barged in without warning, and Eden took them to the living room because it was farther away from the room where Tabor was and he need not be disturbed by their chatter.

But at the doorway Celia Thaxter paused and looked across at the great vase of flowers on the table under the opposite window.

"Oh! Funeral flowers!" she exclaimed with a shudder. "Have they kept all this time? Why on earth don't you throw them out? I just hate the thought of flowers in connection with a funeral, don't you? I think it would be so much better if they could completely break down that idea of sending flowers to a funeral. I always appreciate it when the death notices have the request 'No flowers please.' Flowers seem so out of place when one is in trouble, don't you think?"

Eden gave Celia a wondering look, and caught her

breath. How could she talk that way?

"Why no," she said brightly, "I think flowers are the most wonderful conveyors of sympathy, and I'm always grateful for them. But Celia, those aren't funeral flowers. Those are some roses that Mrs. Mattox my neighbor brought over to me last night. Aren't they lovely? Come in, won't you? Take that chair over by the desk, Celia. It's my favorite chair."

"No thanks," said Celia shivering a trifle. "I'll sit right here by the door. Wasn't this the room you had the funeral in? I thought so. Why don't we go into the library? I always loved that room."

"I'm sorry," said Eden coolly, "but it's right across from the servants' dining room where we had to take Tabor when he was brought in, and I'm afraid our talking might annoy him. He's still in a very critical state."

"Tabor!" exclaimed the visitor. "You don't mean to tell me you kept him *here*? After he was *stabbed*? He was stabbed, wasn't he? How perfectly dreadful! Why Eden, who suggested that? The doctor? He ought to know better. Tabor's just a servant, isn't he? The very idea of your keeping him in the living part of your house where your friends have to come. Hospitals are for such cases! That's what we give all those fairs and teas for, to get money to have free beds for the poor. You could have even paid his way yourself if you felt all that obligation to a mere servant."

"I *preferred* to have Tabor here," said Eden haughtily. "This is his home and he has been our faithful friend through the years. Would you like a cushion, Celia? That chair is rather deep."

"No thanks! I'll make out. But you certainly are keeping up your old college character of being queer! The idea! A servant having all the attention a member of the family would have!"

"Tabor is a member of the family," said Eden definitely.

"But who takes care of him? Not you, I hope. I should think it would take too much time for the rest of the servants to look after him, and I shouldn't suppose they would be willing to do it anyway."

"Any one of our servants would be entirely willing to go out of their way and work overtime if they could help Tabor. They all honor and love him greatly. But of course we have a nurse."

"A *nurse?* Oh! That's different of course, but it must make a lot more work for the other servants. Who pays for the nurse?"

"Celia, for heaven's sake, mind your own business, can't you?" protested Mary Carter.

"I am minding my business. I think it's our business to protect Eden from imposition!"

But Eden did not answer. Instead she turned toward the other girls.

"Is your aunt any better, Carolyn?" she asked.

"Oh, I guess so," said Carolyn Craton indifferently. "She doesn't whine around quite so much. I certainly do think if a person is sick they oughtn't to bother other people with it. It isn't our fault she has asthma. My dad kept us all poor sending her around from one doctor to another and I don't think it's fair to the rest of us."

Eden turned to Mary Carter:

"Has your brother come home yet from the Philippines?" she asked brightly.

"Not yet. He stopped on the way to visit his fiancée. They're going to be married at Christmas. Just think of it. We're all going out there to the wedding. I think it is horrid. Spoils Christmas for me all right. In fact I'm not even sure I'm going. There are seven parties here at home and I'm invited to every one of them. Can you beat that, girls? And what they want to have their old wedding at Christmas for I don't understand. They're just cutting themselves out of a whole holiday every year. They can't celebrate a wedding and Christmas at the same time without losing out. Well, I may decide to take the midnight train home after the wedding and get back in time for three of the parties, anyway. Though if I do that I'll miss out on the western trip dad was going to stake us all to. I am not sure what I'm going to do."

Then the whole group began to advise Mary, one said come home, and one said take the western trip.

"Oh, but you'd better come home, Mary. You don't

know who's going to be here, perhaps Caspar Carvel! Imagine that! His buddie in the army wrote my cousin Catharine about it. They say he's perfectly striking looking, and he looks swell in his uniform. I think it's horrid they are going to have to give up their uniforms when they are discharged from service, don't you? They look so much handsomer in them than in civilian clothes."

They chattered on in the old way about their boy and girl friends, and the service boys, and parties, but Eden caught her breath and began to look troubled. Was Caspar coming back to make her trouble? Till suddenly she remembered her new life, and that this was something more she could trust to her Guide. A quick prayer in her heart "Please take over, Lord!" and her brightness returned.

"I suppose you know all about Caspar, of course, Eden," said the fourth girl. "You always did. But I imagine you'll have some competition from now on. They say he's much improved, and simply stunningly handsome. Looks swell in his uniform and all that, and is perfectly spiffy in his manner. They say the army has done him all kinds of good. Taken away that goody-goody attitude he had. He isn't a sissy any more. He used to be such a lily, but he's all over that. I can testify that he can swear in a regular way now, just like the toughest guy in the camp."

"I suppose," said Eden quietly, "that a thing like war

has either one effect or the other on those who take part in it."

They looked at her in astonishment. The girl who had told this had expected to horrify little quiet Eden, but here she was taking it as if she expected something like this. The others were looking curiously at Eden.

"You and Caspar used to be awfully good friends, didn't you?" asked Celia meditatively. "You used to be pretty thick, I remember."

Eden looked up and smiled quietly.

"When we were children," she said. "You know he lived in the second house below us. But I haven't known much about him lately."

"Oh, but surely you've been writing to him and he to you, every mail that crossed the ocean in his direction. Now don't try to deny that, for nobody here will believe it." This from Celia again.

"No," said Eden quietly, her voice very well controlled, with a smile that was almost amusement on her face. "We haven't been corresponding at all. I think he wrote a letter when he first went over and then he got interested in other things. You know our acquaintance was a mere schoolmate affair, and never meant anything to either of us. But I really haven't been writing to any soldiers during this war. Father has been rather ill you know, and I was with him all the time. I helped him with business letters and a lot of routine work, and had no time for personal letters at all. And even if I hadn't been more than usually busy I'm not sure that I would have been interested in writing to Caspar. As we grew up I think we rather grew away from each other. We didn't always see things in the same way."

"Oh, but that's too bad, Eden," said Mary Carter. "You always looked so swell together. You made a stunning-looking couple and I always supposed that of course you two would be married sometime as soon as Cappie got home from service. It really is a shame to break that up. Such a swell-looking couple!"

Eden laughed amusedly.

"That's scarcely a reason for selecting a life companion, is it?" she asked with a grim little twinkle about her mouth. "But you'll have to change the pattern of your imaginings. There is not the slightest possibility that this one will ever happen."

"But Eden, you'll come to our little party, won't you?" pleaded Carolyn. "It really wouldn't be complete without you, and will just spoil it for us all. You aren't such a stickler for convention. It's to be a very quiet affair, strictly for the service boys, and no one would think it out of good form for you to come with us and help. Even people who are closer to a family death than you are would think it is all right. Anything you do for the servicemen is a sort of religious duty, you know. It is patriotic besides, you understand, and that is even greater than a religious reason, isn't it?"

"Is it?" asked Eden lifting her delicate eyebrows. "*Why?*"

"Oh, mercy! Eden, you don't mean you don't believe in being patriotic, do you?"

"Oh no," said Eden. "Of course it is right to be patriotic, but it rather amused me to hear it compared in that way, putting it ahead of religion."

"But don't you, Eden? Don't you think patriotism is the greatest thing on earth? I think patriotism *is* religion. It is religion made practical. It is religion being *lived*. Don't you see, Eden?" said Mary Carter.

"Well, I suppose it ought to be, but it seems to me that a lot of the things some people call patriotism is just doing what everybody else is trying to do; only everyone is doing it in a different way, and no two agree."

"I don't think you ought to talk that way. See how everybody is sending Christmas boxes to soldiers. Don't you think that is religion, Eden Thurston?" said Carolyn.

"Why, no, not exactly," said Eden. "It's doing a kind act to give the people they love and a few others a pleasant taste of home, but that is not exactly what I call religion. In a way it's the outcome of religion. But real religion is trying to make other people understand what a wonderful God we have, and how He died to save us, and how He wants us to live, our self lives surrendered to Him.

Dying with Him to sin, so that we might have a right to His risen life. I've been interested in studying that. But of course I believe in sending Christmas boxes and all that. Say, Florence, did your sister get home from Italy? She was a WAC, wasn't she?"

"Yes, she got home, but she got married before she came, so she has a home of her own now and we don't see her much any more. But say, I think it's going to be very exciting, having all these servicemen home to our Christmas party. You'll come, won't you, Eden? There's no real reason why you shouldn't, is there? Nobody will think it queer. Your father was always one to want to help every good work."

"I'm not sure I can," said Eden. "I'll see how our invalid is by that time."

"But surely you wouldn't stay away because of a mere servant, would you?"

"That depends on how he is," said Eden smiling. "But say, girls, I have a box of the most delicious chocolates here, the best I've been able to get all summer. Don't you want some? Wait! I'll get the box." Eden sped up the stairs and brought back a full box of candy which one of her friends had sent in to her. And so with delicious bits of confection they sat and talked, and now they turned to present-day news.

"Say, girls," said Florence Holmes, "there are some perfectly spiffy men coming back, and they're not all of them married either. There's a young minister over at the First Avenue church. They say he's very eloquent, and he has stacks of good stories about the war. It seems he was a chaplain."

"Oh, a chaplain!" sneered Celia. "I couldn't be bothered to go out gunning for him. It would bore me to death. Religion again. Eden, you'd better turn your talents toward him. He might just fit in with your ideas."

"Sorry," smiled Eden, "I'm afraid I don't want anybody I have to go out gunning for. That wouldn't be my idea of a good start in life."

"Oh, but she doesn't need to go out and drag them in," said Carolyn. "She has them all provided for her. Look at the new lawyer her old guardian has just taken over. Girls, have you seen him? He's stunningly good-looking, and they say he's not only handsome but awfully clever. I give you fair notice, Eden, I'm going out for that Mr. Lorrimer, and you needn't say that he belongs to you for I won't take no for an answer. My dad says that he's the brightest man he's seen in an age, and he'll make his mark in the world before long and don't you forget it. Here's where I give notice that I've picked him out."

"I'll bet Eden hasn't even seen the gentleman," said Mary Carter. "She hasn't entered the warpath yet. Give her a couple of years more and she'll wake up and take notice."

"It will be too late then," said Celia, "all the eligible

ones will be married by that time. She'll have to take up with some divorced guy, or a widower with seven children."

Eden was smiling at their jokes, and trying to keep back her indignation at some of the things they said, but she kept her poise, and said very little.

"Have you met this Lorrimer fellow yet?" asked Mary Carter, looking her straight in the eye, and hoping to make her change color, but Eden kept on smiling.

"Oh, yes," she said quite casually. "He's very pleasant."

"Is he married yet? Or engaged?" asked Carolyn eagerly.

"Why no, I don't think so. But of course I didn't ask him," she finished amusedly.

"Well, I don't think you were very clever if you couldn't find out in one interview," said Celia. "Me, I always know at once. They bear the stamp right on their faces, bachelor; married; married and divorced; widower. A really smart girl can tell."

"Why bother?" asked Eden amusedly. "Eventually you'll find out if you're interested. And after all young men aren't the only interest in life. What are you all aiming to be? Businesswomen, artists, writers, poets, doctors or lawyers?"

The girls groaned in chorus.

"What do you think we are?" they said. "We're out for a good time. The war has been bad enough while it lasted, though at least it was exciting, and you never knew whom or what you would meet next. But as for settling down into a businesswoman or a doctor or a lawyer, I'm not interested. It would bore me to extinction," said Mary. "What are you going to be, Eden?"

"I'm not sure yet," said Eden thoughtfully. "I think I'm going to wait until God shows me what He is planning for me."

There was a sudden silence then, an awkward silence, the room filled with embarrassment.

"Oh, heavens!" said Celia. "Girls, do you know what time it is? If we don't go this minute we'll be late for that train the two marines are coming on. Want to go with us, Eden?"

Eden smiled.

"No thank you, I believe not," she said. "I promised to help Janet for a few minutes, and I thought I would sit with Tabor for a little while if he is awake. Come and see me again, girls, and thank you for all the pleasant gossip. I find I was rather behind the times with some of it."

"Well, you're a dear, anyway," said Mary Carter, "even if you are terribly puritanical."

"Well, I guess it takes all kinds of people to make up a world," said Carolyn. "But say, Eden, why can't you—oh, not right away of course, but after a little so nobody's formal ideas will be shocked—have a little party and somehow manage to get hold of that young lawyer Mr. Worden has with him. Invite us all, so we can meet him? I've really quite a crush on him. I could go for him in a big way."

Eden smiled gently.

"I'm sorry, Carolyn," she said pleasantly, "but I really couldn't do anything like that. Not now anyway. But I'll be glad to introduce you if I happen to be around when you meet him. Of course I've met him on business."

"Oh, my goodness, Eden, how do you manage to be so calm and collected about everything? Don't you ever get a crush on anybody?"

Eden really laughed then.

"Why, perhaps I did when I was a kid," she said. "I just don't remember. But after all," she laughed, "I've had rather serious things to think of the last two years, and I suppose I'm growing up."

"Oh," laughed Celia, "I hope it's not that bad. Be your age, girl, and don't let a few troubles get you down. If you do you'll get old before your time, and life isn't so awfully gay that you can afford to pass up a good-looking young man."

Celia went over to the mirror, fluffed up her hair, got out her compact and touched up her lips and complexion. Then she turned back with even a more insolent expression on her face than before.

On the whole Eden was glad when the crowd left, and she could draw a long breath and relax a little. Then she hurried back to see how Tabor was, and found that he was better, was lying there quite comfortably, with somewhat of the old expression on his face. That was a relief, though he was still very weak. He had lost a good deal of blood from his wound before they found him, the doctor said. But his concussion was clearing up nicely, and they had pretty well calmed his mind about lying in the servants' dining room and being waited on, when he had always for so many years waited on other people.

But his eyes lighted happily when he saw Eden.

"So sorry!" he murmured. "Make—so—much—trouble!"

"Oh," laughed Eden happily, "that's all right, Tabor. We're glad to have a chance to get it back on you a little for all the years you've waited on us, and I'm quite sure I've made you a lot of trouble ever since I was born. So I'll be happy if I, or we, can do a little something for you. You've been wonderful to us all these years, Tabor, and wonderful to my dear father. I'm so glad you are feeling a little better. We hope you will soon be well again. But meantime be as good a patient as you have been a helper, and everything will soon be all right again."

Tabor smiled.

"Meh lady, you have—always—been—a dear child! I am honored," and the look he gave her was a heartening cheer to her lonely young heart.

The next day Tabor was so much better that the doctor let Mike come to talk with him a few moments and ask him a few questions. Ellery was being searched for most carefully and the authorities were anxious to talk with Tabor to see what his testimony would be.

"It was Ellery Fane all right," said Tabor, rousing at the question, and speaking slowly. "I only caught one full glimpse of his face. Then—it all—went dark—and that sharp pain in my back! But it was Ellery, and I heard him say he was going ta—*kill* me!" The doctor was standing by, and signed to Mike that was enough, so Mike said, "Okay, old friend! That's enough! Glad you're feeling better. So long!" and the session ended. But the search went on, extending over even wider territory as time went on.

Then old friends began more and more to run in to see Eden. Girls she had known all her life. Some brought real joy and comfort and some were unpleasant developments of the modern times. There were only a few that Eden really enjoyed. But much of her time was taken up helping to make the hours pass pleasantly for the old servant. She discovered that Tabor liked to have her read to him. He even asked for a chapter in the Bible Sunday morning and thanked her gratefully when she had finished. And then one day after consultation with the doctor, she took her little radio down beside Tabor's bed and turned on a Christian song service, and the light in his old eyes showed that he fairly felt he was in Heaven.

It was while this was going on one afternoon that Mrs. Rollin Sturtevant came to call, just a formal expression of sympathy in the loss of Eden's father she meant it to be, for she had been away on a trip when he died. But she sat in the little reception room by the front door and waited all of five minutes while Eden was finding the right station for Tabor to listen to.

Then Eden hurried up the hall and came in to welcome her infrequent caller.

"Oh, my dear, did I interrupt you in something?" she asked as she arose to greet Eden.

"Oh, no," said Eden smiling. "I was just finding the right station on the radio for Tabor to listen to the music. He's very fond of the hymn-singing hour."

"Hymns! How terrible! I should think that would be so gruesome! Aren't you afraid you'll make him morbid? And he ought to have some consideration for you, asking for that sort of thing. You can't help hearing it all over the house."

"Oh, but we love it, all of us," said Eden with shining eyes. "I can't see how anybody would become morbid with hymns. Won't you sit over here, Mrs. Sturtevant? This chair is much more comfortable than the one in which you were sitting. You've been on a trip, haven't you? I suppose you had a lovely time."

"Oh, yes, well enough, though we had to spend so much time waiting for trains even when we had reservations. They just wouldn't let us get on our train sometimes, because they had so many of those service boys to take. I declare I don't see why they had to favor them so much. After all, the war is over and they are getting home, aren't they? They ought to be glad to have to wait a little when they know that. They don't own the earth do they, even if they did go off to fight. And of course you know those boys *wanted* to go? Most of them would have been broken-hearted if they had been made to stay at home and do a little honest work. But really, Eden, I was ashamed that I had to be away at the time of your father's funeral. And I didn't know of it until it was too late even to wire flowers."

"Oh, don't think of that, Mrs. Sturtevant. It was perfectly understandable of course when you were away, and especially at this time, with a war just over. But I don't think we ought to begrudge anything to those wonderful boys. And I know they were crazy to get home, and their people were so glad to have them coming."

"Well," said the caller, "from what I've seen of them they're the most ill-mannered set. They think they can do simply anything just because they wear a uniform. But all I can say is I'm heartily glad I never had any sons to send out to war."

"Yes, It must have been pretty hard for the mothers to let them go, knowing they might never return," said Eden thoughtfully, feeling sorry also for any sons that *might* have belonged to this woman.

"Well, I suppose some of them felt that way," begrudged the woman, "but after all they might have died if they had stayed at home. Some do, you know, without even the glory of medals and ribbons and all that. However, I'm glad this war craze is supposed to be over, and I hope now we'll be able to get a few of the necessities of life. Why, I tried to get some hemstitched linen sheets at the store yesterday, where I've always bought them, and do you know, I couldn't get a single sheet anywhere, not even a cotton one. At last I went to a very exclusive shop in one of our best suburbs and found some cotton ones and said I'd take two dozen, and do you know what the salesperson told me? She said that they were not allowed to sell but one pair to a customer. Of course I had a friend with me and she bought a pair too and gave them to me, so I got four. But imagine it! I really don't believe in war, do you?"

Eden smiled.

"I guess nobody believes in war except the people who want to conquer the world, do they? But I'm glad it's over of course."

"Yes, of course you are. Did you have a young sweetheart in the war, my dear? I feel it must have been so hard for the dear girls who had to say good-by and not know whether the boys were ever coming back. It must have been worse for the girls, and young things that got married in a hurry. Did you have a sweetheart over there?"

Eden's eyes fairly twinkled.

"No," she said laughing a sweet little ripple of a laugh,

"I had lots of old friends and schoolmates of course, but no sweethearts. I haven't ever had time yet to think about that."

"Oh, my dear!" said the honeyed reproving voice of the caller. "Well, be thankful you didn't. The world's all before you now and you can take your time to pick and choose. Now, I really must be getting home. I have an appointment with a new dressmaker. Such a pity we can't get our old stand-bys. My old dressmaker who always made all repairs and adjustments has gone into defense work, and is getting some fabulous sum every week. I declare I think it's a crime the wages they paid during the war. But they'll soon find out that won't keep up, and then they'll go whining around for jobs, and nobody will want them back. Well, good-by, and do run over, dear, when you get lonely and want cheering up. I'll be glad to take you over and entertain you. Call me up sometime and let me know when you can come."

"Thank you," said Eden coolly, "but I'm rather busy just now, and I don't get lonely much, only of course I miss my father. Good-by and thank you for coming."

When the door closed on the voluble woman at last Janet emerged from the shadows of the hall with pitying eyes.

"Ye poor lamb!" she said gently.

"Oh, Janet," said Eden throwing her arms around the

kind old nurse, putting her head down on the sympathetic shoulder.

"Oh, Janet, how many more of these will there be? Will every woman on this street think she has to call on me? This one was terrible. She didn't believe in anything, except what was for herself."

"Yes, my lamb. Thur's a'mony like thet!" said Janet soothingly. "Noo, come awa' tae the lib'ry an' have a bite tae eat, an' a wee drap o' tay. I've made soom hot scones! An' then ye ken say good night tae Tabor. He's coontin' on it."

So Eden had her tea and scones and then went and read Tabor his good night psalm, and left him with a smile of peace on his lips.

Eden was very happy that night as she went to her room to read for a little while, and just before nine o'clock there came a telephone call for her from Lorrimer.

"Good evening," he said. "This is your lawyer. Do you remember him? I've been away to Chicago on business for the bank, or I should have called you before, but how are you fixed for tomorrow evening? Are any guests coming?"

"Not that I know of," said Eden, thinking of Mrs. Sturtevant, and sincerely hoping there would be no more such callers.

"Well, there is going to be a meeting in town tomorrow

evening and a very great Bible teacher is going to speak. I thought of you at once when I heard of it. I wondered if you would care to go with me to hear him?"

"Oh, I would love to," said Eden. "How *wonderful!*"

After she had hung up the receiver she went down the hall to Janet's room.

"Janet, I'm going out tomorrow night to a wonderful Bible meeting, with Mr. Lorrimer. So if anybody calls up and tells you they are coming to see me tomorrow night you can tell them that I shall not be at home."

"Thet will be wonner'fu'!" declared Janet. "I'm glad he asked ye. I ken he's a gude mon."

So both Eden and Janet slept well that night.

Chapter Ten

THE NEXT day went on very happily in pleasant routine, with Tabor hourly showing improvement, and the doctor well pleased with the result of his treatment. Eden went through the day much cheered in heart, able to put aside the great loneliness that so often surged over her as she remembered that her dear father was gone from her.

About five o'clock in the afternoon there came a telephone call from Caspar Carvel, and a cold shrinking seized her when she heard his voice. She wished she had asked Janet to answer the telephone. Janet would have settled him. And yet she realized that after all it was her question to settle.

"Yes?" she answered in a cool impersonal voice, not at all as if she joyfully recognized him.

"Hello, Beautiful!" he addressed her, as of old, and waited an instant for a friendly sign, but Eden gave no friendly sign.

"Yes?" she said questioningly. "Is this Caspar?"

There was an instant's silence and the young man tried again.

"Yes, Eden. I want to come and see you this evening."

"That will be impossible," she answered with finality. "I have an engagement for the evening."

"Well, then let me come now. I want to apologize for what I did the other night. I've got some time off, unexpectedly. I find I'm not satisfied until I make it right with you, Eden, you're my old friend."

There was a note of pleading in his voice. "Let me come over to dinner and we can talk while we are eating. I can't be satisfied until I have made it right with you."

Eden was still a moment and then said gravely:

"I'm afraid you can't do that by any talking, Caspar. You dishonored my father, and you spoke with contempt of my God. Those are not little things to be lightly forgiven."

There was silence for a moment, what seemed almost like astonished silence, then the young man spoke again, almost humbly this time.

"I realize that I spoke carelessly, Eden, and I ought not to have done it. You know I've been away from home in a wild environment and I just got into the habit of speaking carelessly the way the others do. I want to talk it over and make you understand that I didn't mean any harm. Let me come over to dinner and we can talk it over."

"That is quite impossible, Caspar. I'm going to be away for dinner and will probably be out late tonight. Besides, it's time you understood that you cannot dishonor a man who has always been your friend and blaspheme the God in whom I believe, and then expect to make everything right by a little talk."

"Well, can't you call off your other engagement and give me the evening?"

"No," said Eden with finality, "not even if I wanted to, which I do not."

"Oh, say now, kid! That's not like you!"

"No?" said Eden. "Well, neither was blasphemy and irreverence like what you used to be when you were a boy. But you'll have to excuse me now. I must go."

"Aw, Eden! Old friend! Don't be like that! Well, say, then, if I can't come tonight how about tomorrow night? I simply must make this right with you before I go back to camp, or I'll just about go to the dogs, and you'll be responsible. You don't want that do you, Lovely?"

"I don't believe that I would be in the least responsible," said Eden coldly. "But if it will do you any good you may come over tomorrow evening about nine o'clock for half an hour. I really can't spare any more time. Good night!" and Eden hung up on the astonished young egotist.

But after she had hung up the phone she was troubled. Why did this have to happen on this day that had been so happy? And had she done right to let him come at all? Yet it had seemed rather awful, too, to refuse to let him apologize. Well, she had at least put it off until tomorrow night, but she dreaded to have it to look forward to. She wished she might have this one evening free from worry.

Then she remembered the new life that she was wanting to live. Could she leave this also to her new Lord?

So when she went up to her room to get ready for the evening she knelt by her bed and said softly: "Dear Lord, here is something again that I don't know how to manage, and can't do anything about. Won't You please take over, and help me to trust it utterly to You? Show me just what to say and do."

Then she arose with a lighter heart and went about dressing.

She was a bit puzzled for a moment what she should wear. Her father had never liked the idea of wearing mourning for the Christian dead. She had no black dresses that were suitable for the occasion, anyway. So she settled on a simple suit of very dark green wool, and a little felt hat with dark plumes to match, that curled about the brim, and softly touched her hair. There was nothing noticeable about her costume, yet she was looking very beautiful, and the young lawyer felt it and stood with admiring eyes as she came down the stairs. That look in his eyes made her feel as if he, too, were glad to be going out with her. Made her feel just happy and relieved. And a sudden thought that her father would have approved of this evening's plan warmed her heart, and helped her to forget Caspar Carvel and his intended call.

The young lawyer had brought his own car to take this little new lady out. It wasn't an expensive make, but it was a good reliable car, and Eden was never critical of cars. Tabor had always been their driver when she and her father went out, or when she went out alone, and she had heard little discussion of makes and models of cars. Her education had not been along such lines. To tell the truth, even if the car had been of a very inferior make Eden would have been inclined to admire it because it was owned by Lorrimer, although she had no idea whatever that her mind was in such a state that this was so.

The church to which they went was a very large one, located in a popular part of the city, and the crowd which was already gathering when they arrived gave promise of being a capacity audience.

They found a seat near the front. Eden looked around on the audience in amazement. There were a great many young people present, both young men and girls, and many of the men were still in service uniform. Somehow she had not expected to see any young people. She hadn't realized that young people were interested in religious things.

And there was another surprising fact: there were also a great many distinguished-looking men present, of all ages. Some of the men she had met, with her father. Three of these latter were on the platform, and seemed to be going to take a part in the service. Her escort presently pointed out the principal speaker of the evening, about whom he had been telling her on their drive down to the city.

He was a fine, distinguished-looking man with a face full of deep spiritual understanding. Eden recognized that at once. There was a twinkle in his eyes when he looked up and smiled at someone that showed he had a real sense of humor.

Eden studied him while the people were coming in, and while her escort was talking with a man who sat in front of them, and evidently knew the lawyer well.

But aside from the few elderly men who had been her father's friends, she knew scarcely anyone in the audience.

Then when the choir of young people marched in and filled the gallery behind the platform, she studied them. They looked like interesting boys and girls, most of them very young looking, with here and there a serviceman or girl.

The organist was a distinguished musician, and it was a joy to hear him play, but Eden was surprised to notice that in place of the usual formal church music there was much mingling of church hymns and even a gospel song or two. It was then that Eden began to realize that this was a different meeting from any she had ever attended before. It wasn't just a formal church service, it was more like a gathering of people who really loved God, and loved one another. It was a sort of heavenly fellowship gathering; she could imagine that Heaven would be something like this.

Suddenly she looked up at Lorrimer and saw that he was watching her, and their eyes met in a lovely smile, as if he had understood her thoughts. She drew in a quick breath of delight. She had never known a fellowship like this and found herself wishing that her father could be there too. Then came the thought that perhaps he was able to look down and see her there and if that was possible she knew he would be glad of her presence there.

The music was very fine, but with no emphasis on its brilliancy. The solos made the words a sermon, and the prayer was tender and moving. Then the speaker was introduced, and from the first word Eden was thrilled.

"They tell us the war is over!" he said gravely. "But we are still in a war with sin. We have been in a gay and happy mood, getting ready to lay down our implements of warfare, and 'beat our swords into plowshares and our spears into pruning hooks,' get rid of rationing, buy all the beefsteak and gas we want, and have a good time. We go to church on Sunday, and sit back contented in what we choose to believe is an atmosphere of peace, and we like to try and think that there will never be a war again.

"But the Christian church is in a warfare today, only our warfare is in the spirit realm, not in the natural. Not against flesh and blood. The Christian has been delivered from the natural realm, delivered from self: good self, bad self, religious self, and all other kinds of self. He has been brought into another sphere, and it is in that sphere he must live and wage his warfare. We must combine our forces against the prince of the power of the air. And one of the first things we need to realize is that we cannot make a single move without orders from on high.

"We are fighting one of the battles in the great war against the enemy, and we are a spectacle not only for the world to see, but also for the angels. They are watching us there on the ramparts of Heaven, and Christian warfare, in order to be effective, must be fought from a Heavenly standpoint, and not from the earthly or carnal standpoint. That being the case we cannot use carnal weapons and devices, such as human organizations and businesslike schemes the world would use. If we do we're neglecting the spiritual, and losing the power that is of God. There must be spiritual warfare on spiritual ground with spiritual weapons, or else we are defeated at the start.

"We are here as a church to take the prey out of the hands of the evil one, that sinners may be saved, saints built up, and a people prepared for the coming of our Lord Jesus Christ in glory and power.

"The very moment Christians get to warring with

one another the church is divided, and we are defeated. The very moment Christians get into a state of judging or criticizing one another with bitterness and unforgiveness toward one another, they are not only defeated in their own lives, but other people are defeated by their influence, and the devil is well pleased. He knows very well that if he can get the church of God to warring with one another they will not war against him. That is why so many prayers by Christians who are judging and criticizing one another are not answered, and why so many lose the sweet experiences God wants them to have.

"God wants you to go after sinners, to be loving and patient with saints, and if you are sharp and censorious you will only drive them away from God instead of winning them. God wants you to show by your life that He has done something in your life, that He has saved you and separated you unto Himself, and given you His own life and His own patience and grace. There are worldly Christians who have no power in their lives. But when you walk with God, and His Holy Spirit has His way with you every step of the way, then He will give you power and answer your prayers. Before you go out to battle get down upon your knees and ask God to show you yourselves. Then examine your weapons. Be sure they are not carnal weapons.

"Long ago when Babylon had sinned and the Lord was going to destroy it, He raised up the spirit of the

Medes to destroy it for Him, and He told them to get ready their weapons, to be sure there was no rust upon them, to sharpen them to work effectually: 'Make bright the arrows; gather the shields,' He said, 'because it is the vengeance of the Lord, the vengeance of His temple.'

"And today when God calls His saved ones to battle against Satan and his wicked spirits, He tells us to 'Put on the whole armour of God.' But today it is not material weapons we have to sharpen and make bright and ready, but the spiritual armour. Among those are mentioned 'the sword of the Spirit, which is the word of God.' 'And above all prayer.' Then go forth and prove that spiritual weapons are mighty to the pulling down of strongholds. And remember that not only men and devils are watching you, but angels are watching also, and rejoicing over your victories."

When the service was out Eden was introduced to a number of the young people and she promised to come to some of their other meetings. Her eyes were shining with new pleasure as they finally said good night and started away.

They stopped on the way for ice cream in a quiet little place where there was opportunity to talk. "Well, how did you like the speaker?" asked the young man, watching Eden earnestly.

"Oh, so much!" she said. "It seemed as if he had been

listening to some of my thoughts and worries and knew just how to answer them. He really told me how to get ready for something I very much dread, and now I'll go home and make my arrows bright for what is ahead tomorrow night."

"Oh," said Lorrimer, thinking what a quick young mind, and what a willing heart this was, "are you having a battle on tomorrow night?"

"I'm afraid so," sighed Eden. "Oh, it's nothing I suppose, but it rather frightens me to think that I may not say the right thing. He said the sword of the Spirit was the Word of God, and I'm afraid I don't know that Word as well as I should to use it as a weapon."

"I see," said the young man appreciatively. "Of course that is the advantage of the Spirit-guided study of the Bible. But if you are Spirit-led He will show you what to say."

"But, I am such a new sort of Christian, do you think I could be guided definitely?"

"You certainly can, definitely," said the young man earnestly. "You have given yourself into His keeping. You can trust Him utterly. I know for I have tried it. You tried it too, just the other day. If you can trust Him with little trifles, can you not trust Him with the great things of life? If you cannot, then He is not a Saviour. He has promised if you died with Him, you can have that resurrection life that He brought you when He rose from the dead."

Eden looked up into his eyes and a great joy came into her face.

"Oh," she said. "Yes, I can trust Him. Thank you."

They went out to the car then, and did not talk any more about it till he took her home. Then just as he said good night he added in a low tone: "And I'll be praying for you."

She felt suddenly happy then. Her prayers might be crude and very new before the great God, even if He did love her, but his prayers would reach to the throne. He was used to praying for things and getting them.

Janet came hurrying form the telephone to meet her.

"It was that little r-r-rat on the wire," she said, "him as was here before. He wanted tae ken, was ye hame yet, an' whan did I expict ye. I said I dinna ken yer business, an' he said, 'Tell her I'll be there bright an' early t'morra night.'"

"Yes," sighed Eden uncertainly, "he's coming again, Janet. I had to say yes. He said he wanted to apologize. But you needn't worry. I'm not going anywhere with him."

"He's nae fit fer ye tae wipe yer pretty feet on," said Janet fiercely.

"That's all right, Janet. I didn't like his actions any better than you did. But I have to be courteous even if he wasn't. I have to accept his apology. But there I stop."

"Boot he'll try his verra best tae get in wi' ye agin, an' be the same ol' frind. He has a way wi' him. He'll make ye feel he's better than he is. He'll tell ye it's yer dooty tae be his frind."

"No, Janet, he'll not do that. Not this time. I think I've learned my lesson. I know what he is. I must see him tomorrow night, but after this he's just a boy I used to know when we were children. That's all!"

Janet looked after her sorrowfully as she started up the stairs and brushed a glittering tear away from her eyes, as Eden threw her a lovely smile.

"Weel, Oim sure I hoop yer richt!" she said with a doubtful sigh, and turned away quickly to hide her emotion.

Chapter Eleven

Caspar Carvel lunged in, in much the same way he had always done in the years gone by, much as if the house were his own old home and he had a right there. As if there were nothing special due for the privilege of coming. One would never have known from the quality of his regular old-time grin that he had come to apologize for anything. And Eden, whose quick eyes had noted this at once, felt her former anger rising, because she could not seem to forget the insolent words he had spoken. But she had spent time on her knees, with her Bible open before her, and had definitely put the matter in her new Master's hands. She felt assured that He would make it plain how she was to deal with this.

"Hi, there, Beautiful!" he began. "At last my perseverance is rewarded by your worthy presence! You certainly have taken on an air of discipline and distance. What's the little old idea, anyway, Lovely?"

Eden did not respond to this garrulous opening of the interview. Instead she went quietly, sweetly about the duties of a hostess, utterly ignoring his question.

"Good evening!" she said coolly as if it were a stranger she was greeting. "Won't you sit down?" she motioned toward a straight chair and went herself toward another at a little distance.

Caspar stood surveying her, a mask of puzzlement on his brow. So, she really must have been angry at what he had said on his last visit. But he slid down on the chair she had indicated and turned to her a puzzled grieved expression as if he did not understand.

"But what's the little old idea, Ede," he complained. "Why the frigidity?"

"I beg your pardon, Caspar. I understood you came here to make apology for your remarks the last time you were here."

"Oh, that! Why Baby! You're not mad yet, are you? You knew I didn't mean what I said."

"It certainly sounded as if you meant it," said Eden quietly, with sweet dignity.

"Aw, now, Baby! Don't get that way! You ought to know me better than that. You know I'm awfully fond of you. I wouldn't hurt you for the world. I just took it for granted that you had grown up to the times, and would understand. Why, excuse me, Baby, but you don't seem to have changed at all. I suppose your father's sickness has kept you cooped up away from the world. You don't seem to know times have changed."

"I certainly realize that *you* have changed," said Eden, still speaking quietly, and with gentle dignity.

"Hi, there, Eden," said the young man, "wake up and be yourself. You certainly can't think you're being attractive carrying on a line like that."

"I was not trying to be attractive," she said, "but I am wondering if this is your idea of an apology?"

The young man put on another act of hurt dignity.

"Apology? Oh! Why yes, sure I said I would apologize if that is what you want. I sure want to make it right between us old friends, and come here the way I used to do. I shall be mustering out pretty soon, and I want to get things on a friendly plane again. Sure!" and he suddenly sprang to his feet and putting his hand on his stomach made a low abject bow. "So, I most humbly apologize."

Eden watched him a moment as he slowly raised his head and gave her an assured smile as if he felt he had done a good job of apology. Then she said gravely:

"Sit down, Caspar, and listen to me. You haven't made an apology at all. You don't even think you have done anything to apologize for. You are not sorry for what you said, you know you are not. And as for things being on the old friendly plane I am quite sure that can never be."

"But what did I do, tell me, kiddo! I really don't understand."

But Eden looked steadily at him.

"Yes, you understand, Caspar. You spoke of my father in an outrageous way, and you spoke of my God in a terrible way."

"Oh, well, kid, I supposed of course you'd understand I wasn't saying anything dreadful about your father. He was just an old man, rather behind the times of course, but nothing to his discredit. You see I didn't really intend any discourtesy to him. And as for the other matter, Eden, you don't really mean to tell me you still believe in all that sentiment about God. Why simply *nobody* believes that any more."

"I do!" said Eden firmly. "And I resent any word said against my God and my Christ. You see I *know* Him. He is not only my Saviour, but He is my Friend and Guide. And it is to Him you will have to apologize if you want to be my friend."

"Great day!" said the affected youth, "is it that bad with you? Why, you're crazy, Eden."

"You're worse than crazy, Caspar. I'm very much afraid you are *lost*. The Bible says: 'For the preaching of the cross is to them that perish foolishness; but unto us which are saved it is the power of God.'"

The young man stared.

"Who put you up to saying a thing like that?" he asked with a sneer. "That's terrific!"

"Nobody put me up to saying anything. I asked God

to show me what to say to you, and this is the verse He directed my attention to. Of course I had read it before, but I felt you ought to know it was there, and that God understands all about you."

Caspar stared again, and then with an impatient gesture he said testily: "I didn't know you were also superstitious as well as behind the times, but don't let's talk any more about this. We'll never agree, I can see that. Perhaps when you have lived a little longer and been out in the real world awhile you'll change your ideas. However, I can stand it, if you'll just keep it to yourself. You'll get over this fad of course, and I'll do my best to help you. Let's change the subject. How would you like me to tell you about some of my thrilling experiences? As a rule I don't care to talk them over with these newsmongers that come around us vets, but you are different. You've known me all my life and you'll understand."

Eden sat looking at him gravely.

"Very well," she said. "Go on."

Almost sullenly, but very pompously he began his story.

It was a thrilling story, there was no mistake about that, and he told it well, except that he did not omit to mention his own courageous part in glowing terms, so glowing that Eden found herself constantly wondering if he were telling the whole truth, and whether some few of the great acts of prowess and courage should not be ascribed to the credit of some of the others of his regiment, but she put the thought aside and listened, watching her old friend, and studying his handsome, weak face, noting for the first time the arrogance of his chin, the shiftiness of his glance. Did his eyes always look so sort of sly, his mouth have that crafty twist, even when he smiled, or had he acquired that during his absence in service?

But at last he seemed to come to the end of his tale. He looked at her proudly ready to receive her praise. This really was what he had come for the first time he called on her. He wanted her flattery, her exclamations of wonder and delight in his bravery, and she had not once interrupted him. He looked up now to receive his due.

Then he found he was looking into an extended silence, and that instead of praising his courage she was merely watching him sadly, studying him, as one would look with troubled gaze at something that used to be of value, but had somehow become ruined. At last, just as he was growing very uneasy and most impatient she spoke:

"And do you mean to tell me, Caspar, that you went through all that terror and awfulness, without once calling on God, or wanting His help?"

"Help!" screamed Caspar scornfully. "Why should I want help? I had to be my own help. I was trained, wasn't I, to fly and to shoot, and to work all the tricks we were supposed to work on the enemy. It was up to me, not

God. I didn't need any help but myself, and why should I cry out to a God I didn't believe in? When I first went into the army I was thrown with a lot of fellows who were outstanding guys. They didn't believe in God. They said it was sissy to believe in such things. When you went into danger you were up against danger *yourself*, and had to make *your own* way out of it. To tell you the truth if I had called on anybody for help I would more likely have called on the devil for help than God. If there was a God who could have helped me, why did He let me get into such awful straits, I ask you?"

"Perhaps to show you how much you needed Him. Perhaps to make you turn to Him. You once chose God to be your Guide and helper."

"Oh, well, I got over that nonsense long ago."

"You mean you are serving the devil now?" asked Eden.

"Perhaps," he answered with a grin, "but forget it. The war is over and I've got a good line on a successful job for myself where I can get rich quick, and we could get married, and if you'd promise to quit preaching you and I could have a swell life, going out among 'em and making up for all the dull life you've lived so far. You'd be surprised how happy I could make you if you'd just give up this line and get a bit gay. Of course not just now, so soon after a funeral in the family. But by the time I'm out of the army and back home and well into my job, I want you to be ready when I call."

Eden did not smile. She only looked at him sadly.

"No, Caspar," she said solemnly, "I have no desire for a life like that. And I could never marry you, knowing how you feel about my Lord and the things of life that are the most precious to me. And anyway, Caspar, there is more to marriage than just having a swell time. I do not love you and have no desire to marry you. I am only sorry that you have lost the faith I used to think you had, and I shall pray for you that God will sometime draw you back to Him. But that is all. You and I do not belong together any more, even as friends, since you have turned away from all that I hold most dear."

A thunder cloud settled down over the weak, handsome face, and made him look more than ever like a frustrated naughty boy. At last he spoke:

"What does this mean, Eden? Is there some other guy you've been going around with since I went away? Somebody you think you are engaged to? Because if there is I'll *kill* him. I *swear* I will. I've always considered that you belonged to me, and always would, and you can't cheat me out of my rights. I won't stand for it."

Eden's face suddenly froze into haughtiness.

"That is no way for you to talk to me, Caspar," she said in her coldest voice. "I have never belonged to you in any way, and you know it. Our friendship was only a childish one; we were just playmates, even when I thought you were a good man. And now that you are so evidently serving the devil I don't feel that I care to see you again. It would not be even pleasant any more."

"You mean that you are engaged to some one else? Some sissy of a guy who didn't have the nerve to go to war? Who is he? I'll go out and find him and make him understand you belong to me. What's his name? I demand to know it."

Eden was very quiet and steady as she answered.

"I am not engaged to anybody, Caspar, and I have not been running around with anybody. I haven't had time. But I see no reason why it should be anything to you if I did. And now I think we have talked enough, and I wish you would go. I don't like the Caspar you have become. Good-by!"

Eden turned to go out of the room, but Caspar hurried to intercept her before she reached the door.

"Aw, ferget it, Ede. Don't go off that way again. This is ridiculous! You never useta be like this!"

"Neither did you, Caspar. You have gone back on all that means life to me, and I can't be friends with you any more. Good-by," and Eden went and stood by the front door to bow him out.

The young man stood miserable with downcast eyes, which he lifted only to look her over, the slim charming figure, the lovely eyes that had so often smiled at him, the pretty hands, clasped so determinedly as he had so often seen them for some mutual scheme of theirs as children, and Caspar was wondering how he came to forget how swell she was, and why he hadn't been writing to her all these months. That would have fixed her as his, and she wouldn't have been so likely to get all these antique religious ideas.

"Eden!" he pleaded, "at least you'll kiss me good-by!" and he made as if to come nearer. But Eden backed away.

"No!" she cried. "Please go away!"

And then a stern old Scotch voice was heard behind them: Janet coming as fast as her feet could carry her in spite of arthritis that troubled her now and then.

"Did ye call me, my leddy? I'm coomin'."

"Yes, Janet," said Eden sweetly. "Please open the door for Mr. Carvel. He has to leave!" and Eden vanished up the stairs, leaving Caspar Carvel to make his dejected way out of the house, evicted for the second time from the place where he had supposed he would always be welcome.

Then Eden went up to her room and flung herself down on her knees with her face in the pillow, and cried to her new Lord.

"Oh, Lord, I didn't listen for Thy leading. I let my own anger rise, and I said angry things that were in my heart instead of following Thy Spirit. Oh, forgive me! I should have said something that would make him understand how wonderful You are, and I didn't in the least convince him, I'm sure. Oh, Lord, please take over, and somehow bring him to a place where he will understand."

Just then her telephone rang, and much distraught, with tears on her cheeks, Eden jumped up and answered it.

"Yes?" she said, struggling to steady her perturbed voice. And then she recognized Caspar's voice.

"Eden," almost humbly, "I'm sorry I made you angry again. I really didn't mean to, and I apologize. But I want to ask you to promise me one thing: Promise me that you will never get engaged to anyone else without letting me know right away. I might change again and get to be what you want, but it wouldn't be fair to me to string me along for years thinking I was doing it for you, and then have you stand me up afterward."

Eden was very still for a minute for she could feel her anger rising, but here was where she must hand herself over to her Guide. A moment more and her voice was steady, clear, and she knew just what to say:

"Caspar, there is just one thing I'll promise you, and I will not promise anything else. I promise to pray for you that you may somehow get to know God. Good night."

Then she hung up, and Caspar, angry and chastened in spirit, went on his devious way back to the world which had led him away from the path where he had started.

And Eden went back to her prayers, and wondered if a prayer uttered from an angry heart could ever help to bring Caspar back to the right way. Then she wondered if he had ever been in the right way at all, and whether perhaps her beloved father had seen this. Perhaps that had been one of the reasons why he planned trips to take her away from this boy's companionship.

She saw now what Caspar had become, as she might have seen before if she had not been so interested in having the good times with him which he seemed always able to plan. She saw it now, and was thankful that God had made it plain to her before she was led into a return of the friendship which might have been a real danger to her. For now as she thought things over calmly, perhaps with the enlightenment of the inward Guide, she realized that she had been looking forward greatly to the return of her old-time playmate. Now she knew that he could never be her old-time friend again. Even if he should change as he suggested, she had lost the sense that he was fine and wonderful, which she had when he went away. But it did make her heart a little sore to look the fact in the face and see that she had no old friend to cherish. He was gone out of her life and could never come back. She would pray for him, yes, but she would leave him in God's hands. It would perhaps not be a prayer of much faith, for Caspar had proved to her tonight more than ever that there was not much there to build any hope upon, and it would be only God who could ever make anything of Caspar Carvel. Perhaps He could. Of course He could, for He was all powerful, but she was sure no words of hers ever could.

When she lay down to rest that night somehow a great burden rolled away from her, and she began to wonder if she had been carrying her disappointment in her old friend about, as a burden on her heart. At least it was now gone. She had laid him definitely in God's hands.

As she dropped away to sleep some pleasant words of Lorrimer's came back to mind, and the look in his eyes as he spoke them gave her a happy thought to drive other worries away. Life was changing for her. It was inevitable that it should change when her dear father was taken away, but she had not been prepared to have the very foundations of her childhood swept away from under her. New friends, new experiences! Frightening occurrences. Mr. Worden was still at hand, and his pleasant new lawyer. That was nice. Janet was still there, bless her, and Tabor was getting well, thank the Lord for that! And she had a new Lord. She could go on from there and live out her life as God would plan. She need not be afraid, even of Ellery Fane and his silly scheming mother.

And so she slept.

CHAPTER TWELVE

AND THE next day there arrived in Glencarroll three sisters from California, cousins of Eden's mother. Three women of the world who were neither old nor young, just enough older than Eden to assume to advise her, just enough younger than her mother had been to pass for semi-companions for a girl alone in the world, just well enough off financially to realize what it would mean to them to have a young girl, financially independent, and generously inclined, under their care and patronage.

They went at once to the Glencarroll Hotel, and called up on the telephone to make their presence known, probably hoping to be at once welcome to the hospitable Thurston home.

Eden had never known them intimately. There had been occasional letters back and forth during her father's lifetime, and once Eden had spent three days at their home in California, but she did not feel that they would be an asset to her life at this time, and so when they called up and expressed their sympathy in her recent sorrow, she thanked them, and explained that Tabor, their old servant, had been very ill, and it just wasn't convenient at present for her to ask anyone to visit them, but she would run over and see them within a couple of hours and find out their plans.

When she had hung up she sat down and thought over what the coming of these unwanted relatives was going to mean to her. It was obvious that she should not invite them to visit her at present, not with Tabor sick and so much for the servants to do. Besides she was in no mood for taking them around to see the sights, as she knew they would wish to go. Here was a situation that would have to be trusted in the hands of the Lord.

So she dressed very soberly and went to the hotel.

The cousins were most effusive, and said they had come to get her and take her home with them. They had talked it all over and decided that would be best for her, to get away from all sorrowful surroundings, where she would be more or less bound to live a quiet life for sometime, here among her father's friends. So they had dropped everything and come after her, before she had had time to make any other plans.

They were very voluble, and each took up the tale when the other left off, until they had placed before her all their plans for showing her a pleasant winter, and making a permanent home for her in their company.

Eden hoped that her telltale face did not make too plain how she would *not* like to accept their invitation, and how she would hate to live with them. But she kept a smile and waited until they had laid before her their whole plan, and then she pleasantly undertook to answer.

"It is very sweet of you to try to make nice plans for me," she said with one of her loveliest smiles, "and I do appreciate your kindness. I remember your pretty home in that sunny land, and I know you would do your best to make me happy. I thank you from my heart for being so kind. But it would be quite impossible for me to leave here at present. There are business matters that I must settle, and there are plans that I have made which must be carried out. Also I have a lot of obligations here, things that Father left in my hands. I could not possibly go away anywhere now."

"But my dear, you have been through so much. Your father's sickness and death must have been very hard on you, and I should think friends and obligations could wait while you have a time of resting and getting back your normal vivacity. You have a right to get away and get new poise after a shock like death."

Eden shook her head and smiled.

"My father's death was not a shock," she said sweetly. "He talked it all over with me months ago, and prepared me for all the changes that would have to come. Of course it was a great sorrow to have to lose him, but I understood, and he and I together planned out what I should do, and how my time was to be occupied. Besides that I have many friends here whom I enjoy, and who mean much to me. I love my home, and our old servants are here. It is the normal place for me to stay. I am afraid I would be very homesick away from here, especially just now. Though I certainly do thank you for your very kind thought of me. I am only sorry that I am not in a position just now to ask you to come right home for a few days while you are in this vicinity. But you see we had a most unpleasant happening. A burglar broke into the house and tried to steal some of father's valuable papers, just the day of his funeral, and our good old butler went out to try and catch him, and got stabbed in the back. He has been very critically ill in the house ever since it happened, and that has somewhat disorganized our household, so that it would not be very convenient for us to try and have guests at present. That is the reason I came over at once, to explain, and to suggest that if you were to be in the vicinity later, say in a couple of months, before returning to the West, you might arrange to spend a few days with me then. I am quite sure Tabor will be well by that time. At least the doctor says he is reasonably sure. Could you arrange your plans for that? You were so kind to invite me when I was in California that I would certainly like to return the favor."

"Oh, my dear! That's sweet of you to plan so far ahead," said Elspeth, the oldest of the three sisters. "But my dear, I can't see any sense in delaying our visit that way. Surely you don't have to keep a sick servant in the house at the expense of your visiting guests. Couldn't you send him to the hospital? He could certainly be better cared for there than in your home, and then we could come right over and be with you for a while until we could persuade you to return with us."

"Yes," said Clarine, the next sister, "that would be much the best arrangement. We don't intend to give up taking you back with us, Eden. We have quite made up our minds, haven't we girls? And you know the Haldanes do not easily change their minds when once they are made up. So Eden, won't you go to the telephone and call an ambulance and have that old butler taken to the hospital at once? Then we can come over and have a really good visit. I can understand how hard it would be to have a sick servant with company, but surely you can get another butler, and if necessary we girls can help until you secure one. Nerissa is awfully good at getting up dainty lunches and even serving them on occasion. Aren't you, Nerissa?"

Thus appealed to, Nerissa, the third and youngest

sister, smiled and assured Eden she would be glad to do anything to help out.

"So, Eden, you see, the best you can do is to get your servant out of the way, and we can go over at once. With this in view we didn't unpack yet. There is a telephone right over on the right of the desk. Go and get it off your mind, dear, while we wait."

Eden sat up very straight and looked at her would-be guests with surprise.

"I'm sorry," she said quietly. "You don't understand. Our servant is much too sick to be moved yet, and we couldn't think of sending him away. He has been a part of our family for years. And it would not be at all convenient for me to have guests at present. I am sure you will understand. If you can plan to come later I shall be glad to arrange it if it is possible. And now, have you pleasant rooms at the hotel? I know they are crowded everywhere, but I suppose you must have secured reservations."

"Well, no, we didn't," said Elspeth. "We were counting on you, naturally, and we really were hoping you would perhaps just toss a few things into your suitcase and start right back with us."

"Well, that is out of the question, and it is equally impossible for me to have guests at present. It will probably be a couple of months before my plans would allow me to send for you, but if you are to be here later there would be some very delightful concerts on then. I know you are fond of music. And there are lectures always."

"Oh, lectures!" laughed Nerissa. "Imagine it! Is that your idea of a good time, Eden? It isn't mine. I want to see some night life. Of course New York is the place for that. Why not come up with us for a little while and go the rounds?"

"Thank you no," said Eden gravely. "I never cared for that sort of thing you know, and certainly not now."

"Oh, you poor little thing. You mustn't be tied to a somber style of life. You are getting older, and you'll need to go out and have good times. We'll see to that when we get you under our thumbs," said Clarine shaking a warning finger at her and tossing her head with a motion that set the floral earrings in her ears jingling.

Eden was beginning to lose her temper now in a hopeless kind of daze, and she took a deep breath and sailed in, making her statements very clearly:

"I am sorry to disappoint you, but you might as well understand that all this is quite impossible. I am staying right here in my home and carrying out the plans my father and I made for my life. I do not wish to go away anywhere at present. I do appreciate your trying to help me, but I do not want help now. So, since I am rather busy at present and find it hard to get away from the house long at a time, or often, suppose you be my guests here at the hotel for lunch, and then you can go on and make your further plans without reference to me. That is the way it will have to be for the present at least."

So finally the three sisters, much surprised that the gentle Eden had so asserted herself and could be so firm, succumbed, and let Eden take them into the hotel dining room for lunch, and then in rather dignified high dudgeon, they took themselves off to New York. Eden, tired out from the experience of the morning went back home wondering. What in the world had happened that all the unpleasant people she knew had to turn up and torment her, right here at home when she was going through so much else? Well, there was probably some good reason why it all had to be. Perhaps her friend the lawyer would have some theory wherewith to explain it.

When Eden went into the house she found Mr. Worden there pacing back and forth in the hall, looking at his watch.

"Oh, my dear, I'm so glad you have come. I very much want to have you sign a paper that will be needed in this matter of the robbery. I want to keep you out of the trial if possible, and I think perhaps this may help, but it should reach the judge at once. Suppose you just sit down and read it over carefully and see if I have made the statement just as it happened."

When they had finished with the paper Mr. Worden folded it carefully and put it in his brief case.

"Thank you, my dear. I'll get this into the right hands

at once. And now, I wonder how you would like a ride out into the country this afternoon? My lawyer and I have to go out to draw up and witness a will for an old man who is not likely to live long, and wants to get his affairs in shape. My wife wants to go too if she can get out of an engagement she made for a committee meeting. So I thought if you would go along that would be some one for Lorrimer to talk to. I will let him do the driving and my wife and I will be real folks for a change and sit in the back seat and luxuriate. Would you enjoy that, or am I barging in on some other more attractive plan of yours for spending the afternoon?"

"Oh, that will be wonderful!" said Eden, the light in her eyes and the flush on her cheeks showing how much the suggestion pleased her. "You don't know how I long to get away from the telephone for a little while. Someone is always coming in on me and wanting to stay with me, or something like that. I've just got away from three cousins from California who are trying to insist on my going back with them to live."

Mr. Worden laughed.

"Yes," he said, "I understood from Janet that you were in the hands of those three 'harpies' as your father used to call them. I was afraid you wouldn't get away from them in time for me to get this paper off in the mail. Well, I'm glad you got back, and I must be hurrying along. We'll be stopping for you at half past two. Will that be all right?

And meantime if any more 'unwanteds' turn up just deny yourself to them firmly and stay hidden till Janet calls you. Good-by."

Eden danced up the stairs with almost real happiness in her eyes—and found Janet waiting for her, anxiety on her brow.

"An' didna ye see them coosins?" she asked. "Wull they be coomin' here the nicht? Whut room would ye lak me tae prepare?"

"They are *not* coming," said Eden. "I told them it wouldn't be convenient now while Tabor is sick. I said they might come back in a couple of months if they happened to be in this region then. I took them to lunch at the hotel, and saw them off to New York on the noon train. Do you think that was awful of me? Besides, what they wanted to do was to carry me off to California, root, stem, and branch, and have me stay with them permanently, and let them steer me through life. Imagine that, Janet! Wouldn't that have been terrible?"

"It would indeed, my lambkin. Boot I'm thinkin' they had a wee bit of an eye toward your siller, my sweet. They kenned ye was generous, I'm thinkin', and they intended to get out of ye onythin' they wanted. Oh, ef I were tae see thim coomin' in the door I'd tell thim nae, they couldna enter. Ye did weel tae hie thim awa' tae Noo York. They dinna belang in this hoose, thet's certain."

"No, they do not," said Eden, "but it seemed ungracious

in me after they had invited me to their home four years ago. Of course father wouldn't let me stay but two days. I know he never liked them. And now I'm so glad they are not here, for I would have had to stay and entertain them. And they don't like anything I like. They want to be going, going, going all the time, and seeing notable people. I'm sure they would have tried to put me up to inviting several parties if they had stayed. Oh, why are such people tormenting me now when daddy is gone?"

"It's because they are canny an' wanttae share yer fortune," said wise Janet, hurrying about to put away Eden's coat and hat.

"But Janet," protested Eden, "there you go spoiling me again. How will I ever get tidy habits if you go around waiting on me, and picking up after me?"

"Oh, ye cheeld! Ye air thet sweet an' gude naethin' can spoil ye."

"There you go, flattering me, Janet. I'm sure daddy never allowed you to flatter me."

"Not whin ye were a wee bairnie, boot ye air growed, the noo, an' what would a poor ole nurse dae, ef she canna wait on her nurslin'? Gang awa' ter yer bed, my wee girlie, an' take yersel' a bit of rest afore the car cames fer ye. Ye'll be nane the worse fer it."

"Lie down, Janet? Why, I'm not tired, and I'm going to have a lovely restful afternoon, riding in the country. It seems wonderful after escaping what I did. Now find me a clean blouse, Janet dear. I promised to be ready by half past two, and it's ten minutes after, now."

So Eden was soon dressed and down at the door when the Worden car drew up.

Lorrimer was driving and looked happy to put her in the seat beside himself. Janet stood behind the lace curtain and watched them drive away, well pleased to see her nursling beside a young man she need not disapprove. It had been hard for her when Caspar Carvel came back from war. She never had approved of him anyway. And she knew Eden's father did not like him, though he was always most kind to him.

So into the beautiful blue of the autumn afternoon they went, the soft green feathers of her hat making a frame about Eden's lovely face, and the pleasure in her eyes softening the lines of recent sorrow that had been so marked when Lorrimer first saw her.

"She is very lovely," he said to himself, "and you must go carefully, lad. She is wealthy, you know, and you are a young man only beginning your fortune. You mustn't allow yourself to get too interested in her. But I certainly am glad she is along with us today."

That was what he thought as he settled himself for the long ride and the privilege of enjoying it with this unusually lovely girl.

Meantime in a far hideout Ellery Fane, in borrowed garments, skulked in an unsavory den and conversed sullenly with former pals, trying to plan how to contact his erstwhile prison abode and find out if his mother had been caught and was still there.

A little later it was discovered that another member of their gang was expected in a couple of days, en route to Mexico, and it would be easy to send out a feeler through him. So Ellery spent time working out in code an innocent telegram to his mother that purported to be from her grandchild, one named Tilly Brandeis, age nine years, begging her to come home in time for her birthday party and to bring her a string of red beads. This with a silly sentence about her curling red hair, innocently conveyed the fact that Ellery still retained one ruby of the booty he had hidden under a patch of adhesive tape over a self-inflicted wound, in his hair, that showed enough blood to imitate the real thing. But of course the message was one that nobody but Lavira Fane could possibly translate. It seemed to be from an innocent little girl who wanted a beloved relative home for her birthday party. And so it was finally showed to Lavira, who wept over it profusely. But she understood that her son was informing her that they were not entirely without funds, and it gave her a clue where to find him if she could manage to get out. The matron watched her while she read it, and saw a look of such satisfaction settle over the sharp face, that she took the telegram away with her and gave it to the chief of police who somehow read something into it, or tried to, and began the frantic search again for the missing thief, Ellery.

It was well that Eden could not know anything about this or the wonderful peace and placidity of the day might have been clouded for her. She was anxious only to forget the awfulness of that night when Ellery Fane walked back into her life and did his best to stay there. It was now just like a bad dream that she only remembered when she sat by Tabor's bed and watched the gentle, patient look in his eyes. Poor Tabor had taken the hard part of this from her and now he was getting his joy out of it, along with the pain, for it was pay enough for him to have that dear child sitting by his side for an hour or two a day and reading to him out of the Bible. Tabor had always been of a discreet turn of mind, and religiously inclined, but he had never been able to get very much out of his personal reading of the Bible. Now, however, when Eden read it he began to understand the love of the great God for him, that He had cared enough even for a poor servant to die for him. To take all his sin and mistakes upon Himself and pay the price in His own blood for them.

All that had been in the Bible all the time, he supposed, as he thought about the matter, only he had never been able to understand it before until that sweet girl-voice had brought the words to the understanding of his very soul. So Tabor thought about it after she had gone out, and was glad she had taken the afternoon off, and gone driving in such nice company.

And just about the middle of that glorious afternoon Caspar Carvel found himself in a very annoying position. He had come down to the shore with a buddie from overseas who had expected to find his family spending the week end in their summer cottage. When they got there they found that a chance invitation had taken them up the coast a few miles for a cocktail party. It was while his friend was hunting his parents that Caspar Carvel was at a loss what to do with himself.

His friend had gone up the street to a neighbor's cottage, somebody who lived at the shore all the year around, and had left Caspar in his parents' pleasant cottage living room. There was a desk well stocked with stationery, pens and ink. He might write a letter, but he laughed aloud at the idea. Whom would he write to? Eden? She wouldn't read it. She would either return it unopened, or else she would tear it up and never answer it. And anyway, what could he say to her? Nothing in her line. Of course he could kid her along the way he had always done, but she wouldn't like it.

No, he wouldn't write a letter. Or say, he might write to that little number that he danced with at the night club last night. He didn't know a thing about her of course except that she smiled at him even before he had looked her over, and she accepted his invitation to dance without hesitation. She wasn't even a hostess in a canteen either. Just a common little girl who was out for a good time. He had asked her name and she said "Cutie Cordell" and she borrowed his pencil and wrote it down with her address and telephone number. Showed what she was. He hadn't been so much attracted either, but what difference did it make? One girl might be as good as another to have a good time with, and after all when she had gone to all that trouble to write out her address it would be too bad to disappoint her.

Following a sudden impulse he seized upon a sheet of handsome letter paper and began to write.

Dear little Sugar Plum:

You see I can't forget you, and so now that I have a few minutes to wait for a train I am taking this opportunity to write you a letter.

You are a cute little number, and I don't wonder that is your name, Cutie! It just fits you.

I just want to tell you that I enjoyed my dance with you. You were super! And I hope you come around the next time I drop into your town. I want to see your pretty eyes. They are like two stars. I shall not forget the sweet kiss you gave me, and I shall be back for another before long. Don't forget me, Cutie, and I'll remember you.

Yours for remembering,

Cappie

Caspar put his letter in an envelope, sealed it, and selecting a stamp from a little open stamp box on the desk affixed it to the envelope. Then he sat back and tried to thing of something comfortable, to quiet the discomfort that had nagged him ever since he had been driven away from Eden's presence.

Of course he knew it was his own fault, and yet he told himself it was the only way to bring that silly girl to understand that she was all out of date, and had to give up her father's queer old ideas and get some new ones, learn what modern people and science had found out about the stuffy old religion that she had been brought up to respect. Of course he could never marry her while she held such fussy ideas. He couldn't be happy with her. But he had learned to know since he had seen her again that there was no one anywhere who came up to her in beauty and utter dearness, and he remembered how sweet she had been sometimes. Suddenly that inward urge made him reach forward and take another sheet of the heavily embossed paper, and start to write again.

Dear Eden:

I am still thinking of you, though I know if you are thinking of me it is probably to hate me. I don't know why I had to be so disagreeable to you, but I just couldn't help it. I felt you must somehow be made to wake up and get wise to the modern way of thinking. But I might have gone a little slower, and not have antagonized you quite so much. For I am convinced that it won't be long before you find out that I am right, and then I am certain you will change your ideas, and we shall be okay as chums and pals again, and perhaps something still closer.

He read over what he had written and decided it sounded very well, and was a good line to go on, sort of sympathetic and loving, and would show her he hadn't given her up for all her hard refusals. He frowned at the paper and decided to write a few more lines.

I don't know when I shall be coming back—perhaps soon, because I have almost enough points to rate being discharged. And it occurs to me that you didn't even take enough interest in me to notice my rank and decorations. I have some you might as an old pal of mine be proud to see. But of course there is always the possibility that I may be picked off in one of these last trips, so if that's my fate, don't worry about me. When you're dead you're dead, and that's all there is to it. I won't have to worry any longer about how an old friend treated me.

But I'm no pessimist, I don't expect to pass out yet. I'm too young, and there's too much left for me to live for. But if I do I guess I'll stand as good a chance as the next guy, so don't worry your pretty head praying for me. I'm not worth it. Besides I don't believe in it any more, remember.

So long, and I'll be seeing you again soon.

Cappie

His friend was returning, coming up the steps. He scribbled his name crazily, put the letter in another envelope, stamped and sealed it, and rose to go out with his friend, feeling most virtuous because he had written two letters. If one didn't "take," perhaps the other would. The way he felt just now it didn't seem to matter much which one. So at the next post box the two letters started on their way together.

CHAPTER THIRTEEN

THE DAY seemed to glow more gloriously for Eden as they drove farther away from the home town, and penetrated into little by-roads where she had not often gone. They passed pleasant farmhouses back from the road with plenty of trees about them, that suited so well their surroundings, fairly glowing in autumn colors. Nice smug villages with neat well-painted houses, and children playing on the street or in the yards. The woman's clubhouse, unpretentious, but well cared for, two or three little churches of different denominations, and then more woods, a modest mountain or two grading down to lovely green hills and more little villages.

And at last they came to the fine old elm-shaded farmhouse where the dying man was waiting for them.

The banker and lawyer got out and went into the house, leaving Eden with Mrs. Worden. They sat in the comfortable car and talked quietly, feeling somehow the shadow of death that was hovering over that house. Mrs. Worden spoke of the old man's wife who had died a couple of years before, and his married daughter who had several children, and his two sons who were both still across the seas. And then they gradually got to talking of people they both knew well in Glencarroll. It wasn't a particularly enlivening conversation, and Eden was glad when at last the two men came back and got into the car, their business completed.

The sun was getting ready for a grand display of flaming sky as they started on their way again, and delicate tintings flashed into vivid colorings as the sun slipped down lower and lower behind the lovely wooded hills. The sky above glowed deeper and dashed into crimson and turquoise and purple and gold, with beauty that made the two young people in the front seat catch their breath with delight in its loveliness. And the older people, too, took their pleasure in it, though more quietly.

It had been planned that they should journey on to a smaller city on the fringe of the mountains to a rather famous inn to take dinner, and they all felt that the day was having a rare ending as far as setting was concerned.

But it was in this time with that glowing, vivid sky above them that Eden and Lance Lorrimer had their opportunity for quiet talk. It seemed that Eden had so many questions, and the young lawyer was the only one she felt could really answer them, because her shyness with him had been broken down by former talks, and because he understood the new life she was striving to enter.

The sound of their going drowned their quiet voices, so that they did not feel that they had an audience, and Lance Lorrimer studied the girl's sweet face and rejoiced to see the devout look of earnestness in her eyes.

She had been almost too shy to introduce the themes about which she had planned to ask him, but suddenly he turned to her and asked, "Well, how did you come out? Were you helped through the hard time you were anticipating?"

She turned a bright face toward him, that nevertheless was touched by a shadow of perplexity.

"Oh, yes, I was helped. I was able to really speak out the truth of what I felt was so. But—"

"But what?" he asked interestedly. "There are no buts where God is concerned you know. Not if you are fully leaving it to Him."

"Yes, I know," said Eden slowly, "but afterward I wondered, was I really leaving it all to God, or was I putting in my own oar, what I thought was righteous anger at somebody? I'm afraid I wasn't gentle enough. He had spoken out against God, and I couldn't just let it go, could I? But do you think it is ever right to be severe?"

"Sometimes," said Lorrimer, trying to follow her difficult utterance. "You couldn't just keep still and seem to agree against your Lord."

"I know," said Eden, "but still it was hard not to be angry at him. I think I was pretty severe, and afterward I felt that perhaps there had been too much of myself and my own personal indignation. But it was a help to know you were praying."

"It was a joy to me to have the privilege," said the young man almost reverently.

It was sweet low talk, and their earnest young faces made a picture of interest to the two older people who sat behind them.

Then suddenly they reached the inn, and the quiet time was over, the lovely day gone, into a blending of purple and gold below a dome of delicate rose and green, with a single star glinting out like a diamond on a lovely fabric.

They had a delicious dinner, a pleasant talk together, and it was a relief to Eden to be away from all the thoughts that had troubled her since her father had been taken from her.

But what would she have said if she could have known that another element was to come into her life on the morrow?

Oh, it was just an old college friend, Vesta Nevin, and her brother Niles Nevin, who boarded the southbound train from Boston that evening, and laid their plans for an outing that was to include a trip to Washington, and places still farther south, Florida perhaps.

"I'll tell you what I'd like to do, Niles, if it won't upset any of your plans," said Vesta as they settled back to wait while their berths were being made up. "I'd like to run down a few hours to Glencarroll and see my friend Eden. It's not so far below New York, at least it's between Philadelphia and New York somewhere, and we could take an early train down from New York and stop off to see her. I know she'd adore to see me, for we were very close friends in college you know, and she's just lost her father. I'd like to be sympathetic enough to stop off and see her and find out what she is going to do now. You met her, too, don't you remember, once at a college prom or something? She's a darling, and pretty as a picture, or was. How about it? Can you humor me?"

"Why sure, Vesta, if you want to. I could hang around and do something while you were chattering," he smiled derisively. "Yes, I do remember some pretty little girl you especially emphasized when you introduced your gang. Wasn't she a lot younger than you? As I remember her she seemed a mere child."

"She wasn't," said Vesta. " She was one of the brightest girls in college, and only three months younger than I was. I hope you don't feel I'm a mere child."

"You'll pass," grinned the brother, settling back against the cushion and looking at his pretty sister admiringly. "Of course we'll arrange to stop off and see her if you like. This trip is your birthday present, you know. A pity if you can't have one stop off to please you."

"But Niles, I want you to go along to the house. I like to show off my distinguished big brother. I won't enjoy it one little minute if I think you are sighing around somewhere getting impatient."

"Oh, I'll go along of course and do the honors, be polite and all that. But say, isn't this the girl that had such a distinguished father, wrote books or something?"

"Yes, wrote books and gave lectures too, and was a rich banker, besides. I don't see how she stands it to have him gone. She was so devoted to him."

"Oh, heavens! Then I suppose we'll have to go through a lot of sob stuff and you know how I detest that," said the young man, looking annoyed.

"I don't think you will," said the sister. "Eden wasn't the sobbing kind. She was always sweet and self-controlled, and you'll like her, I know. She's traveled a great deal, and she can talk well."

"Oh, I suppose you'd think so if you like her. But well, all right, let's take in Glencarroll in our tour. It's better to have it come at the beginning this way, and then feel free. All right. In the morning I'll get hold of some timetables and see how trains are. It's a pity we haven't got our new car. It would be so much easier to take in these side trips that are sure to appear as we go on. But cheer up. It won't be long before I can get that new car, and then we'll take another trip somewhere and try it out."

So the matter was settled very happily and they soon went to their rest. But quite early the next morning Niles Nevin, consulting with the porter, got hold of necessary timetables, and mapped out a workable schedule for a stop-over at Glencarroll.

"We'd better send a wire or telephone, announcing our approach," said the young man while they were in the dining car eating a hearty breakfast.

"Oh, I'd much rather walk in on her and surprise her," said Vesta. "If we announce our coming she would think she had to get ready for us, invite us to stay over or something elaborate, and I'd just enjoy surprising her. She loves surprises."

"But you don't even know she is at home, and if she isn't we could save ourselves a trip and wouldn't have to bother going out of our way."

But Vesta shook her head.

"Sorry, brother, that this is such a bore to you, but I want to go anyway. I want to see where she lives. She's told me so much about her home, and I want to see it even if she isn't there."

"Well, of course if you feel that way, then that's what we'll do."

So about the middle of the morning a taxi drew up at the Thurston home, and the two young people got out and went in.

It was Janet of course who came to the door, as Tabor

was not yet able to sit up, and when she said she would call her young lady, Vesta burst forth with an eager: "You're Janet, aren't you? Eden has told me so much about you, I was sure it was you."

Janet melted at once into cordiality and looked sharply at the visitor's pretty face.

"Yes, I'm Janet, an' yersel' must be Miss Vesta, my leddy's co-lidge roommate. I've seen yer likeness. She's thet fond o' yer bonnie picter, an' she'll be ower glad tae see ye. Coom in an' I'll ca' her."

"And Janet, this is my brother Niles. We're on our way to Florida and we stopped off just to see Eden!"

Suddenly Eden abovestairs heard the beloved voice of her old friend and hurried down to greet her.

It was a glad reunion, for Eden had been very fond of her former roommate, and she had not seen her for more than a year. For the first few minutes the time was occupied with questions and answers, accounting for what each had been doing, and the handsome brother sat by and watched the lovely stranger. For once he thoroughly agreed with his sister's judgment of the right girl for a friend for her. As a rule he had some fault to find with all her girl friends, but this girl seemed not only really beautiful, but she seemed exceedingly intelligent, a good conversationalist with a good sense of humor. Even though she had just been through a severe sorrow she was able to laugh merrily, which was a relief, for he had counted on this visit being quite sad, full of sob stuff. But the recent death of Eden's father had only been mentioned casually, and his sister's words of sympathy had been received with a gentle smile.

"Yes, I knew you would understand and sympathize with me," Eden had said tenderly. "I was sure you would understand how hard it had been for me. But you know, Vesta, we had such a beautiful time the last few weeks together. Dad talked with me about his going, and tried to make it plain just what I would have to meet, and so even yet, though I miss him so terribly, I still feel that I am just on a journey and have to go on until the time comes to meet him again. He made it seem that way. And now, tell me where you have been all this time, and what you have been doing since you left college."

And then the talk floated off into reminiscences of their journeys and interests, and there was hardly a chance for the brother to get a word in edgewise, until he suddenly broke in upon their chatter.

"Vesta, are you still determined to take that twelve-thirty train? Because if so we've barely time to get to the station before it comes."

"Oh, but you mustn't," protested Eden. "We haven't half caught up on old times yet. You'll have to stay here to lunch of course. If I know Janet she's got some kind of a lunch ready. It may not be up to our usual style because our butler has had an accident and has been very sick.

He's better now and we hope will soon be up and taking his part in the household regime, but in the meantime we're taking whatever can be gotten together in a hurry. Do you mind? Yes, here's Janet. They're ready for us. And surely there are other trains. After all this long time apart you *must* stay a little longer. *Please!*"

The young man smiled at the eager light in the girl's lovely eyes, and then his own eyes sought his sister's face.

"We could take the later train, Vesta," he said leniently, to let her know he was not being bored as he had expected.

"All right," said the sister, "we'll wait for the afternoon train, provided you'll consider going with us to Florida. Will you?"

A shadow of gravity came over Eden's bright face.

"Oh! That would be lovely of course, but I really couldn't think of going away anywhere just now. Perhaps sometime later, but I'm not sure."

Then they began to tease her, to present every possible argument to induce her to go with them, but she was firm.

"I really couldn't think of leaving home while Tabor is so sick."

"But isn't he just a servant? Can't you trust the other servants and your doctor and nurse to look after him? I think that's absurd to let a servant interfere with your own plans and happiness."

205

"You don't understand, Vesta," said Eden earnestly. "Tabor is one of us. He has been with my father since my father and mother were married. Before I was born he was here, and we all love him very much. And now that he is getting better he likes me to read to him, and sing for him sometimes. No, I could not go anywhere at present. But I wish you would promise to stop here on your way back. I think we could have some nice times together."

"Well, perhaps we will. But better still, why not come down to us for a while after your servant gets well enough to leave?"

Eden gave a swift review of her unconsidered near-future, hesitated and smiled.

"Well, that sounds pleasant. I'll think about it and see how things turn out. I can't really promise yet. It depends a little on several other people just what plans I can make."

"Oh, now, now," said the young man, "that doesn't sound very hopeful. You haven't any other servants who are coming down with something and have to be nursed, have you? Or you haven't got a young man in the offing somewhere who has a hold on you?"

Eden laughed and shook her head. "No, I hope not, but there are several matters I have to look after, and I'm not sure how long they may take. But I'll really think about it and see if it can be managed."

Afterward, when the pleasant guests had left on the

afternoon train, and Eden was alone, she sat and thought about it a few minutes, and tried to be frank with herself. She decided that the truth was, she just didn't want to go away anywhere, even in delightful company. She wanted to stay here, and go on getting acquainted with this new life.

Then she suddenly remembered that parting fling: "You haven't a young man in the offing somewhere who has a hold on you?" and her face grew sober. Was it possible that Lance Lorrimer was getting too interesting? Ought she perhaps to go away and put a stop to any such interest before it got a hold on her? She didn't know a thing about the young lawyer except that he was a Christian. He might be engaged, or even married for all she knew, and she simply must not allow herself to let her thoughts dwell too interestedly on him. At least not now. Not till she knew more about him. And of course he wasn't interested in her except to help her. They certainly had a right to a bit of pleasant friendship on that score.

But the thought lingered with her, and she had to own that she liked him a lot. She really hadn't thought about him before in the light of a possible close companion, and she mustn't either. Her father's words of warning, her mother's letters reminded her that she must go carefully.

But on the way to the city to take the evening train for Florida, with maybe a stop-over in Washington, the Nevin brother and sister were discussing the recent visit.

"Well, she's some girl, I grant you. I don't wonder you raved so over her when you came back from college. I thought you were crazy, you know, you talked so much about her, and to tell you the truth I didn't see stopping over there today to see a colorless little girl like that, even if her father was famous, and she did have a private income of her own, as you saw fit to emphasize again and again. But now I've seen her I don't wonder in the least. I certainly hope she gets loose from that doddering old servant of hers pretty soon and that we can coax her down to Florida with us. I could go for her in a big way. She's some girl, and I wouldn't care whether she had any old inheritance or not. What's money when you find the right girl? I believe I've found her, thanks to my sister. Now Vesta, are you satisfied?"

Vesta smiled.

"I knew you would like her, Niles. That's why I was so insistent about going. I certainly spent time on you when I was in college trying to get you two together. I couldn't think of any more ideal relative to have as a sister than Eden."

"Well, didn't I always tell you you had good taste, my lady-sister?"

"Oh, don't be silly. I'm just happy to think you liked her. The only trouble is I'm afraid you'll find some dizzy blonde down in Florida and fall for her even harder that for Eden."

Niles gave her a grin that acknowledged he knew his own weaknesses.

"Okay," he said. "I know I've fallen for a good many, but not so hard I couldn't be sure I wouldn't find somebody better. However, you know I'm growing older. The time has got to come when one reaches a maturity. He does get a little sense and realize that he must settle down for keeps. However if you object to my present admiration, I presume I can find someone else to rave over, until we get home at least."

"Oh, stop acting like a fool, Niles, and talk sense. I'm terribly glad you liked Eden, and perhaps we'll get a chance to see more of her this winter. In the meantime, when and where are going to stop in Washington? Or shall we go straight on to Florida where we have reservations?"

So they drifted into talk about other matters. But when Vesta went to her rest that night in a dinky little rooming house in Washington, which was the only respectable place they could find, she lay for sometime turning over the thin little pillow and exulting in the fact that Niles had really admired her beloved friend.

Chapter Fourteen

Lavira Fane was a clever woman. If she hadn't been she would have had many more charges against her than she had, for so far she had pretty well got away with them. A few days in jail now and then, and some old pal with the hope of gain thereby, would turn up to swear an alibi for her, or testify to some utterly false statement.

And it was a help that in addition to her cleverness she could on occasion be most humble, although some people described that humility as "meaching." But she could if necessary deceive even a matron of a suburban prison.

So for the first few days of her re-confinement in the Glencarroll prison she was quiet, subdued, almost humble in her manner, biding her time. Saying to the matron that she really was grateful that she had been caught, for she simply dreaded to be out alone with the authorities against her. She told the matron she never had been smart to get away with things, that she had been brought up to be a good Christian woman, and she did not know how to deceive, and she readily perceived that if one once got suspected of anything it was hopeless. Especially in her present position, here far away from her home and friends how could she hope to get help? No one knew her any more, and no one was ready to help. Not even that little snob of an Eden Thurston would lift her hand to help her, though she was at least distantly related.

So she was a most docile prisoner, and the matron, accustomed though she was to judging tough characters, began to feel sorry for her, a poor old woman, whose son was really the only sinner of course, for now he had deserted her and left her to shift for herself.

She even considered the possibility of suggesting to the authorities that someone might get in touch with the parents of the child who had sent the pitiful appeal to her for a string of red beads. Perhaps someone, if he knew, might shed light on her case, and produce some relatives to take over the poor soul, whom she told the guards was so sad and dejected and quite willing to resign herself to perpetual servitude.

Lavira played this role so well that she was often allowed to come to the kitchen with the matron and help her with the cooking, glad to be of service in her despondent state. That was how it seemed. And so days passed by and the matron was kind to the poor woman, and gave her a privilege now and then, and some bit of extra fruit with her meals, and often called her to help her in the kitchen, which she did quite willingly though most shyly, looking almost frightened whenever the outside door opened near her, and turning that quick furtive look almost as if to run away and hide. And strange to say that matron really began to trust Lavira.

Still, she was a good conscientious matron, and knew the rules of her institution, knew what was expected of her, and took no chances. She had been a matron too long in such places not to know she might be mistaken.

But one evening just at dark, they were baking hot johnny-cake as a special treat. The grocery boy came in with his late Saturday night delivery order, just as the matron was taking out a hot pan of corn bread. Then the telephone rang.

The matron dropped the hot pan on the top of the stove and went to unfasten the door for the groceries. The telephone rang persistently. It was against the rule for her to send a prisoner to the telephone, and the grocery boy was waiting to have the order signed and his basket emptied. The matron looked wildly from the waiting boy to the telephone, and then despairingly to her burning corn bread in the oven. But Lavira was there with all her senses alert, and stepped toward the oven.

"Don't you worry, I'll take the rest of the pans out," she said, stooping with a holder and lifting out the next pan, setting it on the top of the stove. So the matron signed the grocery boy's paper, and turned to answer that insistent telephone which she knew must be her director calling her. It was only a step or two to the phone in the corridor, and the communication was sharp and direct. "Yes, sir! Right away sir!" she answered in a businesslike tone.

But when she turned back to her stove the oven door was still wide open, a smell of scorched baking in the air, the grocery boy was gone, the back door was wide open and Lavira was nowhere to be seen!

The corn bread had to go on burning—discouraged a trifle by the open oven door, and the cold air rushing in from the outside—while the matron dashed wildly out of the door into the darkness calling after the grocery boy to know if he had seen the woman disappear. But the sound of the delivery car rattling down the lane showed her how hopeless that was, and there seemed to be no sign of any dark figures in the alley. The matron rushed back to the telephone and gave the alarm to her chief, her soul filled with fury to think she had been caught with the same prisoner disappearing for the second time.

Lavira had been very quick. She knew how to slither into the shadows, and this time she had been preparing her mind for just such an opportunity as had come with that combination of circumstances, the burning food about to be served, the grocery boy, and the telephone. She had dropped the second pan like a flash and dashed out the open door and down the back steps, taking only time to snatch the old gray blanket from the seat of the delivery car, as she slid across to take shelter around the corner of a garage with its door wide open. It took but a second to fling the old blanket about her and over her head as she hurried along, out of the alley and down another street and another, avoiding pedestrians as much as possible, and dashing on toward a country road she had often sighted when it had been possible for her to look out a window. It was strange what cleverness and planning could do for a woman when her freedom was at stake.

The matron worked fast. She got the whole force on the job at once, and then she went back to get those trays ready for the hungry prisoners, and take out the rest of the corn bread before it was burned to a crisp. As the whole force was on the job she had no doubt but the fugitive would soon be found. She simply couldn't have got far away. But she knew, too, that her own time of reckoning would come. Oh, what a fool she had been! To trust that sly woman! Of course she was not glad to stay. She must have been watching every moment for a chance to get away. She with her son at large, and both of them now free to carry on their machinations. She recalled suddenly that some of the police force thought that the message from the child asking for red beads might have been a communication from the son, and now she was convinced it was, for she recalled the look in the woman's face when she showed it to her, so furtive. The matron was in sore trouble now lest she was going to lose her own job. It had been an easy one in a way, and one that she could not afford to lose.

And so for the second time Mike came to the Thurston home with his crew and got permission to look around the house for any possible hiding place. A few minutes later Mr. Worden was notified and promptly sent his right-hand man, Lance Lorrimer, over to spend the evening with Eden and keep her from finding out about what had occurred, or at least keep her from worrying if it became necessary to tell her.

Eden had been with Tabor, reading a bit of the news and his evening chapter to him, and she came to meet her guest with a shining face, aglow from Tabor's daily thanks for her kindness. It seemed a happy time. And now to have Mr. Lorrimer come and settle down as if he were going to stay awhile made her feel very glad.

He took both her hands in his two hands as he greeted her, and held them for just a second as if he too were glad, and smiled, deep into her eyes.

"Do you mind my coming just to see you?" he asked, almost shyly.

"Oh, did you do that really, *just* to see me? How wonderful! I can't think of anything nicer you could do to please me," she said, with that ripple of welcoming joy in her voice that sounded so genuine. "And you won't hurry right off somewhere in a few minutes, this time, will you? You're always so busy, and a lot of stupid other people always have so very much time to stay and bore me."

He smiled.

"Why, I thought you had a lot of wonderful friends," he said, studying her face wistfully. "They said some came down from New York, old friends."

Eden laughed.

"Now, where did you get that gossip? Surely you haven't been interviewing the kitchen maids?"

He laughed.

"Why, if I remember rightly it came to Mr. Worden through Mike, who, I think, did get it from your own kitchen perhaps. I don't know that I would exactly call it gossip!"

"Why no, of course not," she laughed. "Well, it was pleasant seeing them, but that was all. That has nothing to do with my being glad to see you. You see, there is one difference. You talk about *real* things and they talk about frills and nonsense. Yet of course they are very nice people and I like them a lot. But there is another thing, too, *you* understand about Tabor, and are in sympathy with him, and all my other friends keep commiserating me for having him in the house while he is getting well. They think I ought to send him to a hospital or a nursing home or something! 'Only a *servant!*' they say with a sneer, and that makes me wild. They don't know what he's always been to all of us. But you have seemed to understand. Even Mr. Worden understands a little I think, for he has never suggested that I send Tabor away. Of course I wouldn't even if he had."

"Yes," said Lorrimer with a light in his eyes. "I understand, and I think your feeling in the matter is beautiful. And I am sure that from what little I have known of your wonderful father, he would have understood, too. Perhaps he knows now, and is pleased."

"Oh, I'm so glad to hear you say so," she said eagerly. "I was almost sure you understood."

"Thank you for understanding *me* so well," smiled the young man. "And by the way, how is Tabor tonight?"

"Oh, he is getting well rapidly now, the doctor says, and he seems so happy. The doctor says it has made a big difference having him here. That Tabor would have been very lonely and despairing if he had been taken away. He knows he is getting old, and I'm afraid he has been feeling that his time of usefulness is almost past. I couldn't have stood it to have him go away, and I know he is being cared for as well as he could possibly be in a hospital. We have a wonderful nurse and doctor, and it isn't as if we needed any equipment that we could not easily procure."

"I am so glad you feel that way," said Lorrimer. "Do

you know it was that in you that first made me feel you were different from other girls. You were more kindly and thoughtful, more loyal to those who were devoted to you."

Eden's face glowed with this bit of praise.

"It is good to hear you say that," she admitted shyly, "because so many have talked another way, and almost made me hate them, only I knew they didn't understand."

Then just at that point Janet came to the door, with her deprecating air that she had to interrupt:

"Miss Eden," she said, "sorry to interrupt, but Tabor was wantin' tae know if that was Mr. Lorrimer in here, and if so, might he be seein' him for a wee while. He'll not keep him ower lang."

"Why yes, of course," said Eden. "Mr. Lorrimer, you asked about Tabor and now he wants to see you. Do you mind?"

"Of course," said the young man, springing up. "You'll excuse me for a few minutes, Eden?"

"Of course," she said, and started to go with him, then stepped back as she saw Janet wanted to speak to her.

"That's all right," said Lorrimer, "I know the way to Tabor's room," and he hurried down the hall.

"Ye'll be needin' a tray in a wee while?" Janet asked in a low tone. "Anything special ye'll be wantin'?"

"Oh, I'll leave that to you, Janet. Your trays are always

grand! But, Janet, wasn't there somebody else in to see Tabor? I thought I heard another voice. Had I better go and see? Tabor mustn't have too much company at once."

"It's joost Mike drapped in fer a chat. Tabor's all richt! Better let thim have their talk, Miss Eden."

Eden gave a quick suspicious look at Janet. She was well acquainted with her tone of voice whenever Janet was trying to evade a question, so she spoke quickly:

"Has something happened, Janet? What is Mike here for? He ought not to worry Tabor. The doctor said we must keep him quiet.'

"Tabor's all richt!" said Janet quickly, an anxious smile in her eyes.

"I must go and see," said Eden, and in spite of Janet's earnest "No, no Miss Eden, best leave thim talk alane," she hurried out into the hall and down to the far door where Tabor lay. She appeared just in time to hear Mike say: "I think she oughtta be told, Mr. Lorrimer. She's a sensible lady, and she'll be much safer if she knows all. She should stay in the house which will be well guarded until we can locate the old un. No tellin' what that bird might not try if she's desperate, an' I think she is. Of course we'll put a strong guard around the place tonight."

Then there was Eden standing in the door, and facing Mike.

"Yes? What is it, Mike, that I ought to be told? You tell me. I won't mind what it is. I know you folks will take care of me."

"Yes, my lady," put in Tabor's voice most earnestly, with all the quaver gone, and a look as if he were going to get right up and guard her. "You mustn't go out of the house until Mike says it's safe, Miss Eden! And that's straight! You needn't get worried."

"Of course, Tabor," said Eden quickly, "I'll do what I'm told, but I'm not worried. Now what is it all about, Mike?" She looked directly at the embarrassed policeman, who hadn't an idea she had been within hearing while he was talking.

"Why, beggin' yer pardon, Miss, it's juist that the old un played her cards well with our matron, and she's got out again, an' we don't know but she might come this way. We're not lettin' you out of our sight till we're sure where she is."

"Oh!" said Eden, looking startled, and then regaining her composure, "but she won't come this way again. At least I don't think so. She won't take the same chance twice."

"But she might, that," said Mike gruffly. "She knows there was cloes hangin' in that there tool shed. She might take a chance to see if they is there yet. Ya see she has only prison cloes, and knows they might be noticed. She had got only what she had on when she got away, the matron's

220

apron, an' her own dress. We know what to watch for, un-less she can get a change. She did take the blanket off the grocery boy's delivery truck. She might wrap that around her, but she'd likely take any chance to get those cloes she hid behind the last time."

"Well, maybe," said Eden, looking thoughtfully at Mike. "But really I think we ought not to stand here in Tabor's room talking. The doctor said I was to be very careful that he didn't get excited."

"The doctor knows we're here, Miss Eden," explained Mike. "He knew we needed to ask Tabor some questions, and he said we might come."

"Oh," said Eden, looking from one to another of the men. "That's all right then, I suppose. Have you asked your questions?"

"Yes, Miss Thurston, we found out all we need to know about the one that stabbed Tabor, and he saw the old un take refuge in the tool house the last time. He tried to stop her. That was how Tabor got hurt."

"All right," said Eden cheerfully. "I'm sorry you had to be dragged into this, but I think we ought to get right out and let Tabor go to sleep. It's past his sleeping time now, isn't it, nurse?" to the nurse who had entered with a wor-ried look, and nodded in answer to Eden's question.

"Well, then, we'll say good night and go. Tabor, you needn't worry about me. I'll do just what Mike and Mr. Lorrimer tell me I ought to do, and if I have to go out anywhere I'll take somebody with me, but I won't go until Mike says I can. And now Tabor, you and I will remember that verse we read tonight, 'The angel of the Lord encampeth round about them that fear Him and delivereth them.' Just rest on that, Tabor," and Eden gave the old servant's hand a little pat, and a smile, and led the others away.

They all came out following her as if they had been attending some kind of religious service, and even the policeman walked more softly, spoke in a lower tone to Lorrimer, and kept his anxious gaze downward.

Lorrimer and Mike lingered by the side doorway for a minute or two while Mike outlined the plan of defense, and noted down one or two directions which seemed important. Then Lorrimer came back to Eden in the living room.

"Too bad we had to have that interruption in our pleasant evening," said the young man as they sat down again, with a graver expression on his face than when he had left the room a few minutes before.

"It's all right," said Eden quietly, with a faint smile, "somehow I've felt all along that we were not through with this business yet. I'm not surprised at anything. But I certainly am glad that you were here."

"So am I," said the young man with a tender smile. "But you certainly are a brave girl. Most young women I know would be terribly upset by finding all this out. They told me not to let you know what was going on. They sent for me to make sure I would understand in case we heard shots, or footsteps walking around the house, and it doesn't seem to worry you at all."

"Well, why should I be worried with so many good friends to guard me? I realize of course that Mrs. Fane is an unscrupulous woman, and rather desperate, and wouldn't stop at anything if she were cornered. But I think too she is a coward. Perhaps I'm wrong, but she wouldn't do anything wild like shooting somebody, or kidnapping, unless she was very sure she could get away with it. I think her role is to act like a wealthy woman who was doing a kindly deed. At least that is the way she made her approach here when she arrived."

"Yes," said Lorrimer thoughtfully, "that may be the way she makes her approach, innocent and kindly, but I wouldn't be too sure she isn't familiar with the ways of guns and the like. So please just act as if you knew she was the worst criminal living. That will make it easier for the rest of us."

"Oh, I will," said Eden earnestly. "It is wonderful to be taken care of again. But I'm not afraid, truly."

"Well, of course it is grand to have courage, but re-member we are taking no chances on just courage."

He gave her a smile that made her heart feel all warm and happy, and her face grew bright with a grateful smile of her own.

"Now," he said as he drew up two chairs in front of the fire, "where is that poem you promised last week you would read to me? I've been looking forward to hearing it ever since."

"I'll get it," said Eden turning to the bookcase between the windows and selecting a bright volume, with leaves that looked as if they had had much use.

She turned to the old lovely words:

Where the quiet-colored end of evening smiles
    Miles and miles,
On the solitary pastures where our sheep
    Half-asleep
Tinkle homeward through the twilight, stray or stop
    As they crop—
Was the sight once of a city great and gay
    (So they say),
Of our country's very capital, it's prince
    Ages since
Held his court in, gathered councils, wielding far
    Peace or war.

And so they were off to a pleasant enjoyment and discussion of Browning.

When she had finished the reading his eyes showed his appreciation.

"Yes, I had read the poem long ago," he said, "but you have made it live again, and painted the picture of that colored evening as I never conceived it before. And, too, it gives such a broad outlook on the world, going on through the centuries, doing all the things we are doing today, building cities, enjoying gay times, living, sinning, fighting, loving as we do now, and dying. It makes the world seem so small after all, to think how many years it has been going on and yet our thoughts and impulses are much the same. Still the old Adam cropping up and bringing on wars."

"They had wars in Bible times, didn't they? Does God like war? If not, why does He allow it?"

"No, God doesn't *like* war, but He uses it sometimes to punish His people who are sinning. He allows it to serve His own purposes. He sometimes sent different nations against those who were not keeping His commandments, who had sinned against Him. He sent the Medes against Babylon to destroy it. He sent word to them to get their weapons ready. 'Make bright the arrows.' You know that means to sharpen them, get them ready for use. And 'gather the shields together.' They had to have bright arrows, not rusty ones that would do no good when they hit the mark."

"But how would that apply to us?" asked Eden, puzzled. "That is, Christians. Does He want them to fight too?"

"Yes, He has told us that we are all in a warfare, 'not against flesh and blood, but against principalities, and

powers, against rulers of the darkness of this world.' And
He has told us to 'put on the whole armour of God.' And
the weapon we are to use is the sword of the Spirit which
is the Word of God. I have always thought that that must
be like the bright arrows that were to be kept sharp and
polished and ready for use. And it has seemed to me that
we should be very diligent about keeping that sword polished and ready, those arrows of God, His own Words,
bright and flashing as they speed to reach the enemy. And
of course the enemy is not just people who don't agree
with us, a mistake some make that causes awful trouble.
The enemy is the devil who blinds and confuses people as
to what is the real truth. That is why we ought to be often
studying God's Word, so that it will be on the very tips of
our tongues, ready to be used at a time of need. And the
Spirit will always tell us *when* that time has come, so that
we shall not be wasting its bright flashing at an unseemly
time. There will be times when the foe presses hard when
a few of those bright arrows flashing through the air may
bring great victory."

"That is wonderful. I've never heard anybody bring
out those thoughts before. Bright arrows. God's Word
in my heart, on my tongue, might be that, do you mean?
Might speed the truth and make futile the darts of the
enemy? And with the shield of my faith in God I shall
not be hurt?"

"That's right. You have the idea. I think you had it before I spoke, for that verse you left with Tabor tonight was verily a bright arrow against the fear of worry and trouble. You know many verses like that. God will teach you when to use them. And now, how about a bit of music, some of your sweet hymns. Wouldn't they help Tabor to trust and not worry, and you and me, too, perhaps? First you play some of those sweet hymns your father used to love, and then maybe we could sing:

Be not dismayed whate'er betide,
God will take care of you;
Beneath His wings of love abide,
God will take care of you.

For answer Eden sat down at the piano and began to play softly, the tender sweet melodies her father used to love, and with which she was sure Tabor was most familiar. Lorrimer sat in the big chair near by, just in the shadow, and watched her admiringly. Eden's face was full of feeling, for she was going back in spirit to the evenings when her dear father had sat listening, sometimes chiming in with his sweet tenor that had once been so strong and thrilling.

And now after a few minutes her fingers went softly into the gospel song they both knew and their voices mingled in the tender words, "God will take care of you."

As the last note died softly away they looked up, and there stood Janet with her tray. Hot scones, tiny sponge cakes, hot chocolate topped by whipped cream.

"Mr. Tabor sent ye worrud, thank ye baith fer the singin', an' tae tell ye it were juist like Heaven tae hear ye."

Their faces lighted up.

"We hoped he would like it," said Eden.

"Yes, tell him we are glad he liked it."

They lingered over the delicious repast, making a gala supper of the simple fare, and when Janet came back and saw that Lorrimer was about to leave, she said: "We'll be all richt, dinna fear. Mike's stayin' the night hissel'."

Lance Lorrimer took Eden's hands for a brief clasp, pressing her fingers warmly, smiling into her eyes.

"Good night, dear lady! We'll be praying!" he said, and Janet, bless her heart, smiled to herself at the words she thought she heard with her deaf ears.

CHAPTER FIFTEEN

FOR SEVERAL days the careful guarding of Eden went on, though they didn't say much about it to the girl herself. Mr. Worden had warned them all not to frighten Eden. But Eden was not frightened and she made them all understand that so thoroughly that even Janet realized it. Though she always insisted on going out with her whenever Eden felt she ought to go anywhere.

And the police had an organized guard about the house for, to tell the truth, they had discovered that the garments behind which Lavira had hidden in the toolroom on her first escape were gone this time, though no one had discovered that until the second day. The police didn't tell Eden, but they had a little something more to go on to broadcast her description than at first. And presently they discovered that a person of Mrs. Fane's description and clad in a worn old cloak and a long green skirt and brown veil had been reported hitchhiking along a road two hundred miles to the west of Glencarroll. Another day or two brought word from watching police who had been on the alert since Lavira Fane's disappearance from the jail, that such a woman had been picked up by a kindly farmer-couple and carried on fifty miles farther.

Then silence for two days, and the report of a woman arrested for stealing garments in a store in the northwest. For by this time Lavira's prison picture had been sent about. It was considered an important case, as there were two persons involved in the holdup as well as several valuable jewels which had been found on them. But there was no doubt but that this woman arrested for stealing clothing was guilty for she had the stolen goods in her possession, and so she was held. She gave, of course, another name. She said she was Annette Coleman, lived in a small town in Iowa, had always wanted something pretty, and had intended of course to pay for what she had taken when she got home to her husband.

Investigation showed that there was no living husband, and no home, and no town where she said she lived. And when confronted by her own snapshot from the prison record in Glencarroll, the look in her eyes as she denied that it was her picture, made them sure she was the same woman who was wanted in Glencarroll.

But having got away from the police a number of times Lavira bided her time and made a getaway again, heading this time toward a hideout in a lonely range of mountains where she felt reasonably sure she would find her son, together with the promised string of "red beads" which would amply finance their further movements.

But the police in the Middle West were on the alert and Lavira was soon brought back to police headquarters and put in safe keeping, to await a trial. As her misdemeanor in the department store was the most recent offense, it had priority, and so the woman was held in the western town.

So the days went by and the household of Thurston grew more at ease. Eden forgot her perplexities, and her face took on a more rested look.

Also Tabor was rapidly getting well now. The doctor was letting him sit up for a few minutes each day, and his wound was healing nicely. If things went on as well as this the doctor said he could count on being able to be about pretty soon and perhaps attend to little duties, like opening the door for callers, and setting tables and so on.

Lance Lorrimer was away. When he telephoned to call off a date with Eden to go to a meeting in the city, he said he was being sent away on business, and wasn't sure how long he would have to stay, nor where he might have to go before he returned. Eden felt a great dismay after she had hung up the receiver. It seemed somehow as if something important were gone, and then she reproved herself. How ridiculous of her! She must not get so interested in a young man that his coming and going meant so much to her that she was desolate without him. After all, there were not so many others with whom she could talk about the things that interested her. But she simply must snap out of this and get interested in something to keep her busy.

To that end she decided to join a Bible class that Lorrimer had told her about. It met in the evenings, of course, but she could take Janet with her and go in the car, if the police were still insistent that she should not go anywhere alone till those Fanes were caught.

And then that very first evening when she had decided to make a start, a caller arrived just after dinner, who turned out to be Niles Nevin. He at once announced his intention of taking the midnight train to New York to be ready for some business matters the next day. He had stopped off here, partly at his sister's insistence, and partly for his own selfish desire to spend the evening with Eden. He said he had come to coax her to return with him to Florida when he came back in a couple of days.

Eden didn't exactly like to tell him that she had other plans for her evening, for after all he had come out of his way to see her, and he was her dear friend's brother. Besides, this wasn't the only night she could go to the class, so she settled down to entertain the handsome young dilettante, who had no serious interest in life save an occasional business trip to sign a few papers and look idly into matters of his own personal income. Even that, he considered a great bore, and had no hesitation in saying so. Yet he certainly was good-looking and interesting, could talk well and entertainingly, could describe charmingly a view he had seen, of mountain or river or sea, and depict the frailties and follies of both his friends and enemies in a most amusing way. He could mimic and portray engagingly the people he had met in Florida and on his journeys, and could make time disappear in a flash, so that most amazingly it was time for his midnight train before she realized the evening was half over.

Yet when, as he rose to leave, he began to press her decision again to go back with him to Florida, Eden knew at once she did not want to go. Though she had to own to herself that she had enjoyed the evening, and that she could readily adapt herself to the kind of living he and his sister were evidently doing, somehow she was not in the mood for it now. What was the matter with her? Was it just because her father was gone, and she could not get used to the change and loneliness? No, that could not be it alone, for she had been prepared for that for some time before he left her.

And this was a pleasant young man, one whom she felt could be a delightful playmate. But somehow it was a strange thing. She found as she looked back after the evening was over that she had been constantly comparing him with Lance Lorrimer, trying to match him up with Lance. Why, it was just as if two kinds of life were being held up for her to choose from, and that was so silly. In the first place there was no choice. Lance was away, and he hadn't given any indication that he had time or interest in being a friendly companion except during that one evening when the Fanes were bothering again. And here was a young man who did not hesitate to proclaim his interest in her, and she didn't want him! Yet she couldn't explain to herself why she wasn't interested.

And then the next morning came a brief letter from Lance Lorrimer. It began,

Dear Eden,

I did not ask if I might write to you, because I was hoping that my errand would not keep me so long away. The end is not yet in sight. But I want to tell you how disappointed I am that I was not able to take you to that meeting we had planned to attend.

I hope you found a way to get there. I thought perhaps Janet would go with you, for I knew you would enjoy it. However, if this business ever gets itself over with and I can return, I hope you will allow me to make up for it.

I find myself very glad that you are in our

Heavenly Father's care, and that you know Him and rest in Him. I am not forgetting to pray for you.

Your friend in Christ,
Lance Lorrimer.

Eden went about her morning's affairs humming a soft little song of happiness after that letter came. It wasn't filled with a great admiration, nor coaxing her to do anything for him. It gave no address where she might write to him, and it didn't claim any exclusive interest for himself. It was almost impersonal in its tone, and yet there was about it an atmosphere of deep friendship, of feeling that they were one in their interests, and an assurance that an absence either long or short could not change their relationship. That they would always understand one another.

After she had read the letter and reread it several times she began to wonder in herself if perhaps the main reason why she did not want to go to Florida was just because she wanted to be right here waiting when Lance came back, not to miss welcoming him home. And if that was the case perhaps she ought in honesty to herself and to Lance to go away to Florida and get over this silly idea that her interest must all be in him. She toyed with the thought, and then she read her mother's last few letters over again. But when Niles Nevin came back and stopped to see if she had made up her mind to go back with him to his sister, and said they could get a plane and make a very brief trip of it, she told him no. She simply could not go away now. There were things she must do. Important things. But she hoped they would stop to see her in the spring when they came back. And then she found she was glad when the door closed behind him and he was gone.

"But I'm going to write to you," he warned her, "and I shall expect letters back. I shall demand them. For you and I have just got to get better acquainted."

Well, she told herself, perhaps this was according to her mother's advice, to go slowly in choosing her friends and not jump to a conclusion that a man with a handsome face, and riches, and a pleasant manner was the companion she should choose for life. Let him write—for a while perhaps. She would see what he was like. It might be better to judge a man by his letters than any other way.

And then came the glad day when Tabor was allowed to walk to the front door and look out for a moment. Afterward Eden spent an hour reading to him while he rested. The whole household was full of joy, servants and mistress, because Tabor was to be about among them again.

Niles Nevin was by no means out of the picture. He sent delightful little picture post cards of the places in Florida where he and his sister were visiting, or taking trips, and he wrote brief bits of messages on them, as an intimate friend might write, as if their friendship were thoroughly established. He had always a bright joke or a funny story in each one, and very often he spoke of how he wished she were with them, and how delightful it was going to be when they got back to New York and she came to visit them. Then he began to talk about summer resorts and tried to sell her on several, begging her to say which one she would prefer, and whether she wouldn't begin now to arrange it at home so that she could be away with them all summer? He always took it for granted that she had given them to suppose that was what she would do. Sometimes there was a message from his sister, but most of the letters were from himself, and he didn't seem to mind that she didn't answer right away. He just kept on writing. His method of pursuit was most persistent.

Eden answered a few of the cards, with little bright brief sentences, but when he began to write long intimate letters, proclaiming his interest in her, and his thought of her beauty, she was long in giving even a brief response, and finally grew more and more troubled as his letters continued to come whether they were answered or not.

"You know I'm crazy about you, Eden, and I can scarcely wait till the time comes when I can see you every day, be near you all the time. I spend half my time watching for the postman, and when I find no answer to my last effusion I am disconsolate until the next mail." Sometimes, too, she could scarcely tell whether his attitude might not be all a big joke.

He sent her boxes of oranges and all delicacies of citrous fruits. He sent her flowers and candy, until she had to implore him not to send so much. And finally she settled down to write very brief letters, always thanking him in quite a sisterly way for what he had sent, and telling how busy she was with a Sunday school class of young girls she had taken over for a friend who had gone away on a trip.

As the spring drew near Eden was more and more troubled, for in spite of her insistence that she could make no promises for either spring or summer, the Nevins' letters continued to urge, and then take for granted that she would be with them. They even suggested a trip to Alaska or Canada, and Vesta herself wrote telling of a wonderful resort they had recently heard about in northern Canada; really wild and primitive yet blest with marvelous hotels, with fishing and hunting in plenty, also horseback riding. At last Eden began actually to dread the coming of the brother and sister, for she saw she must make a quick decision that would end all this persistence. They had even suggested that Eden might like to bring Janet with her as a personal maid. They said this place in Canada had many Scotch people in a settlement near by, and an old-time Scotch church that might interest her. But by this time Eden was thoroughly fed up with the whole plan, and wrote that it would be quite impossible for her to go away *anywhere* this summer. She had other plans. Perhaps another year she might manage it, but at present she was not in the market for any kind of a trip.

And then they wrote that they were coming home at once and would stop at her house and take her to New York with them. She had certainly promised them that she would come on their return. There were parties and plays going on in New York that they especially wanted her to attend with them. They were coming up the end of the week, and would expect her to be ready to go on at once with them.

Eden talked it over with Janet, and decided perhaps she ought to go for a couple of days, just to satisfy them, if Janet would go with her.

But Eden was not happy about it. Her soul was troubled exceedingly.

That night she knelt by her bed to pray, and the petition of her heart was: "Here, my Lord, is something I don't know what to do about. I can't just see the way ahead, whichever way I decide. Won't you please take over and manage this for me?"

Then she lay down and slept quietly. She had put it all in God's hands, ready to go or stay, whatever He planned for her.

The next morning there came a telegram from Vesta:

Mother taken seriously ill. Niles and I are taking a plane for home at once. Sorry we cannot come for you at this time.

Lovingly,

Vesta

Eden stood in wonder as she read the telegram, and was startled at the thought of how soon God had settled that troublesome question for her. "Before they call I will answer"—the words rang in her soul. Her kindly heart was troubled that her friend was having to bear anxiety as a part of God's answer to her prayer, but she could not help being glad that she was not having to go to New York at present.

Two days later Vesta called up on the telephone. She said her mother was critically ill with double pneumonia, and while she was just a trifle better that morning, it would be some days before the doctor could tell them what the outcome would be. When she was better, if she did recover, she should go at once to California, and that she and Niles would have to go with her. Their father could not very well leave until he had some business matters in shape. Vesta's voice was very sad, and she seemed glad to talk her troubles over with her friend.

"I'm so disappointed and discouraged," she said. "I had looked forward to a such a pleasant summer with you, and all that traveling. It would have been delightful! And the best of it is that Niles is so fond of you, dear. He's really fallen for you hard! If it hadn't been for mother being so awfully sick I know he would just have hurried to you right away. But you know he's devoted to mother, and if she needed anything he would be at her side at once. He's really sweet, Eden, when you get to know him. That's why I did so want to have you visit us, and get to like him."

"Oh, I like him, of course," said Eden with a degree of fervor. "I like him a lot, and I know I would have had a lovely time, but it did seem rather inconvenient for me to go anywhere just at present, so it's quite all right to have the plans changed, for I really have still some important things to attend to."

"Well, don't work too hard, dear. You are so serious-minded," said Vesta. "And you do understand why I can't ask you to come to us at once, don't you? Mother has been, and still is, so very sick. We have two nurses, and must keep it so very quiet. We couldn't plan for anything at all."

"Why of course I understand, Vesta. Remember I've been through sickness a lot, and I know what it is. I'm only sorry that the interrupted plans had to come through trouble to you and yours. You dear child, I've been pray-ing for you, and for your dear mother. I do hope she will soon be better. And if there is anything I can do in any way to help you, please let me know."

"That's a dear. Of course I will. But I can't see how there would be, unless by and by you could come to California and join us. I'll keep in touch with you, in case we go, and you keep it in mind and try to plan for it tentatively."

"Oh, I couldn't possibly do that, Vesta, not this year!"

"Oh, don't say that. It would be so lovely to have you, if we go. It might be if mother gets better soon that Niles will run down and plan it out with you."

"No," said Eden, "I couldn't *possibly* go this year, but thanks a lot for wanting me."

But Mrs. Nevin did not get better for a long time, and it was a hard siege in the beautiful old New York house, while nurses and doctors came and went, and the son and daughter hung anxiously over their adored mother. Now and then Vesta called up her friend in Glencarroll and had a talk, giving details of the progress of her mother's illness. But no more was said about the trip to California, as the possibility of that was still in the far distance.

In the meantime Niles's letters grew briefer and farther apart. Eden was relieved, and wondered if that didn't mean that Niles Nevin was never meant for her, or she would have wanted him to come, and been disappointed that he could not leave home. For Vesta had said that her mother was so devoted to Niles, and was always wanting him to come and sit beside her bed and hold her hand, when she was conscious.

Eden was very sorry for them all, but somehow relieved that she was not there, and didn't have to do anything about it.

The weeks rolled by, and at last a final heartening word from Lance Lorrimer arrived:

> The important errand on which I was sent is about accomplished and there is some hope that I may return soon. God keep you, dear friend.
>
> *Lance*

It was brief and said little, but it filled Eden with deep joy. Then she began to upbraid herself for caring so much. This was really not right. He had written to her, yes, several times, but the messages were just friendly. She *shouldn't* care so much!

Then she carried her anxiety to her Lord:

"Please take care of this for me, and make my heart right about it. Let me be what you want me to be, dear Lord." And on that she rested.

Chapter Sixteen

THE HIDEOUT where Ellery Fane had taken refuge was near the top of a far mountain, not many miles from the Canadian border, in a deserted region frequented by outlaws, evil men, sharpers and crooks, in trouble. Ellery had come into contact with them when a mere lad, drifting on his own to a large extent, because his mother was too silly and ambitious to get up in the world, to pay much attention to him. These men had used the willing boy to work for them in their crooked dealings, to slide into banks and places of business to unlock a door, or draw back a bolt, just at closing time, and make a way for them to enter when night came. And because he had been the successful assistant in several such raids, and had under their instructions been able to vanish out of the raided district and never be suspected, they had often sent for him to help in more and more "important jobs" as they called them. It was to such a school that Ellery had been allowed to go by his careless silly mother. So now, in the most trying emergency of his hitherto lightly punished career of crime, Ellery took to the hideout, where he was sure to find friends who would "understand," as he told himself, and might help.

He had once been taken with the other men to this hideout, when he was a young boy, after a daring escapade in which he had supplied the part of a missing link. They had not told him where he was going; "just away on a little vacation so that no one would question him," they said. But even as a very young boy Ellery had been alert to all that was going on about him. "Why" had been the biggest word in his vocabulary since babyhood, and he did not easily forget. He had been always listening when the men thought he was asleep and were talking of private matters. So he had a wide glimpse of crime in the raw, and while of course he hadn't gathered it all at once, still it laid a good foundation for a devious life and its possibilities, even as a baby absorbs most of the language of its new world in two short years.

They had taken him away in the night, after three days in that charmed mountain, watching their games of cards, quick to notice the sharp way in which they cheated and won. He drank in their vile talk. The men did not know how much he was absorbing. He was a good-looking child. They liked him, and he was one they could use in their serious business of hoodwinking innocent people.

They gathered him up out of what they thought was a sound sleep one night. They put him in the car and took him home. It was dark. He could not see much, but what was visible he noted and remembered. In the morning he was among familiar scenes and the men were gone. It was a long time before he saw any of them again.

But lately he had been more or less in touch with some of them, and so it was to their distant hideout in his need that he was making his way.

He had an uncanny sense of direction, and he had had years to figure out where that safe place must be, so he dodged contact with respectable people, got rides whenever he thought it was safe, and at last arrived at the mountain, doing a good deal of the way on foot, scouting around and listening, to make sure whether there were any of his old friends there. It was from that mountain hideout that Ellery, when one of the men went down into the world, briefly had sent his message about the red beads. And it was in search of that place that poor Lavira had been trying to make her way when she escaped the second time and was finally caught and held for trial.

So Lavira languished miserably in jail, and Ellery languished on a desolate mountain, waiting for some news from the world where he had once thought his prospects were so bright. And while he waited there was much time for thought. Perhaps Ellery had never done any thinking before, except about how to get ahead of the other fellow and see how much he could get for himself of this world's goods. Yet here he was shut in by great trees that he grew to hate, under a lofty sky, that bright or dim looked down on him with scorn and condemnation. While he was there perhaps some dim notion of what the God must be who had created those trees and that sky, and himself, entered his trivial soul. But if so, it only filled him with resentment and fear.

There was nothing to do up here. Not that he minded being lazy if there was some fun to be had. But there was no fun. Of course he could gamble with those hardened sharpers, but he had little chance against them, for he had never made a specialty of cards. There had always been some practical sly game for him to play for the benefit of the others, before he came up here. Even here he was sent down twice to do a little ticklish job—something connected with a bank. Strangely he went with his heart in his mouth, because now he was beginning to be afraid. If he should be caught in a big thing like an outstanding bank robbery, he was finished of course. For these men had no real fondness for him. The old ones he used to know when he was a child were either dead, shot, or "in for life," and no one would help him out if serious trouble came. And those red beads would do him no good if he couldn't find a friend to cash them in. It wouldn't do for him to try it himself. They would trace the theft to him and that would be the end. He would be a "lifer."

Thus he mused there on that mountaintop with that awesome sky staring down into his soul—he hadn't believed before that he had a soul, but there was no question, now. He had a soul, and he felt already that it was doomed. He cast frightened eyes around, shook his fist at the wide sky, and turned his glance downward. Was that the messenger coming back?

It was!

He strode down the mountainside to meet him, to grasp the newspaper the man held out, and there he saw his own name in large letters, as a suspect in a murder case!

His eyes hurried down the page. There was his own life history written out, staring him in the face. The sky above and the newspaper below, and he caught between! What should he do now?

Quickly his eyes hurried down the page, taking in whole sentences in a word or two. Yes, they had searched out his life. It hadn't been a long life, but there were as many crime situations as if he had been an old man. It was somehow terrible to be confronted by these things he had done; so many of them he had considered mere jokes when he began. He had never faced his life as a whole. One crime at a time hadn't been so bad, but here was a lifetime of them. It is true that some of the crimes listed were not his; they rightly belonged to the people for whom he was working, those older in crime than he was.

But they were charged on him because he had been the blind to save the others. A mere lock tampered with and he was charged with robbery of hundreds of thousands of dollars. A little note delivered innocently it seemed, and he was charged with a kidnaping crime which almost resulted in the death of the child kidnaped, and did result in what promised to be lifelong illness for the mother of the child. A moment's use of a pen in his skilled fingers, forging a check, and a whole family were plunged into poverty. So it read in the words of a skilled columnist.

Suddenly horror, conviction, and fear greater than he had ever felt before, were in Ellery's eyes as he turned to look at the grim messenger who was grinning admiringly at him.

"Well, I see you got away with a good deal, kid! I guess you really rate being one of us at last! What d'ye say, men?" and he turned toward the other men who had straggled down from the cabin where they herded and were reaching for the paper, stretching their necks to read the staring headlines! "Shall we take the kid inta the innermost, and give him a really big job to celebrate with?"

And the voices of the other men were raised in a furtive growl of assent.

Then suddenly there was a hush, as the hand of the old one was raised in a warning gesture. The hush was intense, to men who lived continually under caution driven by fear.

"Psst!" came a low hiss. "What's *that*?"

A dozen pairs of eyes went down the mountainside, in the direction from which the messenger had just arrived, a devious path which they thought was only known to themselves.

Yes, there was a sound! A falling stone! Snapping of dry twigs and branches. A second more and then the quick measured tramping of feet. Horses' hoofs ringing against the rock.

One look! The shadow of dark forms among the trees. But the men had scattered in every direction until there was not a hint of one of them anywhere. Not even in the cabin. They had long been drilled for an occasion like this. They knew where to hide.

But it was Ellery who felt that he was the main target for this arrival of the law. They were coming to take him away forever. The State Police!

He turned with a great gasp, his hands raised above his thrown-back head, and dashed away from the oncoming posse. Then a bullet whistled through the air, a sharp pain went through his left hand, and his right hand sought the gun that was always his companion now. But a second bullet whistled past his ear, a third shot the gun out of his hand, shattered his wrist, and made him know that the end had come. In desperation he turned, dashed straight for the cliff, and was gone! Down, down to the depths of a frightful chasm, where he lay crumpled on the sharp stones below. It was the final resort of all who came to that hideout, in case of discovery.

It was the mounted police who had at last penetrated to the hitherto mysterious hideout of the gang of outlaws. The authorities had been sure for some time that the gangsters were entrenched somewhere in this part of the mountain, and when that day, early in the morning, an unknown westerner, riding a swift horse, came into town, purchased a few eatables, sent a strange code message by telegraph, and then disappeared, they gathered their forces furtively and watched him until he started out of town.

No watching citizens saw them follow him, for they had well canvassed what they would do if there were any chance of following a stranger. They hastened one by one to a place appointed, and keeping in the distance followed the swift horse. So they had arrived just after the messenger had climbed up to the rendezvous.

But now they scattered and searched out the different hiding places about the cabin, set fire to the cabin itself, and shot or disabled all the gang, piling them into the truck they had left just below the last rise of the hill. They were all there save one, and he was lying at the foot of the gorge.

They sent a couple of men down to find his broken body and the next day the papers came out with an account of the raid and capture of all the gang then present, and the death of the man whose crimes had been enumerated in the paper the day before. People read, exclaimed, shook accusing heads, and murmured how everyone ought to be sure their sin would find them out.

But the word did not get back to Glencarroll for several days, except to the police, and the few who had been most interested, and when it finally got into the papers the whole matter was toned down so that the town gossips did not get hold of it. Just a notice that the robber who had tried to break into the Thurston house had been found, and was dead from the effect of a fall over a cliff after he had been shot by the state troopers. Some wise kind friends saved Eden from further gossip-mongers, and the matter passed into the unknown. Eden was only told that the Fanes had been caught and would worry her no more.

CHAPTER SEVENTEEN

BUT EDEN was having troubles of her own, and didn't even realize that she had not seen the paper that morning. Niles Nevin had just arrived and asked to see her, and she was hastening to change into pleasant garments and go down to meet him, wondering if his mother was better or worse, and how she should greet him. She was rather surprised that her immediate conviction was that she still did *not* want to go to New York to visit them. Well, she would try to be pleasant, and friendly, but she would make him understand that she hadn't much time to write letters either.

The young man came eagerly out to the hall to meet her as she arrived downstairs.

"Eden!" he said, "I'm so glad to see you. It has been wretched to have to have you stay away from us so long, and this is the first opportunity I've had to get away from home. One can't say much over the telephone, especially when the whole family, including nurses and doctors, are around, barging in and listening to everything you say. And besides, dad hasn't been well either, and I've had to be down at the office with him a lot. An awful bore. I just hate business. But I knew you would understand why I have been so silent."

"Why of course," said Eden briskly. "I think it is perfectly excusable. You know I've been accustomed to caring for sick people, so I understood at once. And I've been awfully busy myself. How is your mother now? Is she really better? I suppose she must be or you wouldn't be here today."

"Why, I can't say that she's really a whole lot better," said the young man. "She seems terribly weak, and not a bit like herself. But they took her to the hospital today for some special treatment that couldn't very well be done at home, and that let me out. The doctor feels this treatment may help her a lot, and he didn't think I should go with her today, so I ran off the first thing this morning. Of course I'll have to go back tonight for they may bring mother home this evening, but when I got a chance I had to run right down here to see you. There is something that I've been meaning to tell you, Eden, for a long time. In fact the thought came to me when I first saw you, but you've been so stand-offish, and all the time making excuses, that I thought I would wait until you came to see us. That would be a more propitious time. I wanted you to see my home, and know my people, though of course you're fond of Vesta, and that ought to tell you a good deal what the rest are like."

"Yes?" said Eden. "Well, of course I was sorry not to accept your delightful invitation, and I'm sure I shall like your people when I have the opportunity of knowing them, but you mustn't be apologetic. I understood, of course, you couldn't have company when there was sickness in your home."

"Oh, but you don't understand," said the young man earnestly, "I haven't come down here to apologize, or to try to be polite or anything. And I haven't time to be artistic or conventional about it. I *must* get back this afternoon, so I haven't any time to waste. I think if you don't mind I'll just go to the point at once."

"Why yes, of course," said Eden. "What is it?"

"Well, if you want it bluntly, all right. I came over to—ask you to marry me. If it's all right with you I thought we could go ahead and get the knot tied today maybe, and then you could go home along with me. We could have all kinds of a good time. Hit the high spots, you know. It may sound a bit rushing to you, but we certainly have had time enough to think it over, and my mind is made up. Besides it isn't as if it were out of the ordinary. Everybody's doing it now you know, getting married in a hurry. How about it? Are you satisfied to have it that way? If there are any details we can talk them over on the way back to New York. Okay with you, Eden?"

Eden looked at him in startled astonishment, and then when she saw he was awaiting an answer she simply smiled as if he had been joking, and answered very firmly.

"No, it certainly is not all right with me. I have no idea of marrying you, Niles, either now or at any other time. Sorry to disappoint you, but really that's no reason to get married, you know, to have a good time and hit the high spots." She gave him another of her amused smiles and settled back in her chair more at ease than she had been since he arrived.

"Oh, now, Eden, don't be difficult! Don't say you have to get a lot of togs for a trousseau and all that. We both have enough money to get you about what you want in any line afterward, and just now it's an emergency on account of my mother. It seems it's important that I'm along with her on the journey to California and afterward, or she won't hear to going. I guess it's got to be that way. The doctor says he can't cross her now. Her life depends on her being calm and happy."

"Why yes, of course. I should think you'd go of course."

"But I can't go without you, Eden. I'm awfully fond of you, you know, and we've been separated long enough.

I just won't take it any longer. You know you're fond of me, Eden, and we've really been so little together that you haven't any idea how nice I am."

Eden laughed good-naturedly.

"Oh, yes, Niles, I know you're nice. Haven't I lived with your adoring sister for a good many months and heard her sing your praises every waking hour in the day? And I really like you a lot, Niles. But not enough to marry you. I don't think just *liking* is the basis for marriage, do you? And until I find somebody I really love with all my heart, and who loves me that way, I shall not consider marriage."

"You're crazy, Eden. That's ridiculous! I suppose what I feel for you is really what *you* call love, though that word is a bit out of date, isn't it? Really smart people don't use it any more. It smacks too much of what they used to call 'passion' to be in vogue with nice people, don't you think?"

Eden stared at the young man speculatively, and then shook her head.

"No, I don't feel that way," she said decidedly. "I think love is the grandest word in the world. It is used all the way through the Bible. You can't find any higher source than the Bible. And marriage in the Bible is intended to be a picture of the relationship between Christ and His church. Something most dear and precious and wonderful."

"Good night!" said the self-sufficient young man

annoyedly. "If you are going to hark back to antiques like the Bible I don't see that we are ever to agree on real essentials. The Bible doesn't count in these days. Don't you know that yet? Of course I always knew you were religiously inclined, and I shouldn't at all object to that, provided you kept it in the background, but this bringing it up to hinder your marriage to me is a little too much. I couldn't be expected to stand that. You'll have to leave the Bible out of the discussion."

"Then I'm afraid you'll have to leave me out," said Eden. "The Bible is to me the dearest book on earth. It not only is precious, but I have taken it to be my guide in living. So you can see plainly that you and I would never fit together. Suppose we change the subject. What does the doctor say about your mother? Is she really going to get entirely well, and will she be able to take the western trip soon?"

"Why certainly," said the young man crossly. "But I do not think it is pleasant of you to change the subject when I have been trying to make it plain to you that you are the one I have chosen out of the whole world to make my wife, and you act as if you were simply playing with me, as a cat would play with a mouse."

Eden looked at him gravely.

"No, Niles, I am not playing. I certainly made it plain to you from the start that I could not go away this season, and that I was *not* 'crazy' about you, as you say. I am a good friend, if that is what you want, but that is *all*, and I am *not* in love with you. I am not marrying anybody that I do not love."

"Is there someone else you do love?" asked the young man suddenly, looking at her with demanding eyes. "*Is* there? Because I've *got* to know that or I can't go on."

"No," said Eden thoughtfully, "but if there were I don't think it would be a matter for us to discuss. It would be *my* affair and not *yours*, unless I voluntarily chose to tell you. But even if there were such a situation it would make no difference whatever. You see you have made it quite definite that you and I could never belong to each other even if we could love each other, because of what you have just said about the Bible."

"Eden! You don't mean that! You certainly can't be as ignorant and narrow-minded as that."

"I certainly do mean that, Niles. Jesus Christ means more to me than anything or anyone else on earth. You see the reason you think I am ignorant and narrow-minded is because *you* do not *know* my Lord. If you really would come to know Him you would see that you are the one who is ignorant and narrow-minded. Perhaps you will come to know Him some day, really *know* Him, and then you will understand."

"There is no chance whatever that I shall become deluded by that superstitious belief that has blinded your eyes. But what I hope to do is to teach you little by little that you have taken up with an unfounded tradition that is as antiquated as it is unscientific. Eden, I see it might take some time to bring you to a right way of thinking, but I am willing to bear with you until you can come to see things in a right light."

"Oh, really?" said Eden, lifting her brows gravely. "But I'm afraid *I* would never be able to bear with *you* while you were learning what my Lord is willing to be to you."

"Oh, forever!" exclaimed the young man angrily. "Will you stop talking that nonsense and listen to me?"

"I'm sorry, Niles, but I'm afraid you haven't anything to say to me that I consider worth hearing."

"But don't you understand that you will never get married if you go on that principle all your life? You wouldn't be able to find anyone who would agree with you when you talk like that. Do you want to go unmarried all your life?"

"It doesn't seem very important to me. I have no desire to get married just for the sake of being married. And now, Niles, I think we have said just about all there is to say on this subject, don't you?"

"Eden, do you really mean that this is final?"

"I do. I do not think we have anything in common."

"But Eden, you do not seem to understand. Has it ever occurred to you what it might mean to my people if I should bring a girl into the honorable family to which I belong, who had embraced such peculiar beliefs as you seem to have taken up? It isn't as if you just kept it in the background. A little original whim one might stand, but you seem to put it so in the foreground, to make it an oddity that would be hopelessly embarrassing to my mother, and the family."

"And has it never occurred to you how embarrassing it would be to *my* family for me to lend my companionship to one who repudiates my family, its great Founder, and all that He stands for? I'm a child of the Heavenly King, and I would rather die than dishonor my Lord Jesus Christ. And now, Niles, here comes Janet with word that lunch is ready. Shall we go out? I think it is high time to end this unprofitable discussion, don't you? Come and let us talk of something else, for it is all too evident that we are not getting anywhere in this. I know I shall not change. I doubt if you ever will. Tell me please where it is you are planning to go with your mother? Is it the same place she went before when she was so ill?"

And so Janet ushered them into the dining room, and the discussion for the time being was ended, although there was about the young man's expression an offended haughtiness that did not register contentment. He was not a young man who was accustomed to bearing disappointment, or accepting even the slightest deviation from his own planned way.

Nevertheless as the meal progressed, and the talk drifted into more formal conversation, he watched Eden in a kind of amazement. He had never seen a girl like this, seldom seen one who would have so casually turned down such a well set up and altogether respectable, good-looking, wealthy young man as his honorable self, *just for an idea*. Was this only a pose, or was it real? Would it be better for him to drop her for a while and let her see that she couldn't wind him around her little finger this way? He *must* make her understand what was due his family.

So Niles Nevin made the most of his opportunity to impress Eden with his desirability in the small talk that the lunch table afforded. He showed himself a master of adjustability, able to keep a calm exterior and carry on in the face of what he had made to appear utter disaster to all his plans. He would show her that he could be a wise and good companion, able always to be self-controlled no matter what occurred.

Of course, he reasoned within himself that he might give in to her ideas, and easily win her that way, but that would only make future trouble for himself, and it would not be wise to allow her to think even for a moment that he would ever give in on matters that had to do with his family's conventional views and customs. Of course they all belonged to a respectable church, which they attended regularly—whenever it was convenient—never in excess, but they did not stand for unnecessary religiosity. And so although it did not meet with his plans at present to be firm on this subject, he felt that in the end it would finally win a lasting victory over Eden's fanatical views, and show the girl he meant to marry that she must conform to his family's ways of doing things. The lunch was delicious, for Janet knew what New Yorkers liked, and she did not intend to have her dear lady fall short in any matter that was in her hands. Also the meal was *deliberately* served, for she wanted to understand just what this sudden visit from the young man meant. She had never been quite easy in her mind when she considered the possibility of Eden marrying this Mr. Nevin. Somehow he seemed too easy-going to mate with her precious nursling. And yet when she came to think it over she could never quite explain to herself why she felt this way.

So the two young people talked on, pleasantly, politely, and Eden did not hasten matters herself, for she was quite content to be talking, with Janet coming and going, knowing very well that Niles Nevin would not likely revert to the subject of marriage while Janet was present. Niles was very formal, and it was scarcely good form to press a girl to marry him in the presence of servants. So the conversation was pleasant and she had plenty of time to study her guest. She knew now definitely that Niles and she would never be congenial. She would not be able to forget that look in his eyes when he had told her she was narrow-minded and fanatical.

It was late when they at last adjourned to the living room and found comfortable chairs around the fire which the servants had burning cheerfully.

Two chairs were placed invitingly near the fire, and a little coffee table between the chairs bore a fresh box of delicious-looking confectionery. No more inviting setting for a talk could have been found.

Eden came quietly to her chair, trying to be sweet and bright but not feeling too gay about it. She dreaded the next two hours more than she would have liked to acknowledge, even to herself. She was desperately tired of the subject of marriage, especially as relating to Niles Nevin, and yet she could not seem to think of talkable topics enough to tide over this time until the visitor would leave.

Afterward she wondered if the doorbell hadn't rung in answer to her unspoken cry for help. It was Mr. Worden with a paper for her to look over and sign.

She introduced Niles Nevin to him, then listened to his careful explanations and sat reading the paper as he directed, while he chatted with this very nice-looking young man from New York, wondering just what his appearance meant in the picture of Eden's life. Mr. Worden had shrewd eyes, and a logical mind, and he knew just what questions to ask to help him find out what he wanted to know. On the whole he was pleased with the young man, and thought to himself that here at least was no menace to Eden. Though he might turn out to be a menace to the plans Mrs. Worden had been dreaming out for Lance Lorrimer and Eden. But then his wife was always getting up pretty romances for her friends, and she was particularly fond of Eden. She would of course. Well, time would tell.

Eden signed the paper, and chatted a moment with Mr. Worden before he left. As she came back from seeing him to the door Niles met her just inside the living room, and took both her hands in his.

"I've been thinking, Eden," he said in quite a brotherly tone, gently and advisory, "that we have gone about this matter all wrong. And it was all my fault. We began by statements of facts, and by discussion, and instead it should be a matter of action." Eden gave a quick worried glance up but before she could realize what was coming, Niles drew her up close to his breast, one arm around her shoulders possessively. He held her very close, his nice handsome face boldly and firmly on her own, and then his warm lips were on Eden's in a kiss that was most thorough, and he thought convincing.

"There, isn't that better?" he asked, looking down at her adoringly.

Eden struggled for an instant frantically, and then finding that she could not get free by struggling, she said:

"No! No! *Stop* Niles! Please don't do that!" She struggled again, dragging her hands from his clasp by main force, drawing back and turning her face away from another caress which was obviously on its way. "Let me go! You have *no right! Stop!* I thought at least you were a gentleman!"

"What is there about a kiss that you could call it ungentlemanly?" he asked, and then drew her close again with another quick purposeful caress. At least she should understand once for all what his feeling for her was, and he did his best to rouse her own sensibilities. She must be human. She would *have* to remember that kiss. It must be imprinted deep in her soul!

But Eden suddenly struggled free from his embrace and backed to the hall door.

"That will be *all*," she said haughtily, and her eyes were flashing bright with tears.

He stood back a step and looked at her, with a self-confident smile on his lips.

"You *know* you liked that, Eden, now be honest and say yes."

"*No!*" said Eden, "I did *not* like it, and I don't want you ever to touch me again. I don't even want to be friends with you now any more. You knew you had no right."

The young man stood bewildered and looked at her. What strange kind of girl was this that didn't adore to be kissed?

At last he grew dignified, apologetic, quite grave.

"Really, Eden, I see I have been greatly misunderstood. I sincerely beg your pardon. I was merely trying to show you how you had stirred my heart. I thought if you knew you would be human enough to respond. But I see I was mistaken. I do hope you will forgive me, and perhaps sometime when you know me better you will be kinder to me. I'm sorry I have hurt you. Suppose we just sit down by the fire and have a nice little talk, and forget all about this? In a short time now I shall have to go, and I'd rather remember a pleasant talk instead of a disagreement. Are you willing?"

Eden gave him a steady look and then assented, sitting quietly down in her chair, and looking to him to do the same.

"Would you like another cup of coffee? I see Janet has brought it in for us," she said with dignity.

"Why yes, I certainly would," he said affably, and sat down opposite to her, accepting the cup she poured. They looked like two well-bred young people having a pleasant chat. It was a great relief to Eden.

And very soon the time came for the young man to leave.

He gave her a quick look as he rose to say good-by.

"I'm indeed sorry I spoiled the afternoon for you," he said. "I do hope sometime you will let me come back and redeem my character. I want at least to be a gentleman to you."

Eden gave him a pleasant sad little smile, and tried to

be gentle and forgiving, but he saw plainly that she was not pleased with him, and her reaction humbled him. He had come to win her for his own, hoping to mould her over to suit his family, and he found quite definitely that instead he seemed to have lost her.

She gave him a brief handclasp, just the tips of her fingers, and another grave smile when he went out. She tried to say a cheerful word about his mother, that she hoped she would soon be quite well, and that they would have a happy winter.

At the end he asked: "Have you really forgiven me?" and she answered "Why, of course. Just forget it all and have a good time."

But he answered with a quavering smile, quite humbly, "I can see I was never good enough for you!" With one more lingering wistful look he left her, just in time to catch his train.

As she turned to go back into the house Janet met her at the door grimly rejoiceful:

"So, thet's over an' gane, is't? Well, thanks be! He's nae yer koind. Noo, gang awa' an' rest ye whiles ye have a chancet."

Then Eden sat down in her room and looked her life in its face, wondering if she had done altogether right? Would her mother have felt she ought to have waited perhaps, and not sent this pleasant young man away so summarily? Would daddy have approved her action? He had not known this man. But he was, of course, in a class with the people her father knew and liked. Still was he what daddy would have chosen for her, to go the rest of the way with her? Did God approve what she had done? Had she really put herself in God's hands to show her what would be best for her, or had she just acted on impulse? And did *she* approve of what she had done herself?

She went back over the afternoon and her own re-actions to what her would-be lover had said, and she found herself turning away unpleasantly from some of the memories. Not even those wild passionate kisses of Niles had roused any feeling of love for him in her heart. No, she could not have been wrong. She could never have married him, been tied to his reverence for his wonderful family all her life. They might be very wonderful intellec-tually, financially, socially, but *her* family was a *royal* family, known in Heaven.

And so that night she lay down to sleep with a heart at peace, and feeling that she was really glad she was at home in her own bed, with her own dear people about her, even though they were but servants. She was glad she was not on her way to New York to begin a new life of journeying whithersoever an unknown family dictated.

CHAPTER EIGHTEEN

LANCE LORRIMER was on his way home on the midnight train. He had been on a business trip to New England for the bank, and had been working over the notes he had taken while away. He had them in pretty good shape now, and was numbering his pages and tying up his files, so that there would be no confusion when he came to report at the bank in the morning. Suddenly he became aware of what the man in the seat in front of him was saying. It is wonderful how a familiar name can catch one's ear in a place where it is unexpected. And the name that was mentioned had been much in his thoughts during the last few days.

"That Thurston dolly has been getting herself engaged lately I hear. Beats all how the news gets around. I don't suppose I'd have heard much about it if it hadn't been for Sam. He's been substituting on the mail route for Jacoby Winters for the last fortnight ur so, whilst Jacoby had the flu, an' he told me. He said as how this here guy from New York had been writin' letters, an' even post cards. Most of 'em was post cards it seems, else he wouldn't have knowed so much about their affairs. Yes sir, the expensive kind of post cards all photographs and colored pictures on 'em, mostly Palm Beach. He's been writin' them all season. He's seen 'em off'n on. Of course he wasn't supposed to mention it, and he was usually very particular, though of course we home folks didn't count. And so he'd come in to supper and he'd say, 'Well, that Eden Thurston got another bunch o' mail today,' he'd say, 'an' two post cards. My but that guy does waste money! He tells her how he's always watching for her answers, and how the day isn't nothin' when she don't write, an' all that slob ya know. An' he says he's comin' pretty soon, an' he'll tell her more. An' he says they'll have some trip pretty soon, an' fer her not to waste her time gettin' stuff fer the journey. He'll he'p her pick it out when he comes.'"

"You don't say!" the other man ejaculated. "Strange, I've never heard anything about her bein' engaged."

"Well, I guess it's an 'ngagement all righty. Tom said it sounded a lot like it. And they say he's been ta see her twicet this spring. Oncet about six weeks ago, only stayed a day. Then jus' this week. Seems his mother's awful sick, an' they got two nurses. He must have a pile of money. He's figuring on a trip to Californy, mebbe he means the weddin' trip, an' wants her to be all ready when he calls up."

"Does sound like it, don't it? Wal, I'm certainly s'prized. Her papa useta be so keerful of her. But now he's gone, an' she's got money aplenty, it's not strange the young men should come around after her. Pretty girl, too."

"Certainly is," said the other man. "Don't b'lief there's a prettier, ner a richer girl in the hull town of Glencarroll!"

"That's right! But I thought there was another feller she was 'bout promised to. Caspar Carvel, wasn't that his name?"

"Yes, that's his name. But he went to war. Hasn't been seen back in three years, has he?"

"Yes he has," said the other. "I saw him myself just last week comin' out of the Thurston house. Seems to me that girl has got more than her share of men. And I don't suppose that is the whole tale either. A girl as pretty as that ought to have a lot of beaus."

"Yes, but you see that Thurston girl never was one to flirt. She went around with that Caspar Carvel in school years, but I haven't seen her around much with any fella lately. She stuck by that sick father of hers. She never seemed to leave him. She wasn't around anywhere while he was alive."

"Yes, I'll own she was a faithful daughter. And he was a good man, her father. He done his best to bring up that girl right. I guess he done a pretty good job of it too. She's a modest-appearing girl, and I hope to goodness she gets a good husband."

"Well, the guy I saw comin' away from the house seemed like a nice appearin' fella."

"Well, if what you say is so, then I suppose we'll be havin' a high-flyer weddin' pretty soon."

"Seems like! Wal, I wish 'em luck! Say, did you see the price of potatoes is goin' up? An' just after I sold my crop below what I was reckonin' on. If that ain't the doggonedest luck ever. But that's the way things allus hit me."

But Lance Lorrimer heard no more. His thoughts were off on the news he had been hearing. Was this true? Could it all be true? His heart sank.

There was no further gossip in the seat in front of him, but Lance could not get away from it. It was perhaps the first time that he had realized how very much Eden was beginning to mean in his life, and now that it had come in this breathtaking way he took it full in the face and let it roll over him.

He had recognized when he first saw her how sweet she was, and how beautiful, but he also knew how rich she was, and he had not considered her in the light of a possible partner for himself. His years in college, and war service, had put him in too serious surroundings to leave him time for considering romance, and he was not one who looked at every girl as a possible future bride. In spite of the loveliness of Eden he had thought of her as scarcely more than a child at first. And later, when he knew her age, on account of his familiarity with her financial status, he had thought of her as a wealthy young woman, entirely out of his class. For although he had done well so far, and was already in an enviable job with a fine outlook, he was not one who thought of himself so highly that he reached forward to marry a rich wife. It was only when Eden began to ask him questions on religious themes that his interest grew greatly. Even before he realized how much he was enjoying her society, he must have been harboring a happiness that his wisdom and his caution would never have approved in another.

So this revelation that Eden was pledged to another, a man among the wealthy, a fitting one to place her in a notable position, suitable to her worth, was a shock to him.

For a long time he sat with closed eyes and thought the thing over, going back to his first meeting with Eden, her fine reactions to all that had happened. And then those questions she had asked him. How they thrilled him now again as he thought them over. He had never seen a girl before who would have asked questions like that: "Please tell me how I can get to know Jesus Christ? What does the verse mean, 'As in Adam all die, so in Christ shall all be made alive?'" What a companion a girl like that could be for a man! And this man to whom she was supposed to be engaged, was he a Christian man? Would he know how to lead and help her aright? Or would he be a worldly man who would lead her into ways far from God? Oh, the heartache in that thought! Another man to lead her, and how he would like to be the one! How they could study God's Word together! To see her eyes shine at a new thought as he had already seen them once or twice, to share her study and her joy, and her worries! He had never really taken time to go into such beautiful thoughts. Except in a general way he had never dwelt much on thoughts of marriage. He had hoped in a dim way that someday he would have a happy home of his own, but as yet such dreams had not taken definite form. Now, however, in the light of what he had just heard, it suddenly seemed as if a great door had been opened into a beautiful place which he had never glimpsed before, and then the next instant the door had been slammed in his face.

For a little while he lay back with his eyes closed, trying to take deep breaths, and get control of himself. Trying to get into a normal state of mind. Trying to tell himself he wasn't in love with this girl, nor any girl. He was just crazy, thinking such thoughts.

And if he did admire her greatly he certainly wanted her to be happy, didn't he? Happy with the man of her choice. She wasn't for him of course. He had never started out to win her. Perhaps this other man who was said to be engaged to her was an old friend of years, someone her wonderful father had known and approved, in which case he had no right to think of her any more than if she were married. Modern marriage and divorce were not for Christian young people. That girl with the wonderful face, and the light of Christ in her eyes would never give her life to a man of the world, never choose for a life-companion one who was not worthy of being her husband.

But there! There was no use in wasting time arguing about a thing like that. It wasn't in his hands to settle of course, and the only possible business that could be his in the whole matter was that he should look out that his own heart-interest should not be found in territory that belonged to someone else. This love, or possible beginning of love, must be rooted out and stand away where it belonged. No man had a right to barge in and set his love upon a girl someone else had won. Equally of course he should have found out how it was with this lovely girl whom he admired. And yet how could he? He hadn't dreamed of trying to win any girl for himself at that stage of the game.

Well, perhaps this was all just an emotional upset, startled into being, or shocked into being, by hearing this news about Eden in such a crude way from alien unfriendly lips. And perhaps he was just very tired. It all might not seem so important, or so startling, when morning came and normal conditions were restored, with a good night's sleep, and a real breakfast. For he hadn't been taking much time to eat in the past forty-eight hours.

This was all just foolishness of course. He must get this straight at once. Then with his eyes still closed he took the matter to his place of refuge, where he had always found relief from trouble since ever he had surrendered to his risen Lord.

"Lord, You have shown me something that I did not know I was getting into. Deal with me as You see fit. Whatever is for Your glory, will be my best good. I know You can work it out. Help me always to be utterly yielded to Your will."

That was his prayer, and later he slept and awoke much rested.

The morning brought a graver aspect. He had lost nothing, for what had seemed lost last night was not really his, and now he could surely rest this matter in wiser hands than his own. But he must let it rest until the Lord would show him which way to go. Nevertheless, if a way opened for him to help Eden to wider knowledge of the Word of God, he must do all he could for her, no matter how soul-trying it might be for himself.

With that conclusion he went forward into his morning in the home town, went to his bank, went through the round of the day, spent some hours in court, and in the bank. And when the thought of Eden came to mind, as it did during the day, he just laid it down in Other hands, knowing it was taken care of and he need not worry about it. The Lord was able to change his own feelings and make them fitting for His work, or He was able to work out something beautiful, somehow for His glory.

Yet he would not, for his own pleasure, put himself in Eden's way, nor try to seek her company.

So it was that Eden wearied wistfully, and wondered why he did not come again. Then upbraided herself, and tried to be satisfied. She had no business to be so anxious for another opportunity to talk with Mr. Lorrimer. The questions she wanted to ask him she might learn somewhere else, perhaps, or the Lord could show her the answers through His Word. So much she had thoroughly from Him. There were other teachers that could be sent to her, if there were reasons why Lance could not come.

Tabor was up and around the house now, attending to most of his old duties, even driving the car sometimes, and the ghastly night of robbers and alarms was almost forgotten. Tabor smiled and went about like a saint, and the rest of the servants looked on him with almost reverence. Some of them whispered together that he seemed to have a measure of the spirit of their old master, Mr. Thurston, upon him. When Eden heard it she smiled sweetly and told Tabor about it, whereat Tabor was greatly pleased.

But there was one worry that Tabor and Janet had in common, and that was lest one of the two former admirers of Eden would come back sometime, and somehow win her for himself, and that seemed nothing short of a catastrophe.

But one day Eden dug it out of Janet, what it was she worried about and why she couldn't sleep some nights. When finally Janet told her, deprecatingly, Eden laughed.

"Poor Janet! Are you worrying about that? How silly! Why did you think I would fall for either of those boys? You know what Caspar said and did. You surely don't think I would ever go back to being an intimate friend of his? No, Janet never, never, *never!* And as for the other one, he's a nice pleasant man when he gets his own way I guess, but I didn't love him, and I'm glad he's gone to California. I hope he never comes back. I've seen all of him I want to see. So rest your heart. You'll have to find somebody better than either of those two before you can get rid of me. Come on now, Janet, and smile. Let's be happy while we are here on earth. We can't make everything always the way we would like to have it, but Tabor is well, and we are all together again. If I only could get over thinking about those Fanes sometimes nights when I'm going to sleep, I would be satisfied. But the Lord kept us from them before, I guess He can keep us always."

"Sure He can, my dear leddy. He can, an' He wull."

The next day Janet told this saying of Eden's to Tabor,

and Tabor suggested that maybe they ought to tell her now about what had happened to Ellery. He volunteered to ask Mike about it.

But the very next week Mike came down to talk with Tabor.

"And you don't know what's come to the old un," he said to his worried listeners.

"Ye mean that Fane wumman?" put in Janet anxiously.

Mike bowed solemnly.

"The same," he said. "Just three days before her trial was ta come up she sneaked some sleeping tablets out of the matron's medicine closet, and took a big overdose. And when mornin' come she didn't wake up."

Janet, incredulous, stared at him.

"Yeh mean the wumman is *deid*?"

"She is," said Mike, "an' that's one less we've got to worry about. And I think the young lady should be told."

So Janet told Mr. Worden, and Mr. Worden talked it over with Lance Lorrimer, and they decided that it was time Eden knew.

So Janet told Eden. Mr Worden thought she would best know how to tell the story to her nursling without filling her with horror. So Janet went up with Eden's breakfast next morning and began the story:

"Weel, my bonny cheeld, I got a bit ov news aboot yer enemies, the Fanes. Worrud hes coom from thet western jail where the old one was confined, thet she stole some sleepin' tablets from the medicine closet, an' took they-all, an' she has gane to meet her Joodge. She'll not trouble ye any more."

"Oh, Janet! How dreadful!" said Eden. "I couldn't bear the thought they might come around again. But to go in such a dreadful way! Janet, she was an awful sinner, and no chance to repent!"

"She'd hed plenty chances tae repent, my lamb. She dinna *want* tae repent. She *chose* the wrang way, an' this was her way oot."

"Oh, but Janet. How awful for her to take her own life! And now her son! What will he do? He'll be more terrible than ever."

"Oh, boot her son's deid too, my lamb! They caught him some weeks ago, an' tried tae take him, boot he got awa' frum thim, an' joomped off the cliff, an' was killed. So they's baith gane. Ye munna mourn. They was bad uns."

"Oh, but Janet, maybe I should have done something about them. Maybe I should have given them another chance! Perhaps it was all wrong to have them arrested!"

"Ye couldna holp it, my luve. They was wanted on ither charges, ither places, an' the world wasna safe with sooch es they aboot. Ye would have hed nae richt tae let such menacin' rats loose on puir unsuspectin' folks. God Hisself hed give thim chances 'afore, in plenty. Don't ye ken, m'lamb, thet there is soom folks thet deliberatelike jes' *chooses* the wrang, from bairnhood oop?"

"But they could be saved, couldn't they, Janet? God wants them saved, doesn't He?"

"Yes, He *wants* they tae be saved. The screepture says 'He is not wullin' thet ony should perish, but all should coom tae repentance. Boot, if agin, a mon ur a wumman should *choose* tae dae wrang, an' *refuse* tae repent, why agin thet's diffrunt. Boot ye'll hev tae ast soombuddy wiser than Janet. You ask that lawyer mon. He'll tell ye."

"I will," said Eden, her cheeks softly pink, and then began to wonder when and whether she would see him.

CHAPTER NINETEEN

THE TIME of meeting came sooner than Eden expected. Mr. Worden had asked Eden to stop in at the office the next morning to sign some papers belonging to her estate, and go over again the list of articles that had been in that desk. He wanted to make sure nothing was missing. She had said she would be there at ten o'clock, and she was getting ready to go when the telephone rang. Eden answered the phone, as Janet was busy down in the kitchen.

It was a strange voice that responded to Eden's acknowledgement of the call.

"I would like to speak to Miss Eden Thurston."

"This is Miss Thurston," said Eden, wondering. "Who is it, please?"

"This is a nurse at the Camp Howard Hospital." There followed the location. "I am speaking for Lieutenant Caspar Carvel."

Eden's heart went down. Oh, was she going to have another session with Caspar?

"Yes?" she answered sharply, questioningly.

"Mr. Carvel has had a bad automobile accident. He is not expected to live but a few hours, if that, and he is crying out to see you. He says he has something important he must ask you before he dies."

"Oh!" gasped Eden, and tried to take in the purport of what the nurse had said. Caspar seriously hurt. Caspar going to die! She shuddered and back over her memory came those awful words he had spoken about not believing in God the last time she had seen him. Caspar going to die, and not believing in God. Oh, what should she do? Wasn't there someone else at the camp that could tell him?

"Hello? Hello, are you there?"

"Yes," said Eden, "I'm listening."

"Will you come? May I tell him you are on the way? He is frantic to see you."

"Oh, why yes, I think I can go. I'll have to look up trains, or planes."

"There is only one train left today, late this afternoon, and no plane till early evening. Either would be too late. He will not live so long. The doctor told me you would have to come by automobile, and start at *once* if you want to see him before he dies."

"Oh!" gasped Eden. "Why, yes, of course I'll come, just as soon as possible."

Eden hung up with a dazed expression and found Janet standing in the doorway.

"What is it?" she asked anxiously. "Has something happened?"

"Yes," said Eden, "an automobile accident. Caspar is seriously injured, and is calling for me. I'll have to go, Janet. I'll *have* to. I can't let him die that way."

Janet stood silent, grim, considering. She had almost had pneumonia herself and had been ordered by the doctor not to go out of the house till she stopped coughing, but that was nothing to her if she felt it her duty to go with her lady somewhere. And she certainly wouldn't let Eden go alone to a soldier camp with that horrid Caspar down there, even if he were dying. Maybe that was just one of his jokes, to get Eden away from home.

Eden suddenly turned and took up the phone calling for Mr. Worden.

"I can't come to the office today," she bewailed. "Will tomorrow do? I must go somewhere else in a great hurry. Somebody—"

"Wait!" said the imperative voice of Mr. Worden. "Where is it you are going? Perhaps we can work the two things together."

"I don't think that would be possible," said Eden deeply troubled. "I must go down to the Camp Howard Hospital. It is a long drive. I thought I might take a plane, but that would be too late the nurse says. There isn't another plane until late this afternoon, and the doctor says he's going to die *very* soon."

"Die? Who is going to die? Be coherent, Eden. What is all this?"

Eden caught her breath in almost a sob she was so excited.

"Who is this person that presumes to call you at a moment's notice like this?"

"Why it's my old schoolmate, Caspar Carvel. He's been in a smash-up and is badly injured. He can't live very long. The doctor said it was imperative I get there as soon as possible."

"But how are you going to get there?"

"Oh, I don't know. I haven't had time to think yet. I suppose Tabor will have to drive me. I don't know if he's fit. Maybe I can get a driver from the garage."

"Certainly *not*, Tabor isn't fit. It might make a lot of trouble with his wound again. Who is this person Caspar? I suppose I've seen him, but I can't just remember him. Does he mean much to you, Eden? You don't fancy you're in love with him, do you?"

"Oh, mercy no, Uncle Worden. He was just an old schoolmate, but I don't see how I can refuse his call. I think he is afraid to die. He said some awful things the last time he came to see me, sneered at religion, and things like that, and I guess I've got to go right away."

"Well, wait. If you've got to go, you *can't* go alone.

Where do you say this hospital is? Oh, yes, I know. Wait, let me ask if anybody is driving down that way. I insist that you shall not go alone."

"But Janet is sick, and she ought not to go out, the doctor said. I don't mind going alone. I'll likely get home early."

"Just a minute—" Mr. Worden put his hand over the receiver and turned his head to speak to someone, then back.

"All right, Eden. Lance has just come in. He says he's got to drive down that way on business, and he can just as well take you with him. That will be all right if it will suit you."

"Oh, yes, that will be wonderful and help a lot. Thank you for arranging it. I'm ready to go in five minutes. How soon can he go?"

"Right away," came Lance Lorrimer's voice. "My car has just been serviced and I'll be there in five or eight minutes."

Out on the road in Lance's car with the pleasant sunshine and the crisp cold air, it seemed incredible that she was going to meet death, the death of one whom she had known well. And it wasn't like her precious father's death, who had known and been prepared to go for weeks. This was a gay young fellow plunged suddenly into pain and anguish and fear, with no hope for the future.

She drew a deep breath of the cold air, and tried to

stiffen herself against this sinking feeling that kept coming over her. Lance gave her a quick comprehending look and then after he had made her comfortable he spoke:

"Suppose you tell me in just a few words what this is all about and then we won't talk about it if you don't want to. But I suppose I ought to understand the facts."

"Of course," said Eden. "It was an automobile accident, that's all I know. The nurse at the hospital called me up and said Caspar was terribly injured and couldn't live but a few hours, and was calling for me."

"And was this young man a very special friend of yours?"

"No," said Eden. "We used to be together in high school, and he was always my companion then, but not since. He's been off in service for a long time, and when he was home the last time he was *awful*, said he didn't believe in God, called me old-fashioned, and said my faith was nothing but a lot of superstitions."

Lance gave her a clear steady look.

"But you weren't engaged to him?" he asked keenly. "Not *ever*?"

"Oh, no! We were just school friends. We didn't even write while he was away. But when he came back he seemed to think he thought a lot of me, and wanted me to go here and there with him, but I said no, and then he began to ridicule my puritanical ideas, and even said it was my old-fashioned father's fault for teaching me such

things, and that it was time I got away from his domina-
tion. He didn't even know my father was gone, when he
first began to talk. And he said nobody believed in God
any more. Then I told him to go away. I didn't want to
see him any more."

"I should think not," said Lance sympathetically. "I've
heard so much about your wonderful father from Mr.
Worden. But did the young man leave then?"

"Yes, he left but a little later he came back again and
said he wanted to apologize, though it wasn't much of an
apology."

"I see," said Lance, trying to puzzle it all out. "But I
don't understand how it came about that you were called
to the bedside of a fellow like that."

"Neither do I. Of course when he was a little boy
he used to run in and out of our house as if it were his
own, and he was very fond of my father, and my father
of him. But now he's changed. He told me he didn't
believe in God any more. His own father is divorced
from his mother, and his mother is away off somewhere
in California. He isn't much on writing letters, nor are
they, and I doubt if he even knows where to locate them.
He's been off in the war for two or three years, you know.
I suppose in his distress he thinks maybe I am as near to
own-folks as he can figure, and that is why I didn't dare
say no to an appeal from a dying man. I don't think he
probably knows what he wants except that he wants to

see somebody he knows around. I certainly didn't want to come, and I'm awfully glad you were going this way. I feel as if I were on the edge of a precipice."

Lance looked at her and smiled comfortingly.

"I'm glad I could be of some help," he said, trying to speak impersonally, reflecting that this couldn't have been the young man those men on the train had been gossiping about and saying Eden was engaged to, so there must be another one. But that was entirely irrelevant to the present situation. This girl he loved was in a difficulty, and he must do all he could to help her. Also, here was a stranger, a young fellow about to step into another world, and unacquainted with the Lord. That was something in which he of course could be interested, and that was enough for one afternoon. And anyway it was blessed and precious just to have the privilege of being with Eden, and talking of things about which they both agreed.

They were both silent for a short time while Lance watched the troubled expression in the girl's eyes. Then he said:

"Why are you so troubled, if this young man is nothing to you but a childhood's friend?"

She roused and met his gaze, the trouble still in her eyes.

"Because," said she, "I don't know what to say to him. Even if I have a chance I don't know how to tell him what to do in his distress. I never talked to a dying person before, except my father, and he was a happy one. He didn't mind going at all. He was glad he was going to the Lord, except for leaving me. I don't even know how to introduce the subject, and if I do I'm afraid Caspar will sneer or laugh. It is awful to hear a dying person laugh at God! I can think just how that would sound."

"See here, my friend, stop thinking what this experience is going to do to you, and think what a momentous privilege is yours to swing open the gate of Heaven for this old playmate of yours to enter Heaven. Put it that way to yourself, and ask the Holy Spirit to put the right words into your mouth. Then you will have no further responsibility in the matter. If God takes care of it you may be sure all will be well."

Eden sat thoughtful for sometime, her face veiled with a beautiful humility. At last she looked up and smiled, like the sudden dawning of sunshine.

"You're right," she said. "I had forgotten what great power is in my new God, and how He will take over. Thank you for telling me."

A great wave of joy and admiration for this sweet girl went over him, threatening almost to overwhelm him. And for the first time since he had known her his heart thrilled inexpressibly with the longing to throw his arms around her and draw her close. Such a precious child she seemed.

As they drew nearer to the hospital so that they could

sight it in the close distance Lorrimer grew thoughtful and at last he said:

"Now, suppose you tell me what is my part in this next scene. Should I stay in the reception room, or wherever guests wait, or do you want me to go nearer, where I can be at hand if you should need me?"

Eden gave him a quick frightened glance.

"Oh, I wish you could go with me, if you wouldn't mind?" she said wistfully.

An instant tender smile responded.

"Of course I will," he said, and his hand reached out and gave her hand a quick glad clasp.

"Thank you," she said, nestling her fingers happily in his for just a second. "You know," she added after a pause, "he might want somebody to pray. I wouldn't be able to do that very well."

"I think you could, and I think you will, if it seems to be what is wanted, so don't try to force me into the picture unless it comes naturally. But I'll be right there ready to do anything that seems best. We'll trust our Guide to show us what."

So they reached the hospital.

"He's been almost gone twice," the nurse who conducted them told Eden, "and then he would rouse again and ask for you. I'm glad you've come. He seemed so frantic."

He lay amid his wrappings and bandages, with closed

eyes, like one dead. But when the soft footsteps drew near to his bed he opened wild eyes and looked at them, studying each face. The nurse? She had promised him so many times that Eden was on the way. The strange young man? Who was he? A new doctor? And then Eden! His anguished eyes flashed into relief, and a something like hope.

"Eden! You've—come—at last!" he gasped. "You—were—angry—but—you—*came*!"

Then as if the pent-up anguish of his soul had been waiting under compression he burst forth with his trouble.

"Eden! Tell me—how—to die! You know—how—to die! You've *got* to—make—me—understand."

"Yes," said Eden, reaching out to take the hot pleading hand held out to her. "Yes, Cappie, I'll tell you," she said and Lance thrilled with the sweet sound of her voice, like a bell sounding the way above.

"Do you remember," went on the girl, "the day you united with the church? You bowed your head and said, 'Yes, I do,' when the minister asked you if you would accept the salvation that Jesus Christ freely gave you, and take Him as your personal Saviour? Don't you remember?"

"Yes, but I've been bad, Eden. I've—been a—great—sinner! I—didn't—think it mattered much any more nowadays. I didn't think I believed any—more—but it's different—when you come to die! I see it's different now. I'm a *sinner*—Eden. Is there any hope—for me—a sinner?"

"Christ Jesus came into the world to save sinners!"

"I know—I've heard—that—but—do *you*—believe—it's so,—Eden?"

"I do. I believe it with all my heart! And if you will just remember that He is *your* Saviour, you can rest in that. You took Him once. Christ never lets go His own."

"But—I—haven't—lived right—not like—I promised."

"It is not *your* living that you have to trust in, Cappie, but *His dying*. He died to make it sure that you might go Home to Heaven and stand before the Father, free in *His* righteousness, *not* your own, and without spot or wrinkle or any such thing. Will you trust Him to do that for you now?"

The hungry dying eyes looked up to her face.

"But you see I can't—" he gasped out. "I haven't—lived right."

"But Jesus never said whosoever lives right shall be saved," said Eden. "He said: 'He that heareth My word, and believeth on Him that sent me, *hath* everlasting life, and shall not come into condemnation; but is passed from death unto life.'"

Lance watching her, hearing the sweet voice, could not but think how wise in the Word she was growing. The words that she spoke seemed really to penetrate to the dying mind.

There was stillness for a few seconds while the dying man tried to think it out. Then the poor bandaged head shook slowly:

"I'm not good enough," he said with a hopeless gesture of one hand.

Eden lifted her eyes pleadingly toward Lance, who stood just across the bed back in the dimness, and in response to her he spoke in his low clear tone:

"Jesus Christ said, 'I came not to call the righteous, but sinners to repentance.'"

The quick ears of the dying man heard, and he turned his eyes toward the stranger.

"Who—is—*that?*" he asked, looking back to Eden.

"It's just a kind friend who brought me up in his car so that I might get to you quickly. He knows Jesus Christ. He has been praying for you all the way up here."

"He—*has?*" Caspar turned back to the stranger in wonder.

"Will—you—pray—for me—now?"

"I will," said Lance, and stepped a little nearer, half-kneeling beside the bed, where the dying man could see him and hear his low-spoken words.

"God our Heavenly Father, we come to You in the name of Jesus Christ Your Son whom You sent to take the sins of the world. We come to talk with You about this dear young man, who suddenly finds that he is called to meet You. He has just become aware that he is a sinner, and not ready to go. He finds he has no righteousness of his own to plead and all his own self-righteousness that he thought he had has become just filthy rags. He is ashamed to go Home to You that way. Lord Jesus, we know that You have made a way to clothe him with Your righteousness, and let him come home to You forgiven, his sin blotted out by the blood of the Lamb, his mistakes all covered by Christ's righteousness, if he will believe and accept Your free gift of salvation. We ask in the name of Jesus, that You will now forgive and cleanse and save him, as he now repents his sin and cries out to You for forgiveness and help."

It was very still in the hospital room as Lance's voice ceased, and Eden kneeling beside the bed, watching Caspar anxiously, saw his lips moving. Then heard his voice, strangely like the boy she remembered long ago:

"Jesus—Christ—I'm sorry! Forgive—Help—Save—I trust—in Thee. This—is Caspar—crying—to be—saved!"

His voice was clear and distinct as if he would reach high Heaven with his call, and then he sank back on his pillow again. For an instant he opened his eyes and looked around with an almost radiant smile turned on Eden, and then to the stranger.

"Thanks!" he murmured as his eyes closed, and it was very still again.

While they waited still in silent prayer with bowed heads, the nurse came over, and a little later she murmured, "He is gone! Thank you for coming! This would have been awful without you."

As they stood for an instant wondering if there was anything else for them to do, there was a stir at the other end of the room and a stylish person in becoming black came excitedly into the room. She looked wildly about her.

"*Where* is my son?" she demanded. "Don't tell me you have let him die before I got here. Where, *where* is he?"

"That must be his mother," whispered the nurse. "We've spent a lot of time trying to get her, though he didn't seem to care so much. He was more anxious for the young lady to come. Are you a—relative?" she hesitated and looked at Eden puzzled as she asked the question.

Eden gave a slow smile.

"No, only an old schoolmate, but he knew I wasn't far away."

"Well, I'm glad you came before he went. But now it looks as if there might be a stormy time, and he's well out of it."

The haughty lady arrived by the bed and looked resentfully toward the girl and man standing there.

"Who are these?" she asked disagreeably, indicating by her manner that they were intruding.

"Just some acquaintances he asked us to send for," said the nurse. "They were very kind to come a distance in answer to his call."

"Oh, *really?*" said the mother in a supercilious tone. "Well, that was kind of them I'm sure, but now, of course, we shall not need them any more. I'll take care of everything. And nurse, will you let me see whoever represents the hospital authorities at once?"

The two young people thus dismissed walked quietly out and down the long hall, still filled with the awe of their so recent meeting with God, and almost loth to leave alone with such a mother, the dead boy who had needed them so desperately.

Chapter Twenty

Outside in the clear night air with the Christmas stars pricking out above them making bright the darkness, the two found themselves walking along hand in hand.

It was Eden who came to herself first and realized how warm and comforting that strong hand holding hers was. It seemed that it had been there a long time giving her assurance, and a kind of peace. But she did not withdraw her hand at once. It seemed too sweet and natural, too much as if God Himself were there walking with them, showing them great things about life, and revealing to them some of His gracious plans that they had not yet been shown. And this handclasp that held them side by side seemed a part of all that they had been through. A soul had been born into the Kingdom of God, and then passed into Heaven while they watched and took part in the ceremony. It seemed that never again could they doubt and wonder about things as they had done sometimes before.

Then they came to where the car was parked and paused, almost regretting that words must be spoken which might break the harmony of wonder in God's Presence that had been so near, about them.

"Where are we going?" said Eden, coming out of her trance and trying to be practical. "I suppose we've got to have something to eat, haven't we? It will take too long to get back to the city before we get dinner won't it! Of course Janet will get us up something in a hurry if we wait."

"No," said Lance. "We'd better get something to eat sooner. Not here I think. But I seem to remember a nice little restaurant not many miles from here on the way home. Shall we try that? It seems to me we need to rest a little, get quiet, and be refreshed after our experience before we start back. What do you think?"

"Oh yes. I'm not hungry yet. And I'd rather get away from here now. I wouldn't like to risk running into any further contact with that awful woman again. How terrible to have had a mother like that! Poor Cappie!"

"Yes," said Lance, "no wonder with a mother like that that he went to pieces when he got into war. One needs a mother all through life, even if she is only there a few years to start a right foundation. But this woman doesn't seem to have done even that."

"No," said Eden thoughtfully. "Poor Caspar. I didn't understand. I shouldn't have been so hard on him."

"Well, whatever you did or did not do in the past, you certainly undid any mistakes at the end of his life. I felt as if all the words you spoke were bright arrows that went straight to the mark of the enemy. You certainly must have been brightening your arrows since we last talked on this subject. I never heard better chosen words to lead a soul through the dismal pathways of a Christless 'Valley of the Shadow.'"

"Oh, but I thought you said the Holy Spirit was to choose the words. My work was only to get the words into my heart and on my tongue."

"You had the Holy Spirit's choosing. I am sure, in selecting what verses you should learn. I do not doubt that. But I praise the Lord that you worked so diligently to gather them together where they could be used."

"Oh, I am glad you thought I said the right thing. I was terribly frightened. It seemed so daring to meddle with a human being's eternal salvation."

"It is of course if you are on the job alone," said Lance, "but we are never alone on such an enterprise. The Holy Spirit is there to inspire, to guide, and to bless."

"And I was so glad," said Eden, "that you were there. Your bringing in that Bible verse that just so fitted in that spot! I hadn't an idea what to say next, and then your voice came. It was just as if God made a picture of His plan for us and made it there plainly before us. And I was so frightened about a prayer too, for I knew there ought to be one, and I couldn't have prayed like that. You said the very things that ought to have been said, to make him know God was there and was listening to him and waiting for him to come home. Oh, I'm so glad you came."

"And I'm glad I came too. I wouldn't have missed that experience for anything. It will stand out as the most remarkable instance of soul-winning at the last hour that I have ever seen.

"But here's the restaurant. How does it look? Attractive? It's very plain I believe, but I've heard they have good food. Shall we stop?"

"Oh yes," said Eden. "And I believe I'm pretty hungry after all. Chicken and waffles sounds good."

They went inside and found a plain large room, square tables, coarse but clean cloths, and napkins, great pitchers of creamy milk, attractive sweet country butter, plenty of it, glass pitchers of real maple syrup, plates piled high with steaming waffles, unstinted platters of crisp friend chicken, and plenty of hot chicken gravy. A supper fit for a king; no great variety, but everything delicious. There was also homemade ice cream if one had room for such after the other good things were eaten.

"Why, isn't this lovely!" exclaimed Eden. "Why did we never find this place before? Let's come again sometime."

"Why surely!" said Lance with a quick delight at the thought, remembering how he had been trying to school himself to the thought that this girl did not belong to him and probably never would.

But they had a pleasant supper, and made much progress in getting to know one another better than they had ever done yet. That scene in the hospital they had shared would be a link that could never be forgotten. They had been together to the gate of Heaven and escorted a lost soul in, and they could never lose the memory of how frail a breath held earth and Heaven together.

They came out at last and drove homeward through the purple twilight, growing more and more quiet as they approached the city with its blinding lights. They were both saddened by the thought that this day with its nearness was over, and there was no promise of more such companionship ahead. For though there was no real reason for Eden to feel that this was so, she did have a feeling that somehow the old bar between them was coming down between them again. What was it? Some tie that kept him back from the free and easy familiarity that sometimes she had seen in him? She could not tell.

As they drove up to the Thurston house they could dimly see a shadowy form at one of the front windows watching for them. It was Janet of course, true to her lifetime form, looking out to make sure her nursling was safe. It was Tabor who laughed about it sometimes quietly with her.

"I've often wondered, Janet, what you would have done, supposing sometimes she did *not* come home on time. Who would you send for? Would it be the police or the doctor?"

But Janet took it all good-naturedly, and kept her watch just as faithfully.

So Janet sat by the window when they drove up. But that cold little bar had dropped between their two hearts again, and kept Lance from coming in, though he very much wanted to.

He said good night at the door, letting his fingers linger a trifle longer in hers than necessary, and leaving with Eden that wistful, tender, true look that stayed by her even when she was asleep.

But it was Janet who interrupted even this bit of farewell, though she knew better. She opened the front door for them, unnecessarily soon, and burst out with her Scotch speech, anxiously.

"And hoo did ye find Caspar?" she asked excitedly. "Was he really hurt bad?"

"Yes, very badly, Janet," said Lance gravely, "but fortunately we got there before he died."

"Deid, is he? Ye dinna *maen* it! Boot praise be, he's better in the Lord's han's than ever he was down here. And noo, p'raps it'll be possible tae feel sorry fer him without bein' feared ov him."

"Now that's a strange thing for you to say, Janet, whatever can you be meaning by that?" asked Eden.

"Wull, ye maun work it out, my bairn, boot I've ben afeard o' yon lad sence iver he began tae grow a mon, and I'm relieved the Lord has took him over, I canna be sad he's gane. Boot the Lord allus kens best."

The eyes of the two young people met in a tender little twinkle of amusement at the quaint old woman, and their fingers, unaware of relaxed caution, gave sweet pressure one to another that lingered in both their thoughts through the long night hours and came out alive again in the morning, much to the upsetting of the decorum they were allowing their chastened young selves.

CHAPTER TWENTY-ONE

SOMETIME IN the dim watches of the night, the Lord came and talked with Lance Lorrimer in a dream, about the heaviness that was upon his heart.

"What is it, Lance, my son? What is so troubling you?"

"Why Lord, I've got myself into something that is breaking me all up. I have let my heart get all entangled with a girl who belongs to somebody else. I never meant to get into a thing like this. And I've tried with all my heart to break loose from it, but I can't seem to get anywhere with it. I just am loving that dear girl. Now what shall I do? Should I go away where I'll never be seeing her any more, or is this a cross You are meaning me to bear all my life? I know that You are able to furnish the strength to overcome this, and to live to please You, nevertheless, but I seem to have come to a sort of a crossroads where I must know which way to turn. Try as I will, resolve as I may from day to day that I will put myself in her way no more, constantly I come upon a situation where my duty to my job, and my sense of decency make it necessary for us to be thrown together. Yet I could not refuse to go yesterday, even though I knew my desire was so great that I was only tangling my life up further. Yet the outcome seemed to prove that it was right to go. And now here I am again pleading for help for this situation. Will You not make it plain to me what I shall do? It is not fair to her or to me, or the man I hear she is engaged to marry that we should grow more and more near in companionship. I do not know what it is doing to her, of course, but I do know that it is making it very hard for me to go about my daily duties and do them right. If that is what You want, my Lord, it is all right with me, but You'll have to give me grace and strength for this new way."

Then a still small voice spoke deep into his heart.

"Lance, my son, why should you think this girl could not be for you? Don't you know that before the foundation of the world I looked forward to your time, and I planned her for a fitting companion for you? Why is it that you have drawn away from this great joy that I have planned to give you?"

"But, Lord, I have been told that she belongs to another."

"Yes? Who told you? One you knew and trusted? Did you ever try to find out if this was true? Why not?"

"But, Lord, I was ashamed. I have no wealth to offer her befitting her station. I have no great standing in life, either financial, social or intellectual. She is a wonderful girl I know and I would not try to win her away from all those worldly advantages she rates, as the daughter of a wonderful father."

"Lance, when did I ever tell you that these things you have named were important? Money? Station? Social prominence? Worldly advantages? Don't you remember that the silver and the gold are all mine? Have you forgotten that all advantages of the world are mine to give or to take away? Do you think that a child of the Heavenly King should make decisions on a foundation of that sort? Are you mine, to follow Me everywhere, or only Mine when the world agrees with your standards?

"For pride's sake were you letting this wonderful girl slip away from you? Compelling her to go on alone perhaps? Not letting her know of the treasure of your love, which I have created to be a jewel in her life and in yours, to bring you both joy?"

The vision began to fade, but as he woke in the early dawn of a roseate sky, the words that had seemed to be spoken grew clear again. Then his common sense stepped up, and offered humdrum reasoning. But as he rose and prepared for the day, he found a cheerful song was in his heart. Whatever was coming to him in the next few hours he did not know, but he could trust and not be afraid. He somehow felt that the Lord was on his side.

He thought over the situation carefully. Somehow it seemed as if he should find out from someone about whether Eden was engaged or not. But again he put that thought aside. His own wisdom was not best. The magic of the vision was still upon him. This was not a matter of reasoning things out. That was following an inward calling.

Of course he might ask Mr. Worden, just casually, if Eden were engaged. He likely would know if anyone did. And again he might ask Janet. But somehow he disliked to be talking her over with anyone. She was the only one who had a right to give this information, and he had no real right to get the information from any other source.

How he was going to go about this difficult business of enquiry he had not yet settled, but surely a way would open. He must not run ahead of himself and he must not make a set blue print to follow, for if this was of the Lord there would be a way. The main thing was to be prepared with ammunition, and a ring was one of the articles that was always associated with a matter of this sort, wasn't it? A ring, the sign that she belonged to him. How that thought thrilled him. He had never realized that anyone might belong to him. And now that he thought of it, he hadn't noticed that she was wearing a ring on her engagement finger. Wasn't that a sign that she was free? Dolt that he was! Why hadn't he thought of that before? Well, now he was going to find out just where he stood. And he was going the first thing to prepare for the siege in which he was to engage today. This morning he would go to the very best jewelers in the city and choose a gorgeous ring. Thank the Lord he had money enough put away to get a really good one. Not too large, not too showy, but good. One that she need never be ashamed to wear.

Somehow he had never realized before what lovely things diamonds were, how beautiful to handle and watch. As he looked them over and admired, he was reminded that somewhere he had read that the Eden of old, the first Eden, bore flowers made of precious stones, and someone had hazarded the thought that perhaps in the *new* earth gardens were again to bear, both growing blooms, and flowers of jewels again. It sounded fantastic, but with a great God was anything fantastic that He chose to do?

Lance chose at last a beautiful stone the lights in whose facets were rainbow-tinted stars and prisms, and when he took the tiny velvet box containing the lovely jewel, wrapped in white, and put it in a safe hiding place till he could give to Eden his heart was filled with great joy. He had not thought that just a jewel could mean so much to a mere man. But this jewel represented a great love, his love for the girl he had chosen, and whether she accepted it or not did not now enter into the question. That would be for him to find out tonight, but he would not begin to expect disappointment beforehand. He would go forward into this thing just as any other man had to go to win a wife. His own heart told him that she was the right one. He would take it for granted that she was, unless she told him no, and even then perhaps he would keep on trying to win her love. He must not expect everything at once. There were many duties in that day to fill its long lagging hours till evening when Lance might go to try his fortune with his beloved. Yet he did his work tirelessly, and with precision, and took a kind of joy in it because its path led to evening.

He had called her on the telephone as soon as the diamond was safe in his possession, and asked her if he might come to see her for a little while that evening. Her voice had lilted across the charmed air filled with welcome. It almost seemed an echo of the rebuke for his lack of faith from his vision of the night. He marveled at himself that he was no longer fearful to put to the test the great hope of his heart.

"Come early," she had said. "Why can't you come to dinner? We are always hindered by so many things when we set out to have a little talk. But I just hope we won't have any more burglaries or crimes to hinder us tonight."

"Very well, I'll come to dinner. I'll be there at five o'clock. Is that too early? And then you can have dinner whenever Janet and Tabor decide."

The lilting laugh rippled out again.

"How simply super," said Eden. "We'll have a real time together, won't we?"

"We certainly will," said Lance feeling suddenly a great deal younger than he had been since he returned from service. "And if former friends, or hateful neighbors approach and decide to call tonight what shall we do? Shoot them on the spot, or run off and leave them?"

"No," said Eden, "we'll turn all the lights out and let Janet and Tabor tell them we are not at home to callers tonight. Because you see," she said, growing more serious in tone, "I really have a great many questions to ask you. They are things I need to know, and I don't want a hoard of neighbors barging in on us."

"Yes? Well, I have only one question I want to ask you, but it's important."

"Oh, how interesting. What is it about?"

"Well, it's too serious and involves too much to go into it over the telephone. Besides it will take too long and I have work up to my eyes this minute and can't stop to talk about it now. See you around five o'clock, if I can possibly make it. Good-by!"

And if a man can lilt, Lance Lorrimer's voice certainly lilted on that farewell word.

Eden hung up and stared at herself in her mirror. Her cheeks were a lovely rose, her eyes like two stars. A bar of sunshine dashing in at her window sprinkled sparkles on her curly hair.

"Of course," she told herself, "this doesn't mean anything but a pleasant call. I mustn't get silly and spoil it all. He is just tired. He said he was, and he's coming to have a congenial talk. But I like that better than anything else, and I mean to fix things so we won't be bothered with outsiders. I know the Wordens are going to some cousin's wedding over in New York tonight, so they won't come, and there isn't anybody else likely to bother. I'll manage so we won't be annoyed for just one night, even if I have to get Mike and his policemen to help me out." She giggled softly to herself.

She stood there a minute thinking and then she danced down to Janet who was polishing silver in the butler's pantry.

"Janet," she said, and the lilt was still in her voice. Oh, Janet knew a lilt when she heard one. This was the same lilt that Eden's mother once had in the days when Eden's father was courting her. She loved it. For a long time she had been waiting for a lilt like this to come to her beloved nursling, watching and waiting and hoping, but fearing, too, that it might be brought there by the wrong lover. So now she turned sharply at the sound, and held the spoon she was polishing in mid-air while she stared at Eden.

"Janet, I'm having a guest to dinner tonight."

Janet fairly trembled with anxiety. Had that dratted New Yorker come back again, and had he really won her "leddy" at last after all his palavering?

Janet's face stiffened into disapproval even in spite of the soft pretty color on her girl's cheeks, and the stars in her lovely eyes.

Then Eden caught the look in Janet's eyes and broke down laughing.

"Oh, don't put on that disapproving glower, Janet dear. It's somebody you like. I think—I *guess* you like him very much, though you've taken great care not to say too much about him. Janet, Lance Lorrimer is coming to dinner, and to spend the evening, and I want you and Tabor to shoo off the neighbors and try to let us have a little peace. We want to talk awhile about important questions without being interrupted; and we want to read aloud, and maybe sing a little, so if any kind of a mob comes barging in, just say we're busy with some business tonight and can't see anybody. Tell them to come again, and to call up before they come, or something. I can trust you to get by with it."

"Oh, bless the bairn! Thet's somethin' quite diff'runt. Sure, he's yer lawyer, why shouldna he? Whut d'ye want fer the menoo?"

"Oh, something nice. I'll let you order that. There'll have to be scones of course, because he likes them terribly."

"Yis. Scones ov coorse!" beamed Janet. "An' whut will ye wear, my lamb? Let it be somethin' light and gay. Ye ken yer feyther allus craved tae see ye in happy things, as he ca'd thim."

Eden gave her a bright smile.

"Why, yes, Janet. That's a happy thought. I'll wear the light blue wool frock with the white fur on the neck that he loved so much. He used to call that my 'happy dress,' you remember?"

"I mind," said Janet. "It was al'lus the best thing ye wore."

"I'm awfully silly, Janet, don't you think? But I haven't dressed up in so long that it really seems like a sort of holiday night. Just a little evening of business, of course, but why not make it cheerful?"

"Why not?" said Janet with satisfaction, hurrying to finish the silver and get it away so she could go and tell Tabor that there was coming a tiny ray of sunshine into the house after the storms of the winter.

"But this is ridiculous!" said Eden to herself, as the afternoon waned. The house had been put in spic-and-span order, and she had got herself dressed in the soft blue frock her father had loved, with the line of white fur in the round of the neck, and the finish of fur on the comely little sleeves against the white rounded arm. "This is just ridiculous! What a fool he will think I am, if he notices at all. To rig up this way, just for a bit of religious conversation, and maybe a spot or two of business. Just plain ridiculous! But I like it, and I'm going to get fun out of it. And I think daddy would like me to be a little happy too for a while. This is someone daddy surely would like, and I'll sort of feel that daddy is here with us tonight."

Eden had elected to bring her guest to the library, because that was the room where she and her father used to sit so much, and because strangers did not often come there.

So, though Eden had not said anything about it, the servants had an uncanny way of figuring out her wishes, and a little before five o'clock there was a fire laid in the library, and the curtains were drawn close in the living room opening from it. There was but a dim light in the hall, as if the family were all out. Tabor knew his business, and he and Janet were often in league to run the house in the most acceptable manner possible, according to their lights. And their lights were lighted from the taper that their Lady Eden carried as she walked her pretty ways.

"And when it's all over," thought Eden, looking wistfully into her mirror because there was no one else to whom she cared to confide these thoughts, not even Janet, "I'll be most terribly lonesome, I just know I will. Because the other people I know are so silly and uninteresting to me. But maybe I can get acquainted with some of those nice young people we met at that first meeting I attended, and be a 'regular guy' myself. I mean a really happy, *un*lonely Christian. Well, here goes. There is the doorbell. I'll run downstairs and meet my guest."

And so she dawned upon him, running down the stairs in her pretty soft blue dress, with a wreath of sparkle in her hair like little bright leaves from a fairy tree, and her small feet twinkling in her slim silver slippers.

A perfect setting for the diamond! But the thought did not come to Lance at first, only the wonder of her beauty, and the amazing fact that he was daring to come and seek her as his own. And there he stood looking as if she had been some angel suddenly dawning upon him. Of course he hadn't before been seeing her in gala clothing; she had worn just plain go-to-meeting suits.

Tabor had opened the door before Eden was down the stairs and she could see by the way Tabor stood, and the look he gave, that he was doing her guest all honor, as if he were one he greatly admired.

But suddenly Eden felt shy as if this were all at once some august presence, and she had been too forward to be asking him to dinner, when he had only asked to call. Had she been too eager in her approach?

And then she saw that look in his eyes, and it warmed her frightened heart, and brought the bright color to her cheeks, giving her courage to go forward with her pretty program.

So Tabor took his coat and hat and the box of flowers that Lance had brought.

"They say those are Christmas roses," he said, smiling at Eden, as she reached eagerly over to take them. "They wouldn't be my idea of Christmas, but somehow they reminded me of you."

"Oh, how lovely!" she exclaimed delightedly. "How exquisite! They're just the shade of pink I love. Will you put them on the table, Tabor? And here, I'll keep this precious bud to smell. What delicate perfume! It seems as if it were specially made for just this color of rose."

She took one lovely bud and held it in her hands, bending her head to get the fragrance, as she led the way into the living room where she meant to stay till dinner was announced. And as she went a great shyness came upon her, so that she was almost afraid of the evening which she had allowed to mean so much to her lonely young self.

Tabor took the roses ceremoniously and carried the box away gently to Janet as if it had been a baby. And Janet quickly spirited away some flowers she had bought to decorate the table. So Lance's roses shone in all their delicate beauty and filled the good old nurse's heart with comfort. She took an instant out of her ceremonies wherewith she was conducting the preparations for the meal, just to stand with folded arms and gaze at them, as if they had been dropped down from some Heavenly sphere.

"He's all richt," she murmured to herself with shining eyes. "He's a bonny heirted mon."

"What's that, Janet? Did you say something?" asked Marnie who had come in to bring the celery.

"Oh, it's juist thae roses," she explained embarrassedly. "He broucht thim."

"Oh, did he? Aren't they lovely," exclaimed Marnie. And then she went and told the cook, and the cook came to see them. Then came Tabor, and beamed above them all. His household was pleasing him tonight.

Over in the living room the two young people sat politely as if they were almost strangers again, Eden tapping one silver slipper toe and smiling into the delicate rosebud. And Lance watching her silently, and thinking that she did not need a diamond to set her off. She was jewel enough without it. She and the rosebud at her sweet lips. It had been the flower after all, the living flower that had provided the finish to her costume. The *flower*, not the jewel.

The talk they made was not much, just pleasant little fragments of speech, meant to tide them to the great business of the evening, and Eden began to feel her heart fail again lest they were dropping back to be strangers. Only their eyes were not strangers. They looked deep into one another's souls now and again, and their smiles were there, expressing pleasant flattery. Yet somehow they were content to let the time drift slowly by, coming as it would, as God sent it in His beautiful deliberate way.

Then Tabor came in and dinner was announced.

Lance arose and bowing low offered his arm to the lady, showing that in spite of all his forebodings he was to the manner born. And all these little things were noted down in his favor by the two servants whose loving critical eyes were not missing a thing that went on.

It was early when they sat down, but the dinner was served deliberately, and rather formally, in spite of the scones which were on hand as promised. Both servants were pleased that the meal opened with a reverent grace spoken by the guest, with Janet and Tabor standing, and Marnie and the cook standing at the crack of the butler's pantry listening delightedly. Old times were coming back again, and the old master, if he were able to look back to the world he had left would be well pleased.

It was as if those four servants had an uncanny insight into the little white box that reposed in Lance Lorrimer's pocket.

When dinner was over, the two young people were more at their ease, for they would soon be out of the sight of those adoring servants, and by themselves.

They went straight to the library now, followed solemnly by Tabor carrying the crystal dish of roses. He set them down on the old master's desk, as if to represent his presence in the room and grant a blessing on the evening.

Tabor had seen that the fire was lighted and burning brightly before they came in. Eden stood a moment warming her hands and her guest stood cosily near on the hearth.

"Now," she said, "you said you had a question to ask, and I have a lot of them. Suppose you begin, will you? Since there is only one of yours, I'm sure we'll soon get to my questions."

Lance gave a twinkling smile.

"I'm not so sure, little lady," he said. "At least I hope not." He hesitated an instant. The words he wanted to say seemed to come in a rush and then suddenly catch on something in his throat. "But my question involves a statement first. It is short but it means a lot to me." Then he turned and looked deep into her eyes. "I came over tonight to tell you that—I love you! And my question is, 'Will you marry me, dear'?"

Eden was looking up into his eyes with almost a glory look in her own, that gave her assent wordlessly.

The love in the young man's eyes almost overwhelmed her it was so strong and tender. Suddenly his arms went out and drew her to him. For a long moment they stood so, her face against his shoulder, his arms folding her close. Then Lance stooped and laid his lips softly on her hair, eyes and forehead, and finally she raised her head and their lips met.

"Oh, this is *Home*," she whispered.

"Darling!" he said and kissed her again.

Then he drew her down on the seat beside the fire.

"Wait," he said, "I am putting my seal on this contract," he said quaintly. He brought out the little white velvet box from his pocket, took out the ring, and slipped it on her finger.

The firelight caught the heart of the jewel, flung out its many colored facets, and blazed on her pretty finger as if it too had found itself at home.

A long time they sat there in the firelight, and not even Tabor came to interrupt. And Eden never did get to the beginning of her own questions, because they had so much to say about themselves and how and when they first came to care for one another. Then when they had finished they had to begin all over again and tell some things that had been left out.

It was Janet who finally came to the door and interrupted them at last with her inevitable tray. "A wee drap o' tay, t' hearten ye," she said with a knowing smile.

"But this time we don't need heartening, Janet," said Lance with his twinkling smile.

"Oh, see, Janet, Look at my wonderful ring!" said Eden and held out her hand with the sparkling gem.

"Oh, my bairnie, *dear!*" said Janet and took the little hand in both of hers, laying her face against it an instant. Then hurriedly she turned, brushing away glad tears, and made for the door.

"Don't—stay oop too late!" she adjured them.

"Oh, but we haven't planned about the wedding yet," said Eden.

"It's to be right away," called Lance joyously.

But Janet hastened out to tell Tabor and the rest.

Afterward, when Lance finally did tear himself away, Eden found her retainers all trooped together to see the wonderful ring, and watch her happy face.

"Wull, ye've hed a mony chances," said Janet comically, "boot ye've waited wisely an' we all approve."

Eden laughed her little trilly ripple.

"Yes, Janet," she said joyously, "I'm sure he's the right man God meant for me."

"Bless ye, my bairnie lamb!"

They all trooped up as if it were a wedding reception, and bowed, and wished her well, then went to their rest.

And Eden kneeling at her window, looked up to the many stars above, and thanked God for answering her mother's prayer.

WHO WAS
GRACE LIVINGSTON HILL?

THE ROWS of books each contain well-worn spines. Hours of loving time spent curled up with a good book, and each one contains a singular author's name—Grace Livingston Hill. Millions of readers love this pioneer for her spiritual romances. How did she accomplish so much, and what experiences from her personal life were built into her stories? No one writes from a vacuum of experiences. The joys and trials of each person's experiences build something into her fiber. The writer draws on these experiences and combines them with her imagination to write lasting fiction. Grace Livingston Hill was no exception. Born in the nineteenth century, Hill wrote in the days before computers and word processors. Each of her stories was typed with a manual typewriter, but we're getting ahead of her life story. I invite you to settle back and learn from this remarkable woman.

Born on April 16, 1865—the day after President

Abraham Lincoln died, after being shot in Ford Theatre—Grace Livingston Hill entered the world struggling to breathe. Concern and prayers spread throughout the small town of Wellsville, New York, where her father was a Presbyterian minister. Charles and Marcia Livingston's little girl's breathing soon returned to normal, and she lived. Before the child's birth Marcia and Charles had agreed that if they had a boy, Marcia would name the baby and if they had a girl, Charles would name it. Mr. Livingston named his daughter Grace. The sweet joy of celebration for this birth was mixed with his sorrow over the death of President Lincoln.

A Family of Storytellers

From a young age Marcia MacDonald Livingston, Grace's mother, loved to tell stories. Because of their love for stories, Marcia and her sister, Isabelle (known as Belle), were called "The Queens of the Bedtime Tales" by their father. Now as Marcia tucked her own child, young Grace, into bed, she spent hours spinning bedtime tales, often ending with a moral or teaching point. Both Marcia and Belle developed their own writing careers through producing magazine articles. Belle shared her new typewriter with Marcia. At an early age Grace was taught to use the typewriter and soon began to spell short words on scraps of paper. At one point the sisters collaborated on the romance novel *By Way of the Wilderness*.

Charles Livingston was known as an outstanding speaker and also frequently contributed to magazines and religious newspapers through his nonfiction writings.

For Grace's twelfth birthday Auntie Belle created a special gift. Several months earlier Belle had carefully listened to one of Grace's stories about two children. While listening, Belle created a typed version of the story on her typewriter. Now for Grace's birthday, Belle presented her with a bound hardcover copy, which included woodcut illustrations. A printing company in Boston, the D. Lothrop Company, who published most of Belle's books, had created this single book.

As she presented the book to her niece, Auntie Belle said, "Now, Grace, I have some important advice to give you. This is your first book, and I am your first publisher. But in the future you must write your stories down and find a publisher on your own. Your mother and I will help you, but you must discipline yourself early in life to your writing."

THE FIRST BOOK CHALLENGE

Most summers the family spent several weeks in Chautauqua at a conference; but one year because of a move, they weren't able to attend the session. The next year Grace and her mother eagerly made plans to return. Charles brought them back to reality, "If you look at our bank account and what we can save between now and then, combined with the expenses of making a trip from Florida to New York, the costs are impossible." Mother and Grace worked the numbers and agreed they didn't have the money. Then Grace offered, "If I write a book and sell it, can we all go?"

With a smile, her father promised, "If you earn the money to take us all to Chautauqua, Grace, your mother and I will be happy to go with you."

In a matter of days, Grace was writing her story to get it out of her head and on paper. She promised her mother, "I'll show you the manuscript when I've finished the first draft, then I'll ask you for some editorial help."

One chilly evening while Grace's parents sat near the fireplace, Charles could see his daughter writing. He spoke loudly to break into her work, "Grace, stop for a few minutes and come and read to me, dear."

Immediately she responded, "Let me finish this page and I'll be right there." For the first time, Grace's father understood she was going to be a writer. His daughter had the ability to follow through and could even be interrupted without getting upset because she had a clear plan for her story.

When Christmas arrived, Grace had completed her book and rewritten it several times into a lined exercise book. Borrowing a typewriter, Grace and her mother took turns typing the manuscript, *A Chautauqua Idyl*, until it was completed. She mailed the book to D. Lothrop Company, where Auntie Belle had put together her first hardcover book. Only a few weeks later in mid-January an acceptance letter arrived from Lothrop. The publisher sent a copy of the manuscript to the Chaplain of the United States Senate, Edward Everett Hale, and they planned to use his response as a means to introduce the book. His introduction began, "I have read Miss Livingston's little idyl with much pleasure. I cannot but think that if older and more sedate members of the Chautauqua circles will read it, they will find that there are grains of profit in it."

Grace and her mother hurried to church to tell the good news to Charles Livingston. In her excitement to receive the acceptance, Grace hadn't thought about the payment. Now in the church office she re-read the letter and studied the contract. Charles affirmed his daughter had earned enough money to take the family to the Chautauqua conference during the summer months. Grace signed her first book contract and returned it the same day. In the spring of 1887 A *Chautauqua Idyl* was published with twenty-two pen-and-ink illustrations, and the hardcover sold for sixty cents.

LOVE AND LIFE EXPERIENCES

Several years later in 1890 Grace's newest book, A *Little Servant*, had just been published and announced at the Chautauqua conference. She met Reverend Thomas Frank Hill, whom everyone called Frank. He asked to accompany her to the evening vespers service. Educated at Princeton University, Frank came from a family of preachers, and he had a congregation near Pittsburgh, Pennsylvania. Frank and Grace were often together in the group setting of the conference. When they said good-bye, Grace discovered a new feeling—the difficulty of parting from someone. They promised to stay in touch through letters, and their correspondence was steady throughout the next year. During the following summer Grace and Frank spent even more time together. At the end of the summer the Livingstons planned to spend a weekend of their vacation at Frank Hill's home near Pittsburgh, and Grace's father would preach at his church. Before the conclusion of that weekend Frank confessed to Grace that he loved her and planned to give her an engagement ring the next summer. On a clear and cold day, December 2, 1892, Frank and Grace were married in Hyattsville Presbyterian Church.

A short time later the presbytery asked Frank to transfer to a larger church in eastern Pennsylvania, and soon the couple moved to Germantown, near Philadelphia, to work at Wakefield Presbyterian Church. Their marriage and relationship seemed perfect—except for one major flaw, which Grace never talked about until twenty-five years after Frank's death.

Only a day or two after the wedding Grace noticed that Frank suffered emotional mood swings. While his moods weren't violent ups and downs, there was a consistent pattern. He would begin the day nervous and fidgety, then at breakfast seem calm and almost sleepy, and finally normal for the rest of the day. When Grace asked about the nervousness, Frank dismissed it.

One Sunday following Sunday school, Grace noticed that her husband seemed particularly on edge. While Frank contended he was fine, as he sat on the platform preparing to preach, he appeared particularly uncomfortable. Asking the song leader to direct another song, Reverend Hill suddenly walked off the platform toward his office. To help, Grace followed and when she cracked open the office door was surprised to see Frank swallowing a small pill. Looking disturbed to see her, Frank quickly took a second pill and returned the pill container to his coat pocket. Walking over to his wife, he put his hands on her shoulders and said, "I've got to go preach. Pray for me! I'll explain everything later."

Pastor Hill returned to the platform and preached his sermon, completing the service. Several people asked about his health as they left the church. He told about a slight recurring illness under a doctor's treatment with an occasional attack. These individuals wished him well and seemed satisfied.

Later as the couple walked home, Grace asked if her husband was seriously ill. "Do you remember those terrible headaches I told you about when I was a student in Scotland? The doctor prescribed some medicine that helped a great deal. Any time I got a headache, I took one of those tablets, and the headache was gone within a few minutes. Within about three months I realized I couldn't get along without the tablets. The doctors there don't tell you about what they prescribe, or I would have been more careful. He never warned me about the possibility of addiction."

Grace could barely echo the word, "Addiction?"

"Yes, to morphine. I've prayed about it. I've asked God to help me overcome it. I've confessed the sin of using it. But I can't stop." Pausing for a moment, Frank continued, "Sometimes, like today, I try to put myself into a position that will embarrass me too much for me to leave and take one of those awful pills. I thought with you there that I could force myself to stop and that you would never have to know. But nothing works, Grace. Nothing."

Grace learned that, besides herself, only a doctor and Frank's father knew about his struggle. "Frank, I love you. I don't know what I can do to help you, but I will if I can. Keep praying and trusting. You're a wonderful husband and pastor."

Sighing in the painful discussion, Frank said, "I've spent years thinking about this; and I feel that as long as I'm able, I will preach and teach God's Word and leave my personal problems in His hands. I'm sure I'm much more patient with people than I would have been had I not been plagued with this problem."

The couple plunged into the local work of the church. Grace seemed to have boundless energy and continued writing amid housework. On September 17, 1893, Margaret Livingston Hill was born. Four and a half years later on January 24, 1898, Ruth Glover Hill, their second child, arrived. The two girls became close friends.

Less than two years later, early in the summer of 1899, Frank felt pain in his side, and his doctor diagnosed appendicitis. In those days an operation was dangerous and only to be performed as a last resort. Even with a bland diet and reduced work schedule, the pain increased until in November he decided to have the surgery. After the operation his condition worsened, and Frank Hill died November 22, 1899. Grace Hill felt her life was shattered. Yet she trusted God's purpose for this situation. Her parents stayed with Grace and her daughters for a while and helped them relocate to a new house, but eventually they returned to their own home, and Grace turned to her writing. It was now more than a hobby; it was her sole means of financial support. She wrote in short bursts of time while taking care of all the household chores and parenting her two girls.

The following July Charles Livingston grew ill and died. Within two weeks Marcia Livingston moved into the Hill home, and the pair divided the household chores, caring for the children, participating in church work, and writing.

Several years later Grace determined two clear goals. First, she wanted to build her own home, and she purchased a lot in 1904. Second, she decided to change her style of writing so it appealed to non-Christians as well as Christians, yet maintained a clear gospel message. With the popularity of Zane Grey westerns she decided to write a western, and *The Girl from Montana* became a large success. When she heard historical novels were growing in popularity, Grace researched a family story and turned it into the popular *Marcia Schuyler*, which was published in 1908.

Grace's younger daughter, Ruth, recalled her mother's life and work habits over the years, saying, "Mother was very family oriented all her life, and it shows in all her books. She was very friendly and helpful, always ready to drop what she was doing to help when there was a need. Mother took part in many of our activities, yet she was also writing two or three novels a year, averaging 80,000 words each. She certainly got the most out of each day— and night, for often she wrote until 2:00 or 3:00 a.m. 'when the house was quiet.'"

Through the years Grace Hill was in high demand as a speaker and addressed hundreds of churches and public conference centers. Each audience was eager

to hear about her latest book; and from this demand,
Grace summarized each book into as few as five pages
or as many as fifty pages, depending on the amount of
time for her speech. She continued this active ministry
until age seventy-nine.

In 1947, a few weeks before Grace's death, James M.
Neville from *The Sunday Bulletin Book Review* wrote her last
public interview. In part he wrote:

Mrs. Grace Livingston Hill, at 81, published her
seventy-ninth book last month. Religious inspira-
tion blended with "boy-meets-girl" romance has
served Mrs. Grace Livingston Hill as a durable
story formula that has survived the literary fads
and fashions for more than fifty years.

Often termed as one of America's most beloved novelists, as well as the most prolific, Mrs.
Hill's books are invariably overlooked by critics
and reviewers because of her frankly escapist stories and unvarying happy endings.

Mrs. Hill, however, had a direct answer for this
oversight in her Swarthmore home.

"I feel," she said with sincerity, "that there is
enough sadness and sorrow in the world. So I try
to end all my books as beautifully as possible, since
that is God's way—and the best way."

Her method of dreaming up plots, she said, is

simply by noting some incident around her home, in the street.

"Anything starts me off," she continued. "A few words overheard, or more subtle still, an expression on a passing face will set me wondering what story lies behind it, and I go on from there.

"But the magic way to get a story going," she concluded, "is simply to sit down at the typewriter and just go ahead."

A few weeks after this article appeared, Grace died, and newspapers around the country pointed out that her life had spanned from the end of the Civil War to the invention of the atomic bomb. The millions of her books are the greatest and ongoing legacy from the life of Grace Livingston Hill.

W. Terry Whalin prepared this brief biography from the expanded biography by Robert Munce, The Grace Livingston Hill Story *(Living Books, 1990). Munce is the grandson of Grace Livingston Hill.*